Mystery Sachit X
Sachitano, Arlene
Disappearing nine patch : a
Harriet T   se
Th

$14.99
707841

Night Had Fallen...

...by the time Lauren turned onto Harriet's hill.

"Did you see that?" She pointed out the windshield. "Blue flashing lights. Looks like they're on your street."

Harriet craned her neck to see up the hill from the side window, but they'd reached a section of the road that had mature trees and shrubs on both sides, obscuring the view.

"Something's going on at your house," Lauren said as she slowed to make the turn into the driveway.

She pointed, and Harriet could now clearly see two Foggy Point police cars parked behind a red fire truck. She threw her door open and jumped out before Lauren had fully stopped, causing her to slam on the brakes, and began running toward the house. She stopped when James grabbed her around the waist.

"Let me go," she shouted.

"You can't go up there right now. The fire is out, but they have to check before anyone is allowed back in."

"Fire? My house was on fire?" She slumped, and he held her tighter, preventing her from falling to her knees.

Also By Arlene Sachitano

The Harriet Truman/Loose Threads Mysteries

Quilt As Desired
Quilter's Knot
Quilt As You Go
Quilt by Association
The Quilt Before the Storm
Make Quilts Not War
A Quilt in Time
Crazy as a Quilt

The Harley Spring Mysteries

Chip and Die
Widowmaker

DISAPPEARING NINE PATCH

A Harriet Truman/Loose Threads Mystery

ARLENE SACHITANO

ZUMAYA ENIGMA   AUSTIN TX

2016

DISAPPEARING NINE PATCH

© 2016 by Arlene Sachitano

ISBN 978-1-61271-300-7

Cover art & design © April Martinez

"Zumaya Enigma" and the raven logo are trademarks of Zumaya Publications LLC, Austin TX

https://www.zumayapublications.com/enigma.php

Library Of Congress Cataloging-In-Publication Data

Names: Sachitano, Arlene, 1951- author.
Title: Disappearing nine patch : a Harriet Truman/loose threads mystery /
    Arlene Sachitano.
Description: Austin TX : Zumaya Enigma, 2016.
Identifiers: LCCN 2016003069 | ISBN 9781612713007 (trade pbk. : alk. paper)
Subjects: LCSH: Quiltmakers--Fiction. | GSAFD: Mystery fiction.
Classification: LCC PS3619.A277 D57 2016 | DDC 813/.6--dc23
LC record available at http://lccn.loc.gov/2016003069

For Vern And Betty

Chapter 1

Harriet heard the customer entrance of her long-arm quilting studio open as she came downstairs into her kitchen. She paused. She wasn't expecting anyone, but her quilting group, The Loose Threads, met in her studio often enough that most of them had keys.

As if to prove her right, her aunt, Beth Carlson came into the kitchen through the connecting door, followed by Beth's best friend Mavis Willis.

"Honey…" Beth said then paused while she set a glass baking dish on the kitchen counter.

Harriet crossed behind her, opened the coat closet and began rummaging around, her back to her unexpected guests.

Mavis set her worn black leather purse on a kitchen chair and slid out of her jacket.

"I know you've been a little down these last couple of weeks since Aiden left," she said. "But you can't mope around the whole time he's gone. He's probably not coming home for another two months, and he may decide to stay and visit when his friend gets back to Africa, so it could be the end of summer before he comes back. You can't stay holed up in your studio all that time."

Beth turned toward Harriet.

"You haven't come to any Threads meetings down at the quilt shop, and you've refused everyone's invitations to dinner or anything else, so we decided to have a potluck here. The rest of the group will be here in half an hour."

Harriet grabbed her jacket and purse.

1

"Can you take Scooter out in a little while? I've got to go. I don't know how soon I'll be back. I'll call when I know more."

She exited into the garage, leaving her aunt and Mavis standing in her kitchen.

✂ --- ✂ --- ✂

She drove to Smuggler's Cove in record time, turned her car into the driveway of her friend James's restaurant, and braked to a stop. James met her at the back door, dressed in his white chef's coat and hat.

"Thank you for coming so fast—I didn't know who else to call. Cyrano was in his kennel when I checked him fifteen minutes ago. I'm sure I closed the latch—I always double-check. I went back in the kitchen and set some water on to boil, and when I went out to get him and put him back in the office, he was gone. I've got twenty-five women coming for a special lunch in the private dining room, so I can't leave to go search for him."

"Do you think one of the other racing wiener dog owners could have taken him?"

"I doubt it. None of our local group is that competitive. We're all in it for the fun."

"Let me go walk the neighborhood, talk to a few neighbors and find out if anyone's seen him."

"He's wearing his green 'wiener-in-training' T-shirt."

She put her hand on his arm. "Don't worry, we'll find him."

She hoped she wasn't lying.

She set out across the parking lot, pausing where the gravel thinned around a mud puddle. She bent to look and pulled out her phone to take a picture of the faint paw prints on one side of the puddle. Closer examination revealed a child-sized tennis shoe impression.

Harriet clicked a few more pictures before continuing to the sidewalk then to the nearest house. The neighborhood was made up of homes built in the Folk Victorian style. They tended to have simpler floor plans and were less ornate than the classic Victorians in her own neighborhood—the affordable homes of their era.

She stepped onto the porch and pressed the doorbell. Moments later, a short woman with white hair opened the door.

"Hi, I'm looking for a missing wiener dog. He disappeared from his kennel in back of the restaurant…" She pointed back toward James's place. "…about thirty minutes ago."

"Oh, you mean little Cyrano? I can't believe he'd run off. He adores James. And he knows which side his bread is buttered on."

"Have you seen any unusual activity in the neighborhood this morning?"

The woman thought a moment. She pressed her lips together and looked up at a spot on the doorjamb.

"I don't know as it's unusual, but the school bus didn't come today, and I saw a couple of kids playing down the street. Must be some sort of in-service day or something."

"Thank you, that helps a lot." Harriet turned to go.

"Will you let me know if you find him?" the woman asked.

Harriet gave her a half-smile. "Sure."

She walked down the sidewalk, scanning the driveways as she went. Three doors down and on the other side of the street, a child-sized bike lay in the grass. She crossed the street and was heading in that direction when she heard a familiar bark. She picked up her pace, taking the steps two at a time to reach the porch.

The barking increased as she rang the doorbell and then, when no one answered, pounded on the door. Finally, the barking became muffled, and a childish voice called out, "Nobody's home, so you can go away."

"You aren't in trouble," she called back. "Just give me the dog."

"We're not allowed to open the door to strangers," the child replied.

"You're also not allowed to steal dogs. Either send the dog out, or I'm calling the police…." She paused for dramatic effect. "…and your mother."

"What's going on here," a dark-haired young woman in running clothes asked as she crossed the yard and stepped onto the porch.

"I'm looking for a lost dog, and I can hear him barking inside your house."

The woman slid a key into the door lock and opened the door.

"We don't have your dog. I'm allergic to dogs—the kids know that. Liam, Sophie?"

There was a muffled noise, and then James's dachshund Cyrano burst into the entry hall. He ran over to Harriet, jumping up and down and barking. Liam and Sophie stood side-by-side, unable to make eye contact with their mother.

The young woman sneezed.

"You two are in trouble, big time. Not only did you take this woman's dog, but you left the house. I told you to stay in the playroom while I ran around the block. You promised me you would."

Sophie, looking like an orphan in her faded pink unicorn pajamas and purple rubber boots, still refused to look at her mother.

"I wanted to watch a show, and Liam wouldn't give me the channel changer. I went out to find you."

"I thought you'd be mad if I let her go out by herself. She's only seven." Liam was similarly attired in too-short jeans over blue-and-red rocket ship pajamas.

"So you went along to…what? Protect her? How noble of you. Maybe if you'd been that selfless about the show, you wouldn't be in this predicament," their mom told them in a stern voice. "And what are you two doing running around the neighborhood in your pajamas?"

She turned to Harriet.

"These two hoodlums are going to be grounded for weeks. When they're finished with house arrest, would you be agreeable to having them do some sort of restitution?"

Harriet had to try hard to maintain her stern look.

"Cyrano belongs to the man who owns the restaurant down the street."

"You two went all the way to the restaurant?" Mom all but shouted, fear leaking into her voice.

Sophie began to cry, and Liam's lower lip quivered.

Cyrano began wriggling.

"I'd better get this little guy home," Harriet said. "James is very worried about him. He's got a restaurant full of people, or he'd be here himself. You can stop by the restaurant and talk to him about whatever penance you think is appropriate."

"You two go up to your rooms." She turned back to Harriet when the little dog-nappers were out of sight. "I'm Melanie, by the way. I'm so sorry my kids took your friend's dog. Can I do anything for him? Does he need to go see the vet or anything?"

Harriet squeezed the wriggling canine.

"He seems fine to me, but James can let you know if any follow-up is needed."

Melanie put her hand over her heart.

"I can't believe they left the house. It's an in-service day at school. They were engrossed in a game and still in their jammies. I thought I could get a quick run in and be back before they finished. Clearly, that was a mistake. Oh, my gosh, you aren't going to turn me in to Children's Services, are you?"

"I don't think that will be necessary. I assume you aren't going to go out and leave them alone again."

"Never," she promised.

"I'll just take this little guy and get him home."

"Tell your friend how sorry I am."

"I will," Harriet said and went out the door.

✂ --- ✂ --- ✂

She carried Cyrano in through the back door of the restaurant. She peeked through the kitchen door and saw James, up to his elbows in julienned carrots.

"You, little man, are going into your kennel in your daddy's office for now."

She put him in the wire crate and made sure there was water in the dish before returning to the kitchen.

"I put Cyrano in his kennel in your office. Your neighbor up the street, Melanie, is hoping you'll let her two junior criminals do restitution of some sort after she grounds them for a while."

James looked over his shoulder at her.

"I can't thank you enough for finding my little rat. I'll make it up to you, I promise."

"That's not necessary. I'm happy to help." She looked at the arrangement of vegetables he was doing on chilled salad plates. "That looks good."

He held a couple of carrot sticks over his shoulder, and she took them.

"How do you get these so crisp?"

"Chef's secret," he said and laughed.

Harriet sighed."I better leave you alone so you can get your work done. Besides, my aunt and Mavis arrived at my house as I was leaving. I think they're staging some kind of intervention. Since I'm their subject, I better go let them do their thing."

He glanced up at her. "I can't wait to hear the story behind that."

"All in due time," she told him and grinned.

✂ --- ✂ --- ✂

Cars lined her drive when she arrived back at her house. She parked in the garage then took a deep breath before going in to face her friends.

"Hey, looks like the gang's all here," she said, trying to sound cheerful as she came into the kitchen and found her aunt filling the tea kettle. "Did I miss the meeting notice?"

Mavis joined them.

"Honey, why don't you come into your studio. We have double chocolate brownies and salted caramel blondies."

Harriet set her purse on the counter and hung her jacket in the closet then turned to Mavis and Aunt Beth.

"If you put it that way, I guess I could hear what you have to say."

5

"Who said we have anything to say? Can't we just drop in for tea?" Aunt Beth said sweetly.

"Oh, please. You and Mavis could drop by, or even you guys and Connie, but the whole bunch of you all at one time? Never happen. You're here to ambush me about something. If you're willing to give me a brownie and a blondie, I'm putty in your hands." She brushed past her aunt and went on into her studio.

"Harriet, we've missed you," Connie Escorcia said from her seat by Harriet's big table. "You've missed the last three Tuesday Threads meetings."

Leave it to Connie to take roll, Harriet thought. As Foggy Point's former favorite kindergarten and first grade teacher, she couldn't let go of her old habits.

"We were getting worried about you," Robin McLeod added. "I know it's been rough having Aiden gone for so long."

"You look like you've lost weight," DeAnn Gault told her. "Have you been eating?"

Harriet held her hands up.

"Everybody—stop, already. I'm fine."

"You're not fine. I've asked you out to dinner five times, and you've turned me down flat," Aunt Beth, who had followed her from the kitchen, complained.

"And I've called you each night before our Tuesday meeting," Mavis added.

"If any of you would have let me get a word in edgewise, I could have explained. As soon as I say I can't go do something, you launch into how sorry you are that Aiden is gone for three months and how bad he must feel, and how I must feel, etc. etc. etc."

She reached across her large cutting table and picked up a brownie, putting it on a napkin before she sat down on a wheeled chair.

"I didn't say I wouldn't go out to dinner, I said I *couldn't* go. Likewise, I wasn't able to take the time to go to a meeting. If anyone had bothered to ask why, I'd have told them."

She was interrupted by Lauren Sawyer coming into the studio from the porch.

"Sorry I'm late, I just got the message. What did I miss?"

"We're having an intervention," Harriet said. "Grab a brownie and join the fun."

Lauren did as instructed and sat down.

"What are we intervening about?"

"I was about to explain why I've missed the last three meetings."

Lauren took a bite of her brownie.

"You were working on that big order, what's the big mystery?" she said when she'd swallowed. She looked around the table at her friends. "*I* could have told you. Harriet got a big job and was working night and day to finish it."

"Thanks for telling us," Mavis scolded her.

"Don't get mad at me. I missed the last meeting, too." She turned to Harriet. "Why didn't you tell me you were MIA when I brought dinner over? I could have filled them in."

"Geez, enough," Harriet said and laughed. "I was just saying—everyone is so busy being sympathetic about Aiden they haven't given me a chance to tell them what I've been doing, and frankly I haven't had a lot of time to spend on the phone waiting for a chance to talk."

Mavis looked at Beth. "I think we've been insulted."

Harriet ignored them.

"As Lauren said, I've had a big stitching job for the last couple of weeks. A woman in Port Ludlow is planning a ninetieth birthday celebration for her mother. Mom was a big-time quilter in her day, but like lots of people, she'd made many more tops than she could ever quilt, especially since she was a hand quilter and now has arthritis so bad she can't really do any handwork.

"Mom has always wanted to get enough quilts finished that she could give one to each of her seventeen grand- and great-grandchildren. The daughter has a long-arm quilter she uses in PL, but given the tight schedule, she needed to spread the quilts around to several of us hired needles. I agreed to take six, and I've been stitching my fingers to the bone getting them finished and off to the women in her quilt group for binding. They rented a hotel ballroom and are having a big bash complete with news people from Seattle."

Aunt Beth put her mug down on the table hard.

"Why didn't you say so?"

Harriet laughed.

"And before you ask, yes, I've heard from Aiden. His research group has a satellite phone the doctors get to use once a week. He's called me a couple of times."

Mavis and Beth exchanged a glance, and Harriet knew her aunt and her aunt's best friend were calculating how many weeks Aiden had been gone and counting how many weeks must have gone by without a call. She could have saved them the trouble—she'd done the math herself. He'd been gone seven weeks and called twice; once to say he'd safely arrived in-country. So, really, he'd only called once. That was fourteen-point-two percent of the times he had a phone available.

She raised her chin, silently daring anyone to press the issue.

"He's keeping busy doing the project work and taking care of the domestic animals and pets in the village near their research station. He said they spend a fair amount of time each day hauling water and boiling it."

Carla's cheeks reddened, but she didn't say anything.

Harriet didn't want to think about why that was. She was pretty sure she didn't want to know the answer.

Connie stirred her tea and set her spoon down.

"In a way, it's probably good that he's keeping too busy to think too much, but it will catch up with him. He's going to have to deal with what his sister did at some point."

Mavis tapped her teaspoon idly on her napkin.

"Denial is a pretty potent coping mechanism."

Harriet reached across the table and took a blondie.

"As to your point, Robin…" She took a bite, chewed and swallowed before continuing. "…I'd actually rather have Aiden off sorting himself out. Having him either no-showing for our dates or showing up and being so down that we can't enjoy ourselves was getting old. I know that sounds harsh, but I'm tired of all the drama. Speaking of which, what's been going on in Loose Thread-ville while I've had my nose to the grindstone?"

"I finished two more blocks of my crazy quilt," Connie announced.

Carla twisted her napkin between her fingers.

"I started a baby quilt for one of the mothers in Wendy's play group at church. She has four-year-old twin boys, a girl Wendy's age, and she's having twins again in August. One of the other moms is making a quilt, too."

Connie patted her hand. "That's very nice of you to make her something new for the babies."

The talk went around the table, with each quilter reporting on progress or problems on their current project. It stopped when they got to DeAnn.

"I have a mission for us, should we choose to accept."

Lauren leaned forward. "Oooh, tell us more."

"Most of you know I have a younger half-sister," DeAnn continued. "She runs a non-profit that's an umbrella organization for the various smaller missing and exploited children's groups around the state."

"I heard something about that," Mavis said. "Aren't they doing some kind of an event in Port Angeles in a couple of weeks?"

DeAnn took a sip of her tea.

"That's what I was going to ask you guys about. Molly is doing a dinner and auction, and she has two donors who have pledged ten thousand dollars each already."

"Here it comes," Lauren said. "And she wants us to make a…"

DeAnn's shoulders slumped, and she looked at Lauren.

"She was trying to think of a special thank-you present, and we were talking. It was my idea."

"Spit it out," Lauren said.

"Since they deal with missing children, I was thinking it would be cool to give them each a disappearing nine-patch quilt."

Carla, the youngest member of the group, looked confused.

"What's a disappearing nine-patch?"

Aunt Beth explained. "It's a simple pattern that ends up looking complicated. You make a basic nine-patch, kind of big, and then you cut it into four parts. You rearrange the four parts and sew them back together."

"Which direction do you cut it?" Carla asked.

"That's a very good question. You can cut it evenly in half and then cut those halves in half or you can cut corner to corner," Aunt Beth said.

"Cutting four small squares is a lot easier than working with the triangles, if you ask me." Mavis added.

"I'm willing to buy all the fabric," DeAnn continued. "That could be my donation. I mean, besides working on the quilt."

"I can quilt them on the machine," Harriet offered. "I'll sew blocks, too."

"I'm willing to do anything," Robin said.

Mavis and Connie nodded their agreement.

"Me, too," Carla said.

Harriet got up and went to her desk, where she picked up a box of colored pencils and a large sheet of grid paper. She brought them back to the big table.

"Okay, let's see if we can map this out and figure out what we need fabric-wise then decide who will do what."

Chapter 2

The crunch of tires on gravel drew Harriet to her studio window. When she saw James getting out of his white catering van, she went to the door and threw it open.

"What are you doing here?"

He handed her two plastic cold-bins.

"Take those to your kitchen." He skipped back down the porch steps and leaned into the back of his van, coming out with a large cardboard box. "I told you I'd make it up to you for finding Cyrano. And this is nothing. Consider it a down payment." He followed her into the kitchen, carried his box to the dining room and returned. "Do you have a deviled egg plate?"

"Probably. Aunt Beth left a hutch full of dishes in there." She pointed back toward the dining room.

"I made eggs, a fruit salad, and an assortment of pastries for you ladies. Just a light snack," he said and went back to the dining room to fetch the desired serving dish.

"How did you even know I was hosting a meeting this morning?"

"I ran into your aunt at the grocery store last night. She was at the meat counter buying chicken breasts. She told me she was making salad for a work day at your house, and I asked if I could bring breakfast."

"Well, this looks delicious, but you really don't owe me anything."

"I can't begin to describe how shocked I was when I went out to check on Cyrano and discovered he wasn't there. I couldn't breathe, my heart started racing…man…" He ran his hand through his short hair. "If the gate had been open, or if he'd dug a tunnel under the fence, I'd have been upset, but it wouldn't have been so shocking. He was there one minute and gone the next with no indication of what had happened."

"I'm glad it all turned out okay. Melanie thought she could trust her kids to stay in the house while she ran around the block. She knows better now."

James's face became serious. "I don't know what I'd do if anything happened to him. My dream for a lot of years has been to own my own restaurant, and I know that means I don't have time for a committed relationship. If the restaurant is my wife, Cyrano is our child. Until the business is more established, he's all I've got."

"Well, I was happy to help you both. I know I'd be heartbroken if either of my boys disappeared."

"Speaking of that, how are you doing with Doc being gone?"

"I meant my dog and cat, but since you mention it, I'm doing fine. It's actually a bit of a relief. Aiden's life has been in such turmoil since he returned from Africa last year that he wasn't really in a position to be in a relationship—with me or anyone else. Now, instead of being emotionally unavailable but physically present, he's not present on either count."

"I guess that makes sense. It just seemed like you two fit together. Even when things were tough, you seemed like a team."

"Looks can be deceiving, I guess. I always felt like I was on the outside looking in."

"Let's hope that's all behind you and things will be good when he gets back."

"Yeah, let's hope. In the meantime, I have a meeting to get ready for."

He unboxed the pastries, which were on stacked baking sheets.

"Preheat your oven to four hundred and then pop these in for about five or six minutes—just enough to crisp them up—then serve them warm." He looked out the kitchen window. "Your aunt just arrived. I better get back to the restaurant. I can stop by tomorrow and pick up my pans, or if Lauren is coming to your meeting, you could send them with her, since it's not that far out of her way."

"Thanks again for all this, and give your boy a hug from his auntie Harriet."

He picked up his empty boxes.

"Will do. Enjoy." He went out through the studio; Harriet could hear him greet her aunt as they passed at the outer doorway.

When she reached the kitchen, Beth looked around at the pastries lined up on the counters waiting for their turn in the oven.

"He's a useful one to have around." She shrugged out of her coat and hung it in the closet.

"He's grateful that I found his dog even though I'm pretty sure his neighbor would have returned Cyrano as soon as she realized her kids had kidnapped him. I was lucky enough to get there first, hence…" Harriet spread her hands and gestured around the kitchen. "…this bounty."

✂ --- ✂ --- ✂

Connie led the way from the dining room to Harriet's studio.

"I don't think I'll be hungry again until sometime tomorrow."

"Me, either," Mavis agreed.

DeAnn set her bag on the cutting table and pulled out several folds of fabric. She divided the pieces into two groups and pushed one pile to each end of the table.

"I tried to get colors that were close to what we drew up on the plan. I hope it's okay with everyone, but I saw a nice Civil War reproduction fabric in lavender, and I realized that might be a good way to make the quilts slightly different but essentially the same."

"Oh, honey, that's a great idea," Mavis said.

Connie spread out the fabric in front of her.

"How shall we do this? Should we have several big work days, or should we each make a few blocks?"

Robin, true to her background as a lawyer, pulled out a yellow legal tablet and a pen, ready to document whatever the group decided.

"We should be able to each take some of the fabric. Everyone here cuts and sews accurately enough it should all match up."

Mavis felt the edge of the fabric in front of her.

"I agree that we all know how to cut and sew accurately, but that isn't always enough. Remember that black-and-red quilt I made a few years back? I cut a bunch of the pieces at our meeting at the quilt store. My ruler had fallen out of my bag at home, so I used one of the ones Marjorie keeps on hand for people to borrow. It was a different brand than mine, and that quilt had a one hundred and twenty-two pieces in each block.

"You wouldn't think it would make that much of a difference, but the blocks I made from the pieces I measured with Marjorie's ruler were almost a half-inch smaller than the ones I'd made at home. Needless to say, I had to do them all over again."

"Even if we do a work day together, we would need to make sure we were using the same brand of ruler, and even then compare them to each other," Harriet pointed out.

The Threads began pulling out their calendars to figure out when they could meet again.

12

"Is your friend going to cook for us again?" DeAnn asked Harriet. "His pastries are—" She suddenly leaned sideways in her chair, looking past Connie and out the bow window. "I wonder what my sister is doing here."

Harriet got up and went to the door.

"One way to find out." She opened it just as a slender auburn-haired young woman reached the porch.

"Hi, I'm Harriet. You must be Molly, come on in."

DeAnn stood up as they approached the table.

"Molly, what are you doing here? Is everything okay?"

"No. I mean, yes. I…"

Mavis got up as well and went to the new arrival, leading her to a chair next to DeAnn.

"Why don't you come in and sit down. We'll get you a nice cup of tea and a pastry. Then you can tell us what's troubling you."

Aunt Beth went into the kitchen while Mavis was talking. Connie went to the instant-hot-water pot Harriet kept in her reception area, made a cup of tea and brought it back to Molly. Beth returned with one of James's pastries on a plate and set it on the table in front of her.

DeAnn was ripping the edge of her notepaper into little shreds, her foot tapping a silent rhythm on the floor.

"Are you comfy?" she asked glaring at Aunt Beth. "Is everything okay? How did you get that bruise on your jaw?"

Molly sipped her tea and set her mug down.

"My ex-boyfriend Josh clocked me."

"I'll kill him," DeAnn said.

"Did you hear me?" Molly said a little too loud. "He's my *ex*-boyfriend. He hit me, I called the police, they took him away, I took out a domestic violence order of protection, and the next day he was out and trying to make up with me."

"I'll kill him," DeAnn muttered again.

Lauren put her hand on DeAnn's arm.

"I don't think you're helping."

"He follows me to my office, I call the police. They warn him away, and two days later, he's sitting in his car across from my apartment, just beyond the three-hundred-yard requirement with a telephoto lens on his camera."

"Can't the police put him in jail?" Harriet asked.

Molly looked at her."I wish it were that simple. It seems like the only penalty for breaking the order is being chased away by the police. As long as he doesn't hit me again, they don't want to put him in jail."

DeAnn started to speak. Molly held her hand up.

"That's why I'm here. I decided since I need to be here for the event in a couple of weeks, I might as well come now. I can work from anywhere. I'm either on the computer and phone, or I'm traveling to other cities, so it doesn't matter where home base is."

Carla twirled a strand of hair around her finger.

"Won't he just follow you here?" Her cheeks turned pink, but she maintained eye-contact with Molly.

Molly chewed a bite of her croissant thoughtfully.

"He could. But so far, he does his stalking around his work hours, and since he works in Seattle, it will be harder for him. He may show up a time or two, but I'm staying at my parents'. I did stop by the Foggy Point Police Department on my way into town. I gave them a copy of the order and told them where I was staying as well as a description of his car and his license number."

"We know a good domestic violence shelter," Connie said.

"I'm nowhere near needing a shelter," Molly told her. "I promise you, he hit me once, and I told him it was one too many. We broke up on the spot, and the police hauled him away. I really think it will be okay. He's too lazy to drive all this way just to get back at me, anyway. He thinks he's irresistible to women. He'll have another girlfriend by the end of the week."

DeAnn's face brightened.

"I don't like the reason, but I'm glad you're here. The kids will be thrilled."

Molly finished her tea and pastry and stood up.

"I better go, I need to go get settled at Mom and Dad's." She gathered her purse and jacket and left.

"I need to leave early, too," Robin said. "Can we pick a date to meet again?"

After comparing schedules, the group decided they would meet on Thursday, three days hence, at Pins and Needles Quilt Shop, and Robin left. The remaining group began the process of pressing the fabrics and comparing their rulers before they began to cut the first fabric into five-inch-wide strips.

✂ --- ✂ --- ✂

Aunt Beth, Mavis and Lauren retreated to the kitchen while Harriet saw the rest of the Threads out. When she joined them, Lauren handed Harriet her purse and fleece jacket.

"We made an executive decision. Your aunt was pointing out that you haven't been out for lunch or coffee or anything else since you started your big job, so we thought we'd take you to the Steaming Cup for a hot cocoa or iced tea or something."

"Okay."

"Okay, what?" Lauren asked.

"Okay, I'll come out. My project is done, and I don't have to start my next job until tomorrow, at least."

Lauren looked at Mavis and Beth.

"That seemed way too simple."

Harriet laughed."I'm tired of me being home, too. In spite of the drama you all imagined, I really was just working hard." She looked at her aunt. "You should be proud of me for being so industrious. I got paid double my normal fee for rearranging my schedule and for accommodating their tight deadline."

"Oh, honey, we *are* proud of you," Mavis said. "We should have known you wouldn't shut us out if you were upset about Aiden."

"Shall I drive?" Harriet asked before another discussion about her relationship got started.

The Steaming Cup wasn't very busy when they arrived, so the barista waved them to a table after they'd ordered and delivered the drinks when they were ready.

Aunt Beth took her mug of black tea and sipped it.

"I don't know how you can drink cocoa after all the sweets we had this morning."

Harriet took her spoon and scooped a bite of whipped cream from her cocoa, licking it slowly, her eyes closed.

"Mmmmm, this is so good. I've been living on tomato soup and grilled cheese sandwiches for weeks. I've got a lot of lost ground to cover."

Lauren looked up from her own cup of cocoa.

"I have no excuse."

"So, what's the deal with DeAnn's sister?" Harriet asked.

"I didn't even know she *had* a sister," Lauren said.

Mavis twirled her spoon.

"No reason you would. Molly left home for college and didn't live here again from that point on. That would have been ten or fifteen years ago."

"I don't remember seeing her around here for holidays or anything," Lauren persisted.

Mavis and Aunt Beth exchanged a look.

"What?" Harriet asked.

Aunt Beth pressed her lips together before speaking.

"Something happened when Molly was a little girl. She wasn't more than five or six." She looked at Mavis for confirmation. Her friend nodded, and she continued, "She was playing with a neighbor girl…"

"Amber Price," Mavis supplied.

15

"No one knows what really happened. Molly was found wandering in Fogg Park by someone from the homeless camp."

"And Amber was never found," Mavis finished.

"Not ever?" Harriet asked in a hushed tone.

Beth and Mavis shook their heads.

Lauren pulled her tablet computer from her bag and tapped it awake. She entered Amber's name and read the results.

"Wow, looks like they've done a lot to try to find her. They even had that horse search group Texas EquuSearch come and everything." She was silent as she read more. "Looks like Molly has been pretty involved over the years in these searches."

Mavis and Aunt Beth looked at each other again.

"What aren't you telling us?" Harriet demanded.

Aunt Beth sipped her tea, stalling.

"Molly became pretty obsessed," she finally said. "After DeAnn and her brother went away to college, her parents moved the family to her stepdad's parents' farm in eastern Washington. The story was the grandparents were getting old and needed help. We all knew they were trying to get that little girl out of town and away from her obsession about Amber."

Aunt Beth picked up her tea again, and Mavis took up the story.

"The problem was, Molly couldn't remember anything. She didn't even remember that she went to Amber's house that day. She was sure if she could just recall what happened, they could find Amber and bring her home."

"Wow," Harriet murmured.

"No one was happy when she graduated college with a degree in social work and went to work for that missing children place." Mavis picked her mug up and held it to her lips. She set it down without taking a drink. "And now she's running the whole place."

"Don't DeAnn's parents own the video and game store here in town?" Harriet asked.

"They came back after Molly graduated college and went to work in Seattle. DeAnn had come back here and gotten married, and they figured they'd be having grandchildren, which, of course, they did," Beth explained.

"DeAnn's parents never wanted to be wheat farmers. They only went because Molly needed to be away from here," Mavis added. "And they really hoped she would study something that would take her away permanently when she got out of college."

"Wow," Harriet repeated.

Lauren leaned back in her chair.

"I wonder what happened to Amber Price."

"She seems to have vanished without a trace. I remember reading about it in the paper at the time," Beth said. "The police didn't have much to go on. One of the neighbors was a man who had been in some kind of trouble with the law. He was crucified in the press and everywhere else."

Mavis set her mug down again.

"Leo Tabor. That was the man's name."

Aunt Beth nodded.

"Back then, Foggy Point didn't have crime like we do now. We also didn't have as many police officers, and in any case, they never came up with anything, But Leo lost his job anyway. He proclaimed his innocence to anyone who would listen, but eventually, he left town, and that was the end of it."

Lauren tapped a note into her tablet.

"Just out of curiosity, I think I'll see what he's been up to for the last few decades."

"Seems like Molly has turned her tragedy into something positive with her work finding missing and exploited children," Harriet said.

Beth lifted her mug, but it was empty.

"Do you want a refill?" Lauren asked.

"No, I better get going. If I'm going to be working on these quilt blocks, I need to go home and finish the mailer I'm working on for the hospice fundraiser."

Mavis stood and picked up her purse.

"I've got a few loose ends to tie up myself."

Harriet looked at her aunt.

"Before you go, do you know why Carla was so red-faced during the meeting earlier when we were talking about Aiden?"

Beth stared down at the table before she spoke.

"Oh, honey, I'd hoped you didn't notice that."

"Not much gets by our Harriet," Lauren said, and Mavis glared at her.

"What?" Harriet asked.

Beth reached out and patted Harriet's hand.

"I think she was feeling awkward because she told us last week that Aiden calls home every week. He's checking on his dog and making sure there's enough money in the household accounts to pay the gardener and take care of whatever else upkeep needs to be done."

Harriet put on her jacket, grabbed her purse then picked up their empty mugs.

"I figured it was something like that." She carried the dishes to the bussing tub and went out to the car.

Chapter 3

Did I miss anything?" Lauren asked as she breezed into the large classroom at Pins and Needles three days later.

Harriet emerged from the shop kitchen carrying a tray with mugs and a basket of mixed tea bags on it.

"We all just got here ourselves. Do you want tea or coffee?"

Lauren set her quilting bag on the table at her customary spot.

"Tea would be great."

Connie followed Harriet into the room with a carafe of coffee in one hand and a kettle of hot water in the other.

Two ironing boards were set up at the back of the room, and Mavis and Beth were busy re-pressing the fabrics they would be cutting.

"We'll be a minute more," Beth said without turning around. "Drink your tea and entertain yourselves."

Lauren pulled her tablet from her bag.

"I've assembled a list of facts about human trafficking for us."

"Why?" Harriet asked.

"I figured since we're making quilts as prizes for the big donors at a fundraiser to make money for the missing-and-exploited organization, we should know whereof we stitch."

"Isn't that 'whereof we speak'?" Robin asked.

"Whatever. I wanted to know what we're supporting."

Mavis turned from her ironing board.

"We're supporting DeAnn and through her, her sister. That's enough for me."

Lauren looked at DeAnn.

"Of course I'm doing my share, no matter what, but since we have to kill some time…" She turned to look at Mavis and Beth. "…I thought you all might like to know a few fun facts about human trafficking."

"I'm interested," Carla said.

"Thank you. Question number one—Does anyone know which state was the first to criminalize human trafficking?" Lauren looked around the table. "DeAnn, you don't get to play because your sister probably told you already."

DeAnn rolled her eyes. "You have no idea."

"Anyone?"

Harriet raised her hand.

"Since you're asking, I'm going to guess Washington."

"Give that girl a Kewpie Doll. Now, a harder one—Which West Coast city ranks third highest in the country for sex trafficking?"

Robin twirled her pen between her fingers.

"The way you stated that question, I'm guessing it is a trick question."

"It's not Foggy Point," Connie said.

Lauren and Harriet laughed.

"I'm going to guess Seattle," Robin said.

"Correct you are," Lauren said. "With its international port and proximity to Canada and Asia, it's not surprising."

"Molly has told me a lot about missing and exploited children," DeAnn said. "And all kidding aside, I was shocked the first time she told me there are something like three hundred thousand young girls working in the sex trade each year."

Carla tapped on the front of her phone, opening the calculator function.

"Wow, if they were evenly spread over all fifty states that would be six thousand per state."

Mavis carried her pieces of fabric to the big table and laid them carefully across one end.

"Now that we've established it's a worthy cause, shall we begin working?"

Robin pulled out her legal pad.

"I think this might work better if we divide up into two teams, one for each quilt."

Harriet picked her bag up from the floor beside her chair.

"I'll vote for that. I think that will help prevent us from mixing up the fabrics when we get to the sewing stage."

"I like the idea, too." Lauren agreed."The lavenders are pretty similar, and so are the dark greens. I know one set is Civil War reproduction fabric and the other is contemporary floral, but their colors are close."

Robin wrote *Team One* and *Team Two* across the top of her paper.

"Does anyone care which team they're on?"

No one did, so she began writing names under the headings.

"Okay. How about Harriet, Lauren, Carla and Mavis on team one, and Beth, DeAnn, Connie and me on team two?"

"Sounds good to me," Harriet said.

The rest nodded agreement.

"Let's finish all the cutting today," Mavis said. "I brought gallon zip bags to put the strip sets into. That way, everyone can take a few bags home to start work on."

Aunt Beth held up a handful of three-by-five index cards.

"I marked these cards with a quarter-inch line. Each person should take one home and line the edge of the card up with the quarter-inch seam guide on your sewing machine. Lower your presser foot, and then the needle, and if the needle doesn't go through the line on the card, adjust your needle position until it does. This should insure that all our seams are the same."

Connie took her card and smiled at Beth.

"Thank you so much for doing this."

DeAnn picked up the pile of strips she'd cut and carried them to Connie, where they would be matched up with the other colors. She stopped and pressed her lips together before speaking.

"I apologize in advance for my sister. Beth and Connie and Mavis probably already know, but for any of you who don't, she's obsessed with figuring out something that happened to her and a friend when they were little.

"The friend disappeared when the two of them were playing and was never found. Lauren, she's likely to ask you for help with computer searches, Beth, Connie, and Mavis, she'll probably grill you guys about what was going on in Foggy Point all those years ago. Carla, I can only imagine what she might ask you, but believe me, she will ask."

"Don't worry, honey," Mavis told her. "We all understand about family."

"Anyone here hungry?" Jorge Perez, owner and head chef of Tico's Tacos, stood in the hall outside the classroom with two large insulated carry bags. "Señora Beth told me you were working so hard you wouldn't have time to take a lunch break. I decided to bring the food to you."

"Bless you," Connie said.

Lauren got up and went to the door.

"What do you have for us?"

She took one of the bags and carried it to the table. Jorge followed, set his bag beside hers, and they began taking foil-wrapped paper plates from the warm interiors.

"Just for variety, I made you chimichangas served on a bed of lettuce with a side of Mexican rice. The sauce is a mild red sauce, except for Señora Connie, who can take the heat." He said this last with a wicked smile. Connie had lived most of her life in Washington, but she'd been born in Cuernavaca, Mexico.

"I have a boneless, skinless chicken breast on a bed of vegetables for Robin, and extra guacamole for Lauren." He looked at the women seated around the table. "Have I missed anything?"

"Sounds like you've covered everything," Beth said with a smile. "As usual."

He smiled at her with a warmth reserved for her and her alone.

$\diagdown\!\!\!\propto$ --- $\diagdown\!\!\!\propto$ --- $\diagdown\!\!\!\propto$

Connie closed the box of gallon bags and handed it back to Mavis.

"The fabric is cut and bagged. Does everyone understand Beth's instructions about setting your quarter-inch seam?"

Heads nodded as everyone stood and began gathering their tools and fabric and stuffing them into their bags.

"Shall we meet again at our regular time on Tuesday?" Robin asked, pen and paper in hand.

DeAnn's phone rang before anyone could reply. She held it to her ear, listening.

"Okay, got it," she finally said and turned to the group.

"I hesitate to tell you what that was." She sighed deeply. "They've got a late entry to the ten-thousand-dollar-donation club."

Lauren sat back down.

"Oh, geez."

"I take it we're making another quilt," Harriet said.

Mavis sat down again, too.

"Well, if we can figure out the fabrics, we can each take some home and use the pieces we cut today as a guide to keep them the same size."

Marjory Swain, the owner of Pins and Needles, walked into the room.

"I wasn't trying to eavesdrop, but I couldn't help but hear your dilemma. I might have a solution. Given the color scheme you already have going on, I was thinking you could do nineteen-thirties reproduction fabrics. I have the solids that go along with them. I think there's a green that is dark enough for you, and there are multiple lavender prints, and prints with cream or white backgrounds. Would you like me to bring a few bolts in for you to look at?"

They did want, and within a few minutes, they had selected colors and Marjory had taken them into the store to cut. Lauren and Harriet followed her out to the front counter to wait for the fabrics.

"I guess it's good that more people are donating that much money to Molly's cause, but I'm going to be hard-pressed to get three quilts stitched in time for the event with the rest of my workload. I'll be back on tomato soup and grilled cheese sandwiches."

"Oh, wa-wa-wa," Lauren told her with a laugh. "You're not the only one with a real job. I can come help you do prep work, if that would help."

"Moral support will help," Harriet told her then took the stack of cut fabric from Marjory.

It took them another hour, but they cut the additional fabric and divided it between the two teams before they left for the day.

Chapter 4

"Here, let me help you," Harriet told Lauren, who was struggling to carry her sewing machine, a messenger bag that doubled as both a computer carrier and a purse, and her quilt bag up the porch steps to the studio. Harriet took the quilt bag and the messenger bag. "I have a place for you on the opposite side of the table from me."

She had set up two mobile sewing machine tables facing each other at the end of her large cutting table. She was thankful once again that her aunt had designed the quilt studio for maximum flexibility when she'd added the room to the large Victorian house Harriet now called home.

"Do you want some iced tea before we start? It's already made."

She pointed to the pie-crust table that sat between the two wing-back chairs in her customer reception area. A pitcher of tea sat on a quilted table mat, with glasses full of ice on either side.

"You"ll need another glass of ice. I invited Detective Morse to join us before we start stitching. If she lingers, we'll get her to press seams for us."

"I'm sure you have a good reason for inviting her to our sewing night. So, what is it?" Harriet poured tea into the two glasses.

"Go get the other glass of ice; and by the time you're back, she'll probably be here, and I can tell you both at the same time."

Sure enough, by the time Harriet returned, Jane Morse, sometime quilter and full-time Foggy Point PD detective, was sitting in the wingback chair opposite Lauren and sipping tea. Harriet pulled a wheeled work chair over and poured tea into the glass she'd brought.

"Okay, we're all here. Now will you tell us why we're talking instead of sewing our nine-patch blocks?"

Lauren reached into her messenger bag and pulled out her tablet computer.

"As we expected, DeAnn's sister asked me to help her with a computer search. I think I might be the first one she's asked." She looked at Detective Morse. "Do you know about DeAnn's sister?"

Morse shook her head. Harriet gave her a brief synopsis, ending with Molly's arriving early for her fundraising event and the Loose Threads' supposition she was going to involve all of them in her endless search for Amber Price and her own missing day.

"I know that name," Morse said. "When I switched to the cold case unit a couple of months ago, the team went through all the cold cases in Foggy Point for the last forty years. All of them are important, but we evaluate them for signs that the passage of time could help with their solution.

"For instance, sometimes, if a critical suspect has been jailed for something else or even died, witnesses who were afraid to testify before will speak to us. Often we already knew who the perpetrator was; we just needed a witness to recant an alibi or something like that.

"That being said, we looked at the Amber Price disappearance. We have nothing. No one saw anything. There was another child with her, but our notes say that child couldn't remember anything, even with help from a memory recovery specialist. I take it that child is DeAnn's sister?"

Lauren stood up and paced a few steps away before coming back.

"Half-sister," she corrected. "She's DeAnn's half-sister, but that's not actually what I asked you to come by for. Molly did ask me to help her dig for information about that time period in Foggy Point, but before I did that, I did my usual due diligence and ran a background check on Molly herself."

Harriet raised her eyebrows but didn't say anything.

"Hey, you never know. I didn't know if she'd go vigilante if I did find something about who took Amber Price. In my business, you can't be too careful."

"I thought you were a computer programmer and software designer," Morse interrupted.

"I am. That's my day job. You can't imagine how many people come to me for help digging things out of the web. Dark and white."

Morse glanced at Harriet, but Harriet just shrugged.

"Anyway," Lauren continued in an emphatic tone. "While I was talking to her, I casually asked her about her abusive ex-boyfriend. Josh Phillips is his name. I thought that might be useful to know, and, boy, was it.

"Anyway, I also dug around seeing what I could find out about her nonprofit. It seems on the up-and-up, by the way. When I was looking at the web page, it had been updated to reflect the three ten-thousand-dollar donors, but it said the new one wished to remain anonymous."

"Really," Harriet said.

"Really. It seemed a little fishy to me. Most people who donate that much want the publicity. Besides, this is Foggy Point. No one can keep that kind of secret. I thought it was possible it was someone out of our area, but if they're from Seattle, it seems like they'd donate at the event the organization has coming up *there* in another month. Anyway, let's just say I was curious."

She stopped by the table and sipped her tea.

"I'll admit this next part involved a bit of subterfuge." She glanced at Detective Morse. "I called the Seattle office of the non-profit and told the sweet girl who answered that we were personalizing the quilts and I needed the donor's name to put on the embroidered label. I swore I wouldn't reveal it until the quilt was awarded. She confirmed the donor would be attending the auction and dinner."

"And now you are going to betray that confidence?" Morse asked.

"I hadn't planned on it. I was curious, and I expected it to be someone who was publicity shy, or Molly's parents, or something like that."

Harriet leaned forward in her chair. "So, who is it?"

Lauren tapped her tablet awake and turned it toward Harriet and Jane. A photo of a large blond man in a plaid button-down shirt and tan chinos filled the screen.

"And that would be?" Harriet asked.

Lauren turned the pad back around.

"None other than Joshua Phillips."

"Whoa! Molly's abusive ex?" Harriet asked.

"Didn't I see an order of protection against him at the station?" Morse asked.

Lauren sat down and slid her tablet into her bag. Harriet leaned back in her chair.

"I see why you needed to tell someone," she said.

"I wonder if he got some kind of special release to attend the event," Morse said thoughtfully. She pulled a small notebook from her purse and wrote a note. "I'll see if he has friends in high places who might have helped him out a little."

"I thought you should know," Lauren said.

"For once I have to agree. I don't like you guys digging around in police matters, but this time it seems like you found something we would have missed. I'm sure Mr. Phillips was counting on that."

Harriet stood up.

"Want to stay and press seams for us?"

Morse looked at her watch.

"I can do that for an hour or so."

They carried their tea over to their workstations and began making squares for the quilts.

Chapter 5

In spite of spending the previous night stitching into the wee hours, Harriet got up early to go for a run.

"You two behave yourselves while I'm gone," she admonished Fred and Scooter, her cat and his canine protégé. Fred had spent the first few months of Scooter's presence ignoring the small rescue dog Harriet had adopted, and then graduated to terrorizing him.

It had been either a show of dominance by the cat or some sort of boot camp because the result had been a recent rash of team mischief. The cat opened cabinet doors and tossed things like protein bars down to the small dog, who then chewed the packages open so they could both eat the contents. She was contemplating the possibility of installing child-proof latches on the cabinets as she stepped outside and onto her driveway to stretch before her run.

She was touching her toes when she heard the crunch of gravel. She looked up and saw a white late-model sedan approaching. The car stopped, and Molly Baker got out. She was wearing new-looking jeans and a purple hoodie.

"I hope it's not too early to come by," she said.

"I was about to go running." Her intention should be obvious from how she was dressed and the fact she'd kept stretching, but she was hoping saying it would encourage Molly to keep it brief.

Molly came over and stood opposite her.

"I was talking to my sister last night, and she told me that you've solved a number of crimes in this area since you moved here."

Harriet was trying to think of an appropriate reply, but Molly held her hands up in a "hear me out" gesture.

"I know you're not a detective or anything—DeAnn told me. And she said you only investigated when it was someone you knew and the police were wrongly accusing them or something like that."

"That's all true. I don't want to be a detective, either. I'm a quilter. On a few occasions, when someone close to me has been threatened, I've asked a few questions and talked to a few people."

"And it resulted in the right person going to jail," Molly stated. "That's all I'm asking. The police say they've exhausted all evidence regarding Amber's disappearance, and they all tell me to be happy I survived and to go out and do something wonderful with that gift."

Harriet spread her feet apart and bent to touch her ankle with the opposite hand.

"That's not bad advice."

"I can't move forward until I know what happened. I mean, what if *I* did something to Amber. We were always climbing on trees and stuff. What if she fell and hit her head, and I got scared and hid her body."

Harriet straightened up and put her hands on Molly's shoulders.

"Molly, you were—what? Five years old? What five-year old could have pulled off that sophisticated of a plan? Besides, they probably searched with dogs. They would have found her. They found *you* miles away from where you were playing, in Fogg Park. You couldn't have walked that distance."

"I suppose. It doesn't ever go away, though." She balled her hands into fists and pressed them into her temples. "I have to know what happened."

Harriet sighed. "I'm not sure what I can do that the police haven't al-ready done, but I suppose I can see what Lauren turns up and go on from there."

Molly blushed. "I guess Lauren told you I asked her for help, too."

"Foggy Point is a small town, and the Loose Threads don't have many secrets from each other."

"I suppose not."

"Now, I really do have to go run."

"I'm sorry I kept you."

"No problem."

Molly got back in her rental car and drove away. Harriet looked at the sky and wondered what she'd just gotten herself into.

Harriet couldn't help but notice that her ten-pound weight loss made running up her hill a lot easier. She wanted to think she could keep it off, but her aunt's Jekyll-and-Hyde behavior when it came to food would make that difficult. One minute Beth was admonishing her about her gluttonous eating habits and the next was bringing over her latest dessert concoction. She never knew which version of her aunt would walk through the door when they got together.

Her phone interrupted her musings.

"Hello?"

"Can you go with me to a wiener dog race meeting?" asked James. "We could go for coffee and then the meeting. I'd come get you in about an hour."

Harriet did a quick mental review of her day's schedule.

"I can do that."

"See you in an hour."

She stared at her phone for a minute after the screen went dark. James's sister was his usual partner in dog racing, but Harriet had subbed for her once before when she'd had to miss a race due to her child's illness. It was curious he hadn't mentioned what the problem was. She slid her phone into her pocket and walked the remainder of the way to her house.

Harriet came outside and locked her studio door when James pulled into the driveway.

"Thanks for coming with me on such short notice," he said as she climbed into the passenger seat.

"Is Maggie sick? Or one of the kids?"

James hesitated before answering then blew out a breath through his teeth.

"Something is going on with her, and I'm not sure what, but it isn't good. She resigned from Team Cyrano. The whole wiener dog race thing was her idea in the first place. Now she doesn't want to be away from home—at all."

"How are things with her husband?"

"She won't talk to me about him. But then again, she's always been tight-lipped about her relationships. We'd only met her husband a few times when she announced they were getting married. I see her, and I see my niece, but we never see Dan." He turned the car on. "Whatever's going on, the net result is Team Cyrano is down a member."

Harriet looked at her hands. She had a feeling James wasn't going to come out and say it, but he was clearly asking her to replace his sister on the race team.

"How much of a time commitment would it be?"

James smiled as he guided his brown BMW SUV toward the Steaming Cup.

✂ --- ✂ --- ✂

"The whole idea of the wiener dog races, besides having fun, is marketing," he said when they were seated and had their drinks in front of them. "It gives the participants an inexpensive way to promote their businesses. You may have noticed the team shirts all have sponsor names on the back.

"In our case, my restaurant is the sponsor. There are social events before race day, and our Northwest organizing committee is even talking about a sister-city type program between the towns that hold the qualifying races. Today's meeting is for sponsors and teams to sign up and to discuss the first event. We don't have to stay for the whole thing."

Harriet laughed. "So, this…" She gestured at the table.".…was all a set-up? Why didn't you just tell me you need me to sign on?"

He had the good grace to blush.

"If I'd asked you right off the bat, you might not have gotten in the car. I know you have a weakness for chocolate."

Harriet looked down at the cocoa he'd ordered for her without asking.

"Here I thought you were just an unassuming nice guy. I'm going to have to file this away for future reference. 'James is more devious than he looks.'"

"Have I heard a yes in there yet? I brought along a box of my home-made truffles. Do I need to deploy them?"

"Yes, I'll help you, and yes, you definitely need to deploy the truffles."

James sat back in his chair.

"Boy, you are one tough negotiator."

"Now, it's your turn. I need some help with something."

"Uh-oh. Am I going to have to pay the price for my manipulations?"

"This won't be hard. You grew up in Foggy Point, right?"

"I've been here my whole life, except for the ten years when I went to culinary school and then my apprenticeship in New York."

"What I'm going to ask you took place before that. Do you remember when a little girl named Amber Price disappeared? You would have been in your teens when it happened, I think."

He stared out the window.

"I think I do remember that. Wasn't there another girl who was found but couldn't tell them what happened?"

"Yes, that's the case. It turns out the one who survived is my friend DeAnn's half-sister. According to DeAnn, her sister has had a lifelong obsession about it. She's here in town for a fundraiser right now—she works for a

30

non-profit that deals with missing and exploited child cases. She's starting to ask our quilt group members to help her."

"If the police couldn't figure it out then, what are you supposed to do all this time later?"

Harriet took a sip of chocolate and set her mug down.

"You begin to see my problem. Since she's DeAnn's sister, I have to try. Lauren is digging on the Internet, and I said I'd ask around."

James leaned toward her.

"Maybe I *can* help. My mom has a friend who lives in that neighborhood and has forever. I didn't pay much attention at the time, but they talk about everything, so if there was any talk on the street, my mom probably knows."

"Can you ask her?"

"It'll be better if I hook you two up. If *I* ask, she'll talk for thirty minutes, and I won't remember it all, and half the stuff won't even relate to the question at hand."

"That would be great...I think."

"So, what are you quilting on this week?" he asked her, changing the subject.

They discussed her stitching and his new menu items, and before she knew it, they were leaving for the race meeting.

✂ --- ✂ --- ✂

Harriet was looking forward to a quiet evening of takeout and binge-watching a British mystery series on TV. The only decision was which cuisine it would be. She pulled a collection of menus from her kitchen drawer and spread them out on the countertop.

Fred rubbed against her ankle, and she reached down and scratched his ears.

"What do you vote? Do you want to lick up after Thai?" She looked at him for any indication of interest.

"I hope you're talking to one of your pets," Mavis said as she came in from the studio carrying a covered dish.

"Did we have a plan I don't remember?" Harriet rocked back on her heels. "Please tell me this isn't another intervention. Is Aunt Beth on her way? No offense, but I can't do this again."

Mavis's shoulders sagged as she walked past Harriet to the stove, where she set her dish down.

"I can just leave this with you, then." She started for the door.

"Wait. I'm sorry." She stepped over and put her hand on Mavis's shoulder. "I'm sorry," she repeated. "Let me take your coat. Come in."

31

The older woman shrugged out of her light jacket and hung it in the coat closet.

"Maybe I am being too pushy. I saw your face the other day when you found out Aiden's been calling Carla every week. I just thought...well...I thought you might not want to be alone on a Friday night."

"I appreciate your thoughtfulness, but I'm talked out when it comes to Aiden. I know it's terrible, what his sister did to him. I know he has to recover, but once again, he's choosing to do that alone, without me. I understand that, I really do. The whole year he and I have known each other, he's had terrible things happen, and it's all been done by people who supposedly love him.

"He and I met and fell in love, but it wasn't enough. At every turn, he chose to shut me out. I know it's probably selfish, but I want to come first. I want to put him first in my life, and I want him to put me first in his."

"Oh, honey, that's not selfish, that's how it should be."

They stood in silence for a long moment. Harriet looked over at the foil-covered dish.

"So, what did you bring?"

"It's my famous chili-cheese-dog casserole. You should pop it in the oven for about fifteen or twenty minutes—it probably cooled a little on the drive over, and it's best piping hot."

"I'll make us tea while it warms up. I was planning on binge-watching *Black Coat* tonight. The new season started three weeks ago, and I haven't gotten to watch any of them yet. If you haven't seen them I think I'd like some company."

Mavis brightened. "Oh, honey, I haven't—my cable's been on the fritz, and they had to order me a new box. I'd love to stay and watch if you really don't mind."

"Say no more. It's a small price to pay for dinner delivered to my door."

"If you have a little lettuce, I can throw a salad together."

"I can do you one better. I've got salad in a bag."

Mavis smiled. "Perfect."

Chapter 6

Harriet was munching on an antacid when Mavis arrived the next morning. She slid the roll of tablets into her jeans pocket.

"Good morning, and thanks again for bringing dinner last night."

"You don't have to hide those Tums. I know I got it a little too spicy last night."

"But it tasted so good."

"It did, but hand 'em over. I could use one myself."

Harriet laughed and did as she was told.

"How many blocks did you finish," she asked.

Mavis pulled a stack of nine-patch blocks from her bag and set them on the kitchen counter.

"I finished ten."

"As Lauren would say, 'Aren't you the overachiever'."

"Well, honey, I knew you had to get back to machine stitching on your regular customers' quilts, and Lauren has *her* day job, and Carla has that little girl and big house to take care of. I figured I'd take the pressure off the rest of you. Besides, it was nice to just stay home and sew."

Lauren had joined them as Mavis was speaking.

"How very thoughtful of you. And perceptive. Harriet and I worked together, and even with Jane Morse pressing seams for us, we still only got ten done between us."

Harriet looked out the kitchen window.

"Carla's arriving. Let's go to the studio. I'm dying to know if all our careful measuring resulted in blocks that are the same size."

"How can you even question it?" Lauren asked.

33

"That would be 'experience with our group'," Harriet shot back.

Mavis shooed them through the connecting door and into the studio.

"You two behave yourselves, Carla's about to walk in."

Mavis opened the door to let their youngest member in. Carla's black hair was pulled back from her face and braided.

"Oh, honey, your hair looks cute pulled back like that."

Carla blushed.

"Wendy kept fighting me about putting her hair up or in barrettes or pretty much any way except hanging down. I finally realized she was trying to look like me. So, now I'm braiding my hair every day, and most days now she doesn't argue about hers."

"Well, whatever the reason, I like it." Mavis told her.

Carla set her bag on the cutting table and pulled out a stack of blocks.

"I only got five blocks done," she announced. "Our kitchen sink got all plugged up, and I ended up having to call the plumber last night. He had his puppy with him, and Wendy played with it while he snaked our drain. She was so excited she didn't go to sleep until ten. All she could do was talk about 'puppy'."

Harriet put her blocks on the table next to Carla's.

"I only got five done, too, and my excuse isn't nearly as fun as a puppy."

Lauren pulled hers out.

"What she said."

Mavis joined them at the cutting table.

"We're in good shape. We only need thirteen more nine-patch blocks. With four of us here, we should be able to do that today and probably cut them all up, too."

Harriet gathered the individual stacks of blocks and started piling them into a single group.

"Let's not prolong the agony." She lined up the edges of two blocks. "Well, look at that."

Lauren leaned in for a closer look, and then held her hand up to Carla for a high-five.

"Just like I said, they match perfectly." She laughed.

Harriet smiled.

"Yeah, just like you said."

Mavis selected two rotary cutters from a box on the work room shelf and handed them to Harriet and Lauren.

"Here, you two cut strips, and Carla and I will sew and press them."

✂ --- ✂ --- ✂

Harriet arched her spine and put a fist in her lower back. She and Lauren had cut all the basic strips and were now cutting the seamed units Carla and Mavis were making into rectangles.

"Anyone ready for a break? I have a box of lemon cookies and could make tea."

Lauren stood her iron on its heel.

"Count me in."

Carla got up from her sewing machine and arched backward at the waist. She paused and looked out the window.

"Who's that?" She pointed to a blue car coming up the driveway.

Harriet came to her side and looked where she was pointing.

"I don't recognize the car or the guy driving it, but that looks like De-Ann's sister Molly in the passenger seat."

Her guess was confirmed when Molly got out of the car and approached the door, followed by a slight, dark-haired man.

"I'll go get the cookies," Mavis said.

"Come on in," Harriet said as she opened the door. "You remember Carla and Lauren."

Molly raised her hand slightly and wiggled her fingers in acknowledgment and then stepped to the side, revealing her companion.

"This is my friend Stewart Jones. We crossed paths at the Foggy Point missing children's office. I'm borrowing office space there until the fundraiser."

"Nice to meet you," Harriet said and then looked at Molly. "We were just taking a break from sewing on the donor quilts. Would you like to join us?"

Molly and Stewart agreed, so she led them to the kitchen, followed by Lauren and Carla. Mavis had pulled the kitchen table from its normal position against the wall so they could use all six chairs.

"So, what's *your* interest in Amber Price," Mavis asked Stewart when introductions were complete and the reason for the unannounced arrival explained.

"Well," he said slowly, "she is, or was...would have been...my foster sister. Sandra Price was my foster mom until I aged out of the system, but I came to live with her after Amber had already disappeared. That family did so much for me, I guess my hope is if I can finally give them some kind of closure about Amber, it will in some small way pay them back for all the support and kindness and everything they've done for me."

Molly cleared her throat.

"Speaking of Amber, the reason we came by is to see if you've had a chance to investigate."

"I think you're overestimating my powers as a detective," Harriet protested."Besides…" She glanced around the table at her friends. "…we've been spending our free time making the donor quilts for your fundraiser."

"I'm sorry, I knew that. And I know I only asked you yesterday. I'm just so desperate for answers. I feel like this has been hanging over my head my whole life." Tears filled her eyes, and Stewart Jones reached over and put his hand on hers.

"So, what do you do?" Mavis asked him, giving Molly a chance to compose herself.

The tea kettle whistled, and Harriet got up to retrieve it. She poured hot water into cups for everyone and carried them to the table, two at a time. When she was finished, she got a small basket of mixed tea bags from the cupboard.

Stewart looked up at her as she handed him the basket.

"I'm a poet. And before you ask, yes, I'm published, and, no, it doesn't pay the bills. I work as a convenience store clerk at that store down by McDonald's. Out on the highway."

Molly sniffled and dabbed at her nose with a crumpled tissue.

"I've read his work. It's really very good."

Carla passed the plate of cookies across the table to Molly and Stewart, and they busied themselves selecting a couple and passing the plate on to Lauren.

"I've started researching Amber's disappearance," Lauren told them. "So far, I'm learning a lot of background information. Pretty much all the theories that didn't pan out."

Mavis set her cup down.

"So, Stewart, how did you happen to be at the missing children's place? I mean, Amber's been gone for a long time."

He leaned back in his chair.

"You're right—the Carey Bates Missing and Exploited Children's Organization was only formed five years ago. Twelve-year-old Carey Bates went missing from Foggy Point, only to be found being sold as a prostitute in Seattle. They brought her home, but she ran away repeatedly until one time she didn't come home. She had died of a drug overdose in her pimp's hotel room.

"I heard about them the first week they opened, and I went to let them know about Amber. I've checked in with them once a month ever since."

Harriet leaned forward.

"Have they ever had anything for you?"

He hung his head and closed his eyes briefly before looking back at her.

"They've done age progression pictures every year. They post them on missing children sites, but so far, nothing has turned up."

"I was glad Stewart was there," Molly said. "My ex, Josh, showed up to deliver his donation to the fundraiser. It was terrible." Her face turned red as she spoke. "Can you imagine? *He* took out a restraining order against *me*!"

"What?" Harriet asked.

"I know, right?" Molly continued. "He got a judge somewhere to believe that he—all six-foot-three, two hundred-and-sixty pounds of him—was abused by *me*. It's a nightmare."

Lauren took a sip of her tea and set her cup down.

"So, what happened?"

"He drove up and parked in front of the office, and then had his attorney, who was conveniently in the car with him, come in and demand I leave so he could safely come inside and make his donation."

"That takes some nerve," Mavis said.

"I was lucky Stewart had come in just before that. I was in my office, and I got so upset I couldn't even speak." She looked at Stewart. "Stew took me by the hand and led me out the back so I didn't have to see Josh. We went to the coffee shop and talked for hours. When we went back by the office he was gone."

Harriet got up to get the box of cookies to refill the empty plate.

"He just conveniently had his attorney with him?" she asked.

Molly took a cookie from the proffered plate and took a bite. Stewart answered for her.

"Supposedly, his attorney is also his AA sponsor."

"You don't believe him?" Lauren asked.

"He told the secretaries in the office his whole long sob story about how his life had fallen apart when his girlfriend had become abusive. He told them he'd begun drinking excessively, and one night he'd seen one of those reality shows on TV where families do interventions on their substance-abusing loved ones. He realized he was disappointing his mother, so he stopped drinking cold turkey and called AA the next morning."

Harriet was twirling her teaspoon between her fingers. Her hand froze.

"Wait. This doesn't make sense. If Molly was so abusive to him, why is he in Foggy Point donating all this money to her fundraiser?"

Molly took up the story.

"He claimed he was doing it to try to help me. He said he hoped if they found out what had happened to Amber, I could…" She made air quotes with her fingers. "…recover—I guess."

"That was big of him," Mavis said. "He was going to help you stop being an abuser? That's got to be a first."

Molly's shoulders pulled up toward her ears, and her jaw tensed. Mavis looked at her.

"Honey, we all know you're not an abuser. Anyone can see that. Never you mind what your crazy ex says about you. He's doing all those theatrics to try to get a reaction from you. It'll be hard, but your best move is to ignore him."

"That's what DeAnn said when I called her."

"She's right," Harriet told her.

Mavis stood up.

"I don't mean to chase you out of here…" She stopped for a moment and smiled. "I guess I do mean to chase you out of here. If we're going to manage another quilt, we need to get back in the studio and finish the one we're working on."

Molly stood up and carried her mug to the sink.

"I've got to go back to work, too. Hopefully, Josh left when he realized I was gone."

Stewart picked up his keys from the table where he'd set them.

"If his car is there again, we'll drive on by, and I'll take you home or wherever you want to go."

Carla cleared the rest of the table while Harriet and Mavis escorted their guests through the studio and out the door. Lauren pulled out her tablet as soon as they were gone.

"What are you doing?" Harriet asked when she returned.

"We have a new player in the mix. I figured I'd take a quick look and see if anything popped."

Harriet stopped folding the inner bag in the cookie box.

"And?"

Carla came over from the sink, drying her hands on a towel. Lauren spun her tablet around so they could see what she'd found.

"He wasn't lying about being a poet. He's got three books published by a small but respected publishing house. He has a schedule of readings listed." She pointed with her finger to a calendar on the webpage. "Looks like he stays on the West Coast. Mostly the Northwest, it seems."

She clicked the sleep button on the side of the tablet, and the screen went dark.

"It would appear he's who he says he is."

Harriet closed the cookie box and returned it to the cupboard.

"I'm glad, for Molly's sake."

Carla folded the kitchen towel and set it on the counter.

"Me, too. Seems like she's got her hands full with that other guy."

Mavis popped her head in from the studio.

"Are you three going to do any more quilting today?"

Harriet led the way back to rejoin her.

"We've got to hustle if we're going to make another quilt," she scolded. "Before we go home, we need to finish the rest of the nine-patch blocks and cut them into fourths. That way we can decide how we want to re-arrange them, and each of us can take some home and sew them together. If everything works right, we'll each have one-quarter of the quilt top finished next time we meet."

Lauren picked up her ruler and started lining it up over a strip set.

"What are we going to do about the third quilt?"

Mavis looked up from her sewing machine.

"Beth is going to stop by on her way home to give us a progress report for her group. If they're at the same point we are, we'll divide the third batch of fabric, and each team will make half a quilt top."

"Geez," Lauren grumbled. "Some of us have real jobs, too."

Harriet looked over at her.

"Hey, stop feeling sorry for yourself. I've got to quilt all these as we fin-ish. And *I* have a day job, too."

"Yeah, yeah, yeah."

Lauren focused on making a precise slice through the fabric, and that was the end of that discussion.

Chapter 7

Lauren was taking pictures of the block layout they'd agreed on when Aunt Beth arrived.

"Looks like great minds think alike," she announced when she saw the arrangement of blocks on the cutting table.

Harriet joined her aunt and studied the layout.

"Is your group at this point, too?"

"We didn't finish all our nine-patch blocks, but we went ahead and cut what we had into fourths. We only need five or six more parent blocks. Connie is going to do them tonight, and she can catch up to the rest of us in sewing them together. DeAnn's had a few family obligations with her sister being home."

"Are you busy Monday?" Harriet asked.

"I have to get my tire fixed first thing, then I'm going to be sorting clothes in the church clothes closet for the rest of the day."

"Can I borrow your car while you're working? Mine needs to go in for a brake job. They said they have the parts on hand and can finish it in one day if I bring it in early."

Mavis gathered the blocks into four stacks after Lauren had finished taking a reference picture. She stopped and looked at her friend.

"What's wrong with your tire?"

"It appears someone slashed it."

"*What?*" Harriet said, louder than she'd intended. "When did this happen? Why didn't you tell me?"

Lauren put her phone in her pocket and bumped Harriet with her elbow.

40

"We might find out if you'd stop asking questions and let the woman speak."

Beth glanced at Lauren and then back to Harriet. She sighed.

"We better sit down for this."

Harriet turned and led the way to the kitchen.

"How about iced tea this time?"

"Works for me," Lauren said. She went to the cupboard and dug around until she found a box of ginger snaps.

Carla glanced at her watch.

"I have to go pick Wendy up in about twenty minutes."

"This won't take that long," Beth assured her.

"The situation is complicated," Aunt Beth began when everyone was seated around the table with a glass of tea and a cookie. "Jorge has a customer who has had a major crush on him for a lot of years. He has done nothing to encourage it, but she comes into the restaurant almost every day."

Lauren leaned forward. "Is she that lady who always wears a fluorescent pink tube top that's about three sizes too small, even in the dead of winter?"

"Now, honey," Beth scolded. "We shouldn't make fun of those less fortunate than us."

"I'm not making fun, I'm stating fact. I don't know how she doesn't end up with frostbite in the winter."

"Her name is Juana. Juana Lopez-Montoya," Beth continued. "She has an imaginary romance with Jorge. She tells people in the restaurant that she's his fiancée, and they're getting married in the spring. Most people understand the situation, so no one pays her any mind. The problem is, she apparently sees me as a romantic rival and has been telling everyone who will listen that I'm trying to steal 'her man'.

"Jorge has gone to talk to the people at the group home she lives in, but they haven't made any headway. They can't stop her from going out, and they can't convince her that she's not marrying Jorge."

"That's pretty awful." Harriet said and sipped her tea.

Beth took a bite of cookie.

"She stepped her game up today. This morning, I found my front tire was slashed. Bernice across the street saw her by my car when she went out to get her paper. She went over to see what was going on. Juana took off on her tricycle, but the damage was already done."

"Did you call the police?" Carla asked.

"Bernice called before she called me. They said they'd have an officer go have a talk with her and her social worker. They suggested I park my car in the garage instead of the driveway."

Lauren laughed. "Well, that would have been more helpful advice *before* she slashed your tire."

Mavis wrapped her napkin around the base of her glass before she picked it up.

"It's a tough situation. No one wants to see Juana put in jail or the state mental hospital. She doesn't fit the profile for either place, and most of the time she does well enough. Her mother's in hospice with lung cancer. I've seen her a few times with Pastor Hafer. There don't seem to be any other relatives. Juana was working at the shelter workshop, but they lost one of their bigger contracts so she's been laid off until they can get more work in."

"That's awful," Harriet said. "I feel for her, but that doesn't make it okay for her to go after my aunt." She clenched her teeth for a second. "What if she'd decided to slash *you* instead of the tires?"

"Beth can get a restraining order, if she hasn't already." Lauren drank a swallow of tea.

"Yeah, look how well that worked out for Molly," Harriet shot back.

"I did fill out the paper work for a restraining order, but I doubt a piece of paper is going to make a difference to a lovesick woman."

Carla took her glass to the sink.

"We probably should ask Robin. Maybe she can do something legal with Juana's social worker, so they have to take more responsibility for her."

Mavis smiled at her with approval.

"That's a good idea."

"In the meantime, to answer the original question…" Aunt Beth turned her attention to Harriet. "If you'll meet me at the tire place first thing Monday morning, they can put my new tire on, and I can follow you to your car place. We can drop your car, and you can drive me to the church. Then, my car is all yours until four o'clock."

"Works for me."

Mavis stood up.

"I'll divide the fabric up for the third quilt tonight, and then I can pass it out to everyone after church. Everybody going to be there?"

"Wouldn't miss it," Lauren said, and the rest of the group agreed.

$\times$ --- $\times$ --- $\times$

Sunday morning was blue-sky beautiful in Foggy Point. The temperature was mild enough the Loose Threads had left their customary fleece and rain jackets at home and were able to gather outside the main doors to the church.

Mavis opened a large flowered bag and started pulling gallon plastic zipper bags from its interior and handing them to each of her group members.

"I divided the fabric evenly so each of us will be making four parent nine-patch blocks. I'll make the extra one. I was thinking, if everyone agrees, we can cut them and then sew the daughter blocks in the same setting we used on the other quilts. That way we'll only need to do a couple more seams when we get them back together."

Carla looked at her bag and then back up at Mavis.

"Are we going to put a border on any of them?"

"Good question," Lauren said, causing Carla's cheeks to redden. "I looked on the Internet and there's no clear precedent. Some people do, some don't."

"Maybe we should wait until we have the tops together," Harriet suggested. "Do we have enough of any of the fabrics we're already using for the blocks?"

"We have plenty of the green left on this last one," Mavis said.

"I think that's true for all three of them, but I agree, we need to see how they look when the tops are together," Beth suggested. "Green may not look best. Unless there was a run on our lavender or creme choices, we should be in good shape. The bolts were new or nearly so when we bought the fabric."

Robin tucked her fabric into her shoulder bag.

"If that's settled, I've given some thought to Beth's predicament."

The Threads who knew about the tire slashing interrupted her for a moment to explain the situation to those who didn't.

"Okay to continue?" she asked finally, and everyone stopped talking. "I think I'd like to talk to Juana's social worker tomorrow. First of all, she needs to attempt to counsel the woman about her behavior. But second, I'd like to suggest that they find her something to do at the shelter workshop as an alternative to us pressing criminal charges against her. I know they lost a contract, but I think they'll make an exception."

Aunt Beth sighed.

"Oh, honey, that's a brilliant solution. I don't want them to take her to jail, but she can't be left to do who-knows-what else if they don't do *something*."

"While I'm talking to the social worker, I'll ask if they can put any sort of tracker on Juana. I know that sort of device is available for dementia patients. Maybe they could put something in her purse so they can tell if she's headed out your way."

Harriet nudged her aunt.

"I'd still park in the garage," she said in a quiet tone.

"I would, but my door clicker doesn't work anymore," Beth replied.

Lauren leaned in from Beth's other side.

"I'll come over and check it out. You might just need a new battery. Will you be home later?"

Beth agreed she would as the rest of the group went back to debating the border vs. no border issue then eventually left to begin the rest of their Sunday.

Chapter 8

Harriet was feeling pleased with herself. The Honda dealership had called to see if she was going to need a ride in the courtesy shuttle they provided. She was able to leave her car and get a ride to Aunt Beth's early enough to try out the new coffee cake recipe that had just come out of her oven.

"What are you doing here so early?" Beth asked.

She explained the change in plans and settled at her aunt's kitchen table.

"I'm guessing Lauren got your garage door fixed, since I don't see your car."

"It was crazy. She brought a can of lubricant and sprayed it on those rail things the door rolls into. All of a sudden, my door opener worked."

Harriet smiled.

"She's a technical wizard, that one. I'm assuming Jorge put your spare tire on last night. If not I better go out and do that."

"Of course he did. And you shouldn't make fun of Lauren," Beth scolded. "She's very handy, and you know I like to keep things in working order."

"She can take it. And since when did you start closing your garage door?" Harriet took a forkfull of coffee cake. "This is really good."

"I'm learning from Jorge. Everything's better with butter, according to him."

"He may be on to something."

"Speaking of being on to something, do you have any ideas about Molly's problem?"

"Not really. It's on my list today to check in with Lauren and see if she's been able to find anything out about Leo Tabor. He's that guy that was run out of town for being a sex predator right after Amber disappeared."

"I think that would be barking up the wrong tree."

"Why do you say that?"

"He worked at The Vitamin Factory for Avanell. Well, not directly for Avanell, but she knew him."

Avanell was Aiden's mom and Aunt Beth's best friend next to Mavis. She'd died the previous year.

"So, what did she say about him?"

Aunt Beth rubbed her finger up and down over the curve of her teacup handle.

"She couldn't exactly say anything, being that he worked at her company and anything he might have revealed to her would have been confidential."

"Okaaay." Harriet drew the word out. "What did she say to make you think he didn't have anything to do with Amber?"

"She said she couldn't tell me what had really gone on with him, but things were not what they seemed regarding his sexual predator conviction. He told her how it came about, and she believed him. She said there was evidence to support what he'd told her, but again, it was all confidential."

"That's all very mysterious."

"I know she felt strongly enough about it that she told me she gave him a good severance check and a glowing recommendation when she couldn't talk him into to staying."

Harriet tilted her chair back.

"Well, heck. He was my only line of inquiry so far."

Beth pursed her lips.

"Don't get all riled up. He might still be a source of information if you handle it just right."

"I'll be the soul of discretion." The front chair legs thumped as she leaned forward."Tell me more."

"One of the reasons the police questioned him in the first place is because he'd taken Amber to the station before. He lived one street over on the corner where the neighborhood street crossed a much busier Stephens Street. Apparently, Amber was always wandering around, and he'd brought her back to her house more than once.

"Finally, one day he drove her to the police station and told them maybe they could convince her mother to keep her home before she got run over."

"Do you think this could be as simple as she got run over, and some-one panicked and hid the body? I mean, we know the girls were playing together. Maybe they were both hit, Amber was killed, and Molly was un-conscious. Whoever did it could have buried Amber and left Molly near the homeless camp where she would be sure to be found."

Beth toyed with the edge of her napkin.

"I suppose anything's possible. Without anyone finding Amber's body in all these years, though, I'm not sure how you'd prove it. Beyond that, I don't know how you'd figure out who did it. It's been something like twenty years."

Harriet rested her chin in her hand and stared out the window.

"I assume Molly was in the hospital after they found her. Did she have a head injury?"

Aunt Beth looked up at the ceiling as she thought. Finally, she shook her head.

"I just don't remember. It's been so long. I would have thought DeAnn would say something if her sister'd had any permanent damage from a head injury."

"I think I'll check with Detective Morse and see if they considered the accident possibility."

"If that girl got hit in the head, it might explain a lot."

Harriet took her plate and cup to the sink and rinsed them off.

"We better get moving. You've got clothes sorting, and I've got chores, and we need a new tire before we can do either one."

Chapter 9

"What are you doing here at this time of day?" Harriet asked Lauren as she sat down opposite her at the computer table in the Steaming Cup.

"I'm trying to work."

Harriet picked up her frappuccino.

"I can move."

"Sit down. It's not you. I'm done doing anything productive anyway. For reasons unknown, the boat sales people below my apartment are working on a motor in the parking lot. They have a repair shop out on Miller Hill so why they're working in the parking lot today I'll never know. It involves a lot of motor revving, which makes it impossible for me to work. I put my earphones on, but I could feel the vibration, and I swear I could hear it a little bit, too."

"Hopefully, it'll only be for today."

"They better be done when I get home. Enough about me, what are *you* doing out and about?"

"Catching up on everything I put off while I was doing those quilts. My car's in the shop, my dining room drapes are at the cleaners, I picked up Scooter's prescription dog food, took my cans to the recycling depot... need I go on?"

"Sounds awful."

"It felt good to get some things done. I started the day at my aunt's. I've got her car while my brakes are being fixed. Anyway, she told me a little more about Leo Tabor."

"The pedophile who was run out of town on a rail?"

"Yeah, only Aunt Beth says that Avanell told her things were not as they seemed. She didn't tell her what, but she was on Leo's side. Then she said apparently, Leo had found Amber wandering the neighborhood on numerous occasions and finally took her to the police when she was out on the main road by herself."

Lauren picked up her coffee and took a sip.

"So, maybe she was run over?"

"Yeah, that was my thought. Amber is killed, Molly gets knocked out, someone gets scared and covers it up."

"It's still bad, but not nearly the sort of bad Molly is thinking."

Lauren tapped a few keys on her laptop.

"I did a little digging on him after we talked last time."

She turned the computer around so Harriet could see her notes on the screen.

"He came back to Foggy Point. He and his wife worked overseas for six years—she's a teacher, and they both taught English in Thailand. Looks like they rented their house out and then moved back in when they came back. It appears they're retired now."

"Aunt Beth thought he might be willing to talk to us if we approached it right."

Lauren smiled.

"You know I'm the soul of tact. As my mother always said, 'a closed mouth gathers no foot.' Speaking of which, don't turn around, but the happy couple just walked in and headed to a corner table."

"Which happy couple?"

"Molly and her published poet."

Harriet rolled her eyes to the ceiling and blew out a breath.

"Are you free now? If you are, maybe we can swing by Leo's and see what he thinks about the accident theory."

"I'm done here."

"Let's get out of here before Molly notices us. I don't think I can do another 'No, I haven't found out anything yet' conversation."

✂ --- ✂ --- ✂

Leo Tabor lived in an older, well-kept yellow house with a small front yard bordered by landscaped flowerbeds. A white picket fence extended on either side of an arched, gated entry. Harriet lifted the latch and led the way to the covered porch.

A chubby balding man dressed in khaki work clothes opened the door when she knocked.

"Can I help you?"

"My name is Harriet Truman, and this is my friend Lauren Sawyer. We're friends of a woman named Molly Baker, and she's asked us to look into an incident that happened when she was a small child."

Leo—Harriet assumed that's who he was—stiffened, and his jaw muscles tightened. He slid his hand to the doorknob.

"My aunt, Beth Carlson, suggested we talk to you. She is…was a friend of Avanell Jalbert," she said in a rush.

At the mention of Avanell's name, Leo relaxed slightly but kept his hand on the doorknob.

"What is it you want from me?"

Harriet took a deep breath. She knew if she didn't word things just right, he would slam the door in her face, and that would be the end of any cooperation from him.

"Aunt Beth told us that Amber was in the habit of wandering the neighborhood unaccompanied. She said you'd even called the police about it."

Leo's shoulders sagged.

"Would you like to come in?" he asked and held the door open.

Harriet looked at Lauren and, seeing no objection, went inside.

"Wow," she said as her eyes adjusted to the light. Quilts were draped over the backs of the sofa, the side chairs, and hung on a multi-quilt display rack. Most were Baltimore Album style and appeared to have been hand-quilted. On one wall, there were Mola-style reverse-appliqué pieces.

"My wife Janet is a quilter."

"I'm surprised I haven't seen any of her work at the local shows."

"Would you like some iced tea or lemonade?" He looked at them and they both nodded.

"Lemonade would be nice," Lauren said and Harriet nodded her agreement.

"Janet is working in the back garden. I'll go get her."

Lauren stepped closer to the display rack.

"These are incredible. The hand stitching is so uniform."

Harriet joined her for a closer look.

"Would you believe I stab stitch?" a woman said from a doorway that led to the back of the house. "I'm Janet."

She held her hand out to Harriet, who took it. Janet's handshake was firm but not painfully so. She nodded to Lauren, who was standing a few paces behind Harriet.

"You're Beth Carlson's niece, yes?" Harriet nodded, and Janet looked past her to Lauren. "I'm sorry, but I don't think we've met."

"I'm Lauren Sawyer. Harriet's friend."

Harriet gestured to the quilt display box and then the wall.

"These are beautiful. I'm surprised we haven't seen your quilts in any of the local shows."

Leo came back from the kitchen carrying a tray with frosty glasses of lemonade.

"That would be because of me."

"Now, Leo." Janet smiled as he turned to look at her. "I was there, too."

He handed her a glass of lemonade then offered glasses to Harriet and Lauren.

"Sit down, make yourselves comfortable." He moved a couple of throw pillows off the sofa, clearing more space. He and Janet sat in matching overstuffed chairs opposite the sofa.

"I might as well tell you my story. It will make things easier to understand."

Harriet caught herself before she leaned forward. She took a deep breath and tried to relax.

"It all started in nineteen-sixty-seven. 'The Summer of Love,' as it was called. I was eighteen and on my own for the first time. I lived in San Francisco and worked for the parks department, picking up garbage. I was to start college in the fall."

Janet picked up the story.

"And I was fourteen going on thirty, a booster child in a family of overachievers born ten years after my youngest brother. My parents lived in Redwood City and worked in what would become the high-tech industry."

"My parents were Marin County liberals," Leo interjected.

Janet continued.

"My parents thought I was going to the library to study when I was really going down to Haight-Ashbury, telling people I was eighteen and calling myself Sunshine. I followed some people to Golden Gate Park. Jefferson Airplane, Grateful Dead, Big Brother and the Holding Company—they were all there playing music. Lots of people were high on drugs.

"A small group of people were taking their clothes off. They started trying to rip clothes off of the people standing around them, and I was in their line of sight. I was wild, for a fourteen-year-old, but I wasn't ready for that."

Leo set his glass down.

"I saw that Janet was scared, so I stepped in and put my arm around her like she was my old lady. They backed off, and we walked away from the gathering."

Janet's eyes twinkled.

"He was my knight in shining armor. We talked until dark and made plans to meet again the following day."

51

"I still thought she was my age. We talked, but she carefully omitted any reference to age or school or anything that would give it away."

"Because my brothers were so much older," Janet continued, "I could talk like I was older than fourteen. They took me to movies that weren't suitable, and I read books I found in their rooms. I thought I was hot stuff."

"It was love at first sight for me," Leo said and gazed at his wife with affection.

"We saw each other as often as I could sneak away," Janet said. "Besides the library, I was supposed to be volunteering at the free clinic, and I had a girlfriend who would swear I was at her house. Leo rented a room in a commune house, and well, with all that freedom and lack of supervision, one thing led to another, and several months into our relationship we found ourselves in a family way."

Harriet could see where this was going.

"So, your parents charged Leo with statutory rape?"

"And everything else they could come up with," Leo said. "We were told we could never see each other again. Her parents didn't want anything to do with our baby, but fortunately, my parents, bless their liberal hearts, went to court and were awarded custody of our son."

Janet clapped her hands softly together.

"It was a stroke of genius, really. The courts allowed me visitation rights, which, of course, Leo's parents happily agreed to. Leo was always the one who brought Bradley to our meetings after he got out of jail."

"That must have been awful," Lauren said, speaking for the first time.

"It wasn't so bad. They let me serve in the county lockup, and I was out by the time our baby was born. They had vocational training, so I became a firefighter, and Janet's parents sent her back to school. She graduated with honors from San Francisco State with a teaching degree. We did okay."

"As soon as I was old enough, Leo and I got married. We moved first to Port Ludlow and then Foggy Point when Avanell hired him. We had three more boys, and everything was great until that business with Amber Price."

Leo shook his head.

"Some reporter found out I'd turned her in to the police, and when he dug into my background, he found the statutory rape conviction, and that's all he needed."

"I'm sure you've probably heard the rest," Janet said softly. "We moved out of Foggy Point, and then, when the boys were all away from home, we went to teach English in Thailand. A whole group of soon-to-be retired teachers were going, so we had friends, and it worked out.

"We've been living quietly under the radar for the last few years—which is why you won't see my quilts on display anywhere around here."

"Now, we're sitting here waiting for the other shoe to drop," Leo ended their tale.

"Thank you for sharing the truth with us," Harriet said. "I can't imagine how hard it's been for you."

Lauren sipped her lemonade and set her glass down on the coffee table.

"Just for the record, Beth told us you had been wronged, and that was enough for us." She looked at Harriet, waiting for her to continue.

"What we came here to ask you is if you think Amber and Molly could have been victims of a traffic accident. When we heard that Amber wandered, we wondered if it was possible that someone hit the girls with a car, killing Amber and knocking Molly out. Maybe whoever hit them panicked and buried Amber in the woods, and when they realized Molly was still alive left her in the park where someone would find her."

Janet and Leo looked at each other for a few moments. Leo rubbed his chin.

"I suppose it could have happened like that," he said thoughtfully.

"The timing would have had to be perfect," Janet added. "Traffic wasn't like it is today, but there was a pretty steady flow. That's why we finally called the police after we found Amber for the umpteenth time, wandering unsupervised. I won't say it couldn't have happened like that, though."

Harriet chewed her lip.

"The problem is, how do we prove it?"

"I supposed that's always the problem in this sort of situation," Janet said.

They all picked up their glasses at the same time and laughed.

"What kind of quilting do *you* do?" Janet asked.

Lauren got out her tablet and called up pictures of her latest quilt and, with a little looking, found one of Harriet's, too. Leo went outside to work in the garden, and the women talked about quilting through another glass of lemonade.

Chapter 10

Harriet adjusted the mirrors of her aunt's small car for the umpteenth time while Lauren put on her seatbelt.

"I don't know how she sees anything in this little death trap."

Lauren chuckled.

"That's because you drive a tank. Smaller cars have smaller windshields and smaller mirrors. Besides, your aunt has a rear camera on order. They made them standard this year, but her car just missed it."

"How do you know that when I don't?"

"She asked me about it at coffee when you were busy working. She didn't want to bother you. You'll be happy to know this car has a five-star crash rating, too. And before you ask, I looked that up for her before she bought the car."

"Good, I guess."

Harriet backed out of the Tabors' driveway and headed back toward the coffee shop.

"I'm going to swing by the police department and see if Morse is in. Do you want to come with?"

"Let's get my car first, since it's on the way. I'll meet you there."

✂ --- ✂ --- ✂

"Would either of you like coffee or anything?" Morse asked when they were seated in a small interview room at the Foggy Point Police Department.

Harriet couldn't help but notice that the walls were heavily insulated with black soundproofing that had large chunks missing. The industrial Formica-topped table was scarred, and included a heavy metal loop she assumed was for attaching the manacles of feistier interviewees. The table was also bolted to the floor.

Lauren looked around at their surroundings but kept her mouth shut.

"I don't know about Lauren, but none for me. We just drank a bunch of lemonade with Leo and Janet Tabor."

Detective Morse leaned back in her chair, took a deep breath, and blew it slowly out.

"I'm afraid to ask what you were doing there."

Lauren sat back in her chair and looked to Harriet.

"It was your idea, you can explain it."

"Aunt Beth and I were talking this morning," Harriet began. "She told me that Avanell Jalbert had told her Leo was falsely accused and in the process mentioned that Amber Price wandered the neighborhood a lot, including making it all the way to Stephens Street. Leo even took her here once in the hopes the police would call children's services or something.

"Anyway, we wondered if the police at the time considered the possibility that the girls were hit by a car, with Amber being killed and Molly knocked unconscious. Maybe the driver panicked and buried Amber then left Molly where she'd be found."

Morse furrowed her brow and pressed her lips together.

"I don't remember seeing that in the file. I'll look again. Short of an eyewitness, I'm not sure how you'd prove it. Traffic cameras weren't generally in use back then, and I'm guessing Foggy Point wasn't on the forefront of that political hot potato in any case. I guess we could check and see if there was a car lot or any other business that might have had security cameras.

"Even so, the chance of them having tape—and it would be tape that long ago—is almost nil. The only hope would be if they saw something, didn't want to be involved, but saved it for reasons unknown. I wouldn't hold my breath on this one." She flipped a page in her small spiral notebook and wrote something. "I will check it out, though. We haven't got anything else at this point."

"Molly keeps asking Lauren and me to help her. We were hoping there might be a simple explanation. Not that someone killing and burying Amber is simple, but an accident would be better than…I don't know, I guess it's all awful."

"Molly's been down here several times, too. Unless we come up with a previously unknown witness or find Amber's body, I'm afraid she's going to be disappointed."

Harriet stood up.

"Thanks for listening to us. I know you're doing everything you can."

Morse and Lauren got up as well.

"Listen, if you have any other ideas, feel free to share," Morse told them. "Like I said, we're getting nowhere. I'm working with a retired detective who was on the force back then, but he said after they cleared Leo Tabor, they didn't come up with anything. If there'd been forensic evidence, we could apply new tests that have been developed since then, but we've got nothing."

"If Amber's mother didn't watch her closely, I suppose anything could have happened," Harriet mused.

"Unfortunately, being an overworked single mother who didn't watch her child as well as her neighbors would have liked is not a crime in this town. Apart from Leo bringing Amber to the station and calling a few times, Sandra Price was never investigated for child neglect. She had her hands full, and people were pretty sympathetic."

"We better be on our way," Lauren said. "We have quilts to make, and presumably, you have criminals to catch."

Morse chuckled.

"Let me know when you're ready to start binding the quilts. I'm pretty fast." She looked at Lauren. "And before you say something snarky, I'm *good* and fast."

Lauren held her hands up.

"Hey, I didn't say anything. As long as you're the one with the gun, I'm not saying anything about your binding skill."

Harriet laughed at that.

"Come on, I need to finish my chores so I can give my aunt her car back."

&⊱--- ⊱--- ⊱

Harriet went home to check on Scooter and then to Pins and Needles for quilting thread for her machine. She chose a pastel variegated thread that had lavender, green, yellow and cream segments. In case the Threads didn't like her choice, she picked up more off-white, pale lavender and pale-green thread, too. She could always use the solid colors for her customer quilts if they weren't needed.

She stopped by the grocery store and was just putting her purchases away at home when James drove up in his white restaurant van. She opened the door before he reached the small porch to her studio.

"This is an unexpected pleasure. Is that chocolate I smell coming from the box in your hand?"

"You're getting to be like Pavlov's dog. Yes, this is a chocolate box, but they are individually wrapped inside, so don't tell me you can really smell them."

"You're right, my mouth is watering in expectation of your chocolates. You are ruining me for anyone else's truffles."

"I should hope so," he said and laughed."This is a test box of new flavors. If you're willing, I'd like you to try them. Not all at once, I hope. Eat one, write down what flavor you think it is, and then look at the paper under its spot in the box. I want to see if the flavors are easily recognizable."

He followed her into the kitchen and put the candy on the shelf in her refrigerator.

"Those aren't actually why I'm here. The restaurant is closed today because it's Monday. I was going to go visit my mom with a little dinner snack and thought I'd see if you want to come with me. I figured it would give you a chance to ask her about her old friend and the gossip on the street."

"That would be great," Harriet said. Then her shoulders sagged. "I have one little problem. I have to get my car at the dealer's and leave Aunt Beth's at her house. She got a ride home from her volunteer work, so I was going to pick her up to go get my car."

"What if I follow you to her house, and then take you to get your car. You can follow me to my mom's from there."

"That will work. I'm sure Aunt Beth is tired from sorting clothes all day."

"It's a plan, then," James said. "Let me call my mom real quick and give her an estimated time of arrival."

Chapter 11

Harriet looked out the front and then the side window as James drove into his mother's neighborhood.

"Gosh, this reminds me of some of the villages in the Netherlands. You don't usually see such steeply pitched roofs in this climate."

James looked around as if seeing it for the first time.

"I guess that was the idea. It's one of those planned deals. We lived in an old Victorian like everyone else when I was growing up. They finally got tired of taking care of such a big old place. This is their downsize house."

"They must have a great view of the docks and beyond."

James turned the car into a sloped driveway and parked.

"Let's go in, and you can see." He got out and opened the side door of the van, and pulled out an insulated box. "I hope you're hungry. I'm trying out a new recipe. My mom is always my most honest critic, so it has to pass her first."

Harriet got out, and James led the way up six steps to the front door, which opened as they reached the landing.

"Hi, you must be Harriet." James's mother was a slender woman with graying sandy hair and blue eyes. She wore blue jeans with a cotton blouse topped by a linen V-necked sweater. She held her hand out, and Harriet shook it.

"Nice to meet you."

"James has told me a lot about you. Sounds like you've had your fair share of trouble since you moved back to Foggy Point. I'm Kathy, by the way. Here, let's sit in the front room while James fusses in the kitchen."

She led the way to a sitting room to the right of the front door while James went the opposite direction, presumably to the kitchen.

"Your home is beautiful," Harriet said. "I was just telling James I didn't even know about this neighborhood. It reminds me of Europe."

"That was the developer's idea. His plan is to 'gentrify' this old industrial part of Foggy Point. Up until two years ago, this whole block was some sort of ship repair yard. It hadn't been in business for more than ten years. The houses are all built to green standards and also for aging in place. There are two stories, but the second pantry in the kitchen is wired to be converted into an elevator if that becomes necessary."

"He did a great job, and your view is spectacular."

"Thank you. Now, James said you had some questions for me."

Harriet explained how DeAnn's sister had come to town and was anxious to figure out what had happened to her.

"DeAnn told her about some of the unfortunate situations we've run into since I've been back, and now her sister thinks our quilting group is somehow going to be able to solve a mystery the police have been working on for twenty years."

"My friend Lois lived on the same street where that other little girl went missing. I guess your friend's sister lived on that street, too. Of course, it was all in the paper, but most of the attention was on the other girl—Amber, I think, was her name.

"I called Lois when James said you were interested in what happened. We don't know anything that wasn't in the newspaper, but I can tell you Lois never thought that man Leo did it. It was disgraceful how they crucified him, and all along he had an alibi, if I remember right.

"Anyway, Lois and I have no proof, but we always suspected another neighbor—Gary Alexander. He had been in prison for domestic battery and had just returned. His wife took him back. He took anger management classes while he was in prison. Of course, he beat her again, and I think he went back to prison; but that's another story, and it happened years later."

"Is there evidence to suggest he was involved with the little girls?"

Kathy sighed.

"Not really. Lois just didn't like him. I suppose Amber's dad could be a possibility. The parents' marriage didn't last more than a year after she went missing, if they were ever married in the first place. He never was around before she went missing, so maybe they weren't. I've read articles that say it's not all that unusual for the family of a missing child to fall apart afterward."

"I'll tell my friend Lauren about both possibilities. She's a computer whiz. If there's anything about either of those guys in the public record or anywhere else on the Internet, she'll be able to find it."

"I wish I could tell you more. Lois said her neighborhood was pretty average. Everyone kept their yards nice. No one had wild parties or anything. Once a year, they had a block party, and she said up until Amber disappeared, everyone went. Of course, Leo moved away, and Sandra didn't participate for a few years, but Lois says she eventually started coming again."

"Like I was saying before, if the police couldn't come up with anything in twenty years, I don't know what Molly expects a bunch of quilters to do. We're trying because she's DeAnn's sister, but I'm not holding out much hope."

"I wish I had more to tell you, but Lois really didn't know anything."

"What was Foggy Point like back then? I was mostly in boarding school, so I don't really have a lot of memories."

"You were a child in any case. Well, it was smaller…"

Kathy entertained Harriet with stories of Foggy Point twenty years before. She got out a scrapbook to illustrate her tales. Before Harriet knew it, an hour had passed.

She pointed to a picture.

"James is so cute in his little baseball uniform. How old was he?"

Kathy looked at the ceiling while she thought.

"He must have been five, maybe. He was always into sports. As you might guess, you could have knocked his dad and I over with a feather when he turned down a full-ride sports scholarship to go to culinary school. Speaking of his dad, you'll have to come back another time when my husband isn't off fishing with his cronies."

"I heard that crack about culinary school," James said as he came across the entry hall and into the living room. "Your dinner is served."

Harriet sniffed.

"It smells good, whatever it is."

He made a deep bow and gestured with a broad sweep of his arm, directing them to the kitchen.

"This way, Madame et Mademoiselle. Since we are a small party tonight, dinner will be served in the small dining room."

Kathy led the way.

"James is trying to tell you we're eating in the kitchen nook."

"What are we having?" Harriet asked.

"We are having my first attempt at Frogmore stew," James told her.

Harriet and Kathy looked at each other.

"I can tell by your confused looks that you don't know what Frogmore stew is. Let me enlighten you." He pulled out first his mother's chair then Harriet's as he spoke. "Frogmore stew is a classic Low Country South Carolina dish also known as a Low-country boil or Beaufort stew. Basically, it

60

has shrimp, corn on the cob, new potatoes and, in my recipe, hot sausage and a bunch of secret spices." He smiled. "I'm hoping to add it to my summer menu once a week. If the shrimp hold up, I'll be able to use Puget Sound-caught shrimp, and that will be a big draw."

He placed a basket of breads in the middle of the table and got a dish of butter from the refrigerator. He served the two women then watched their reactions as they took their first bites. Only when they smiled and gave him a thumbs-up did he sit and serve himself.

✂ --- ✂ --- ✂

Harriet leaned back in her chair and took a deep breath.

"That was so delicious. I ate way more than I should have."

"Thanks," James said. "I was pretty sure it would be a hit, but you never know."

A distinctive chime sounded from Harriet's pocket.

"Excuse me for a moment. This is my aunt." She stood up and went into the functional part of the kitchen as she answered her phone. "Aunt Beth?"

A man spoke. She felt the blood drain from her face. James came over and took her free arm, leading her back to her chair.

"What's wrong?" he asked when she'd ended her call.

"It's my aunt. There's been some sort of accident."

Kathy stood up.

"Go, take her to her aunt. I'll clean up here. Call me when you know something."

Chapter 12

Harriet dialed Mavis and Lauren as James drove her to the Jefferson County hospital.

"They'll meet us there," she said.

"Do you have any idea what happened?"

"The paramedic said her car went off the road on a steep curve on Miller Hill Road. I have no idea what she was doing there. He said she was lucky in that her car was stopped by a tree a few feet over the edge. I guess someone was driving behind her and saw it happen, so they called nine-one-one."

"Did they say anything about how she is?"

"He did say she was in good enough shape to refuse transportation until he called me."

"I'm sure she'll be fine." James was quiet for a moment. "Actually, I have no idea, but that's the kind of thing my mom says in these situations."

He reached a hand over and took Harriet's. His was soft and warm, she noted. He kept his eyes on the road while he spoke.

"I know I'm not Aiden or Tom, but I'm here as long as you need me to be."

Harriet looked at his profile as he drove.

"I appreciate that."

They rode in silence the rest of the way to the hospital. James dropped her at the emergency room entrance then went off to find a parking spot. Harriet hurried through the automatic doors and went up to the information counter.

"I'm here to see my aunt, Beth Carlson," she told the young woman sitting behind the computer.

"Room three," she said after typing in the name and checking the database. "Go through the right-hand door, and the nurses can direct you."

"Thanks," Harriet said as she turned and hurried for the door.

"I'm looking for Beth Carlson," she repeated to the nurse standing behind the command center when she reached the emergency area. The woman stepped out from behind the circular computer counter and led Harriet past a series of curtained rooms, each marked with a large screen-printed number.

"Here we are. Number three." The nurse held the curtain aside so Harriet could enter.

Aunt Beth was sitting on the gurney, her short legs dangling over the side. A young-looking dark-haired doctor was wrapping her left arm in a stretchy bandage. Her chin was purple.

"I'm fine," she said immediately after she saw Harriet.

"Aunt Beth." Harriet said went over to stand by her. Her eyes filled with tears of relief. "What happened?"

"Now, that's a very good question. Was my car steering okay when you drove it?"

"It was fine. No warning lights came on or anything."

The doctor scooped Aunt Beth's legs up onto the gurney.

"Let's have a look at that ankle," he said and began removing her right shoe and sock.

Once she was repositioned, Beth continued her story.

"I didn't feel like cooking, so I thought I'd get Chinese takeout." She put her good hand over her mouth and gasped. "Call the restaurant, and tell them what happened. Then call Jorge and see if he can run over and get my dinner."

"I'm sure the restaurant will understand, under the circumstances."

"I still haven't eaten, and I still have a hankering for some good Chinese food."

Harriet knew her aunt well enough to make the calls. She knew she'd never find out what happened if she didn't.

"Now, please, what happened?" she asked when she'd finished.

"All I know is, I was taking the shortcut to town over Miller Hill, and when I came to that steep downhill curve, my power steering went out. It happened so suddenly, I couldn't get the wheel cranked around quick enough to make the turn. I went over the side and, luckily, slid into a tree. My ankle injury was from stomping on the brake so hard."

"Seems weird that your power steering would quit on you all of a sudden. Your car isn't that old."

Before Harriet could ask any more questions, Mavis and Connie arrived. She moved aside as they stepped to either side of the bed.

"Are you okay?" Mavis asked.

Beth looked first at her and then at Connie.

"I'm fine. I can't say the same for my car."

Connie looked at the doctor to see if he was listening, but he was busy opening another stretchy bandage. She lowered her voice.

"Do you think someone sabotaged your car?"

"The name Juana Lopez-Montoya comes to mind," Mavis whispered.

"You think someone did this on purpose?" Harriet said in as normal a voice as she could manage.

All three women glared at her. She dropped her voice an a level or two.

"We should have the police here if you think someone did this on purpose."

"That skinny blond patrolwoman came when the ambulance did," Beth told them. "She's having my car towed to the impound lot. She said they'd have a look at it and see if there's any indication something was done to it on purpose. She said the age of my car plus my tire slashing incident made her interested enough to check things out."

"Do you think Juana is capable of something this sophisticated?" Harriet asked, looking at all three women.

Connie narrowed her eyes.

"I've tutored her in the past." She took a breath and blew it out slowly. "I'd have to say it's a definite maybe. I know when she worked at the shelter workshop she used small tools. The question is whether she could put together a plan that involved finding Beth's car and waiting until no one was watching her. I'd say she's more impulsive than that."

"But what if she happened to see it sitting somewhere? I think that car is the only silver Beetle in Foggy Point. And I was doing errands today in it. I was parked in various locations all over town."

"You're assuming that whatever was done took a while to fail?" Mavis asked.

Harriet thought for a moment.

"I guess so."

"I'm with Connie," Beth said. "Juana is jealous of my relationship with Jorge, but I'm not sure she could plan and execute something like this."

"She could have done it after I dropped it off. Was your garage door still open?"

Aunt Beth sagged against the raised end of the bed.

"I didn't close it when you left because I knew I was going out to get dinner."

"Could she be stealthy enough to pull that off?" Mavis wondered.

Connie pressed her lips together and shook her head.

"Anything's possible, but I'm just not seeing it."

"If it isn't her, who could it be?" Harriet asked.

Aunt Beth and her friends were quiet.

"Yeah, that's what I thought, too. If not Juana, we don't have a clue."

The curtain was pulled aside, and a nurse leaned into the cubicle.

"There is a very anxious man in the waiting room asking for you. Since he isn't a relative, I told him I'd have to ask you first." She looked at Harriet, Connie and Mavis. "And some of you will have to step outside to make room."

Harriet did so, followed by Connie. Mavis sat on a wheeled stool in the corner. The doctor had finished wrapping Aunt Beth's foot.

"You're going to have to use a knee scooter for a week or so," he told her. "You need to keep your weight off your ankle, but your arm isn't going to let you use crutches. I'll have someone bring one by to see if you can manage it." He continued with instructions about pain medication and how she needed to stay home for a few days.

Harriet held the door for Jorge as she went back into the waiting room.

"She's fine," she told him. "I think she'll be glad to see you, though. Mavis is with her."

"*Diós mio*," he said and stormed down the curtained aisle.

Lauren stood as Harriet approached the reception area. James was across the room plugging quarters into a drink machine.

"Since you're out here and letting other people in, I'm guessing your aunt is going to be okay."

"She sprained her ankle pushing on the brake and has some sort of soft-tissue injury on her opposite arm, but otherwise, she's fine."

Lauren's shoulders visibly relaxed.

"Well, that's a relief."

Connie pulled her keys from her purse.

"I'm going to go over to Beth's and make up the hide-a-bed in the TV room. The doctor said she isn't to climb stairs for a few days. I'll take her dog out, too."

Harriet turned toward her.

"Thank you so much. I know she'll will be grateful for the help."

Lauren followed Connie with her eyes as she departed.

"So, what do you think happened?" she asked when Connie was out the door.

Harriet noticed that James was lingering at the drink machine, clearly giving them time to talk.

"Maybe an accident, maybe not."

"I'll wait till later to hear about why you're here with the cute chef."

Harriet rolled her eyes but didn't take the bait. She felt her silenced phone buzz in her pocket but ignored it.

"The police towed the car to the impound lot, so I think they're treating it as a crime until they prove otherwise."

"The police *have* looked, and it appears it was intentional," said Detective Morse. Harriet and Lauren had been so intent on their conversation they hadn't noticed her come through the automatic entrance doors.

"The tow-truck driver took a quick look as he was loading the car and pointed out a cut serpentine belt to the on-scene officers. It was cut about three-quarters of the way through, so it would drive a little way before it broke. He says the belt was nearly new and showed no signs of wear to account for the break. He also said the break was too clean to be anything else but on purpose. Of course, we'll have our forensic people double-check his conclusions, but in my experience, if Marco says it was cut, it was cut."

"It's hard to imagine anyone wanting to hurt my aunt."

Lauren smirked.

"You mean except for the crazy lady who slashed her tires?"

Morse looked at Harriet.

"With all the trouble you and the Loose Threads have gotten into in the year or so you've been here, you can't think of anyone who might want revenge?"

Harriet's eyes got wide.

"Relax," Morse said. "I think that's unlikely. But you need to stay mindful of the dangers of involving yourselves in other people's troubles.

"Even though current cases are not my responsibility right now, I did follow up with the officer dealing with Juana. I don't know if you've heard, but Foggy Point is following some of the larger cities in developing a behavioral health unit to better deal with people who commit crimes as a side effect of mental illness. The hope is we can get them appropriate help before they end up in jail. So far, we have one officer and one counselor, but it's a start. Anyway, I know they put a tracker on Juana yesterday, and they're following up with trying to get her working again."

Harriet sighed.

"I drove Aunt Beth's car today. I was all over town doing errands."

"Welcome to my world," Morse said. "You think police work is all car chases and shoot-outs, but really we spend a lot of time at our desks combing through data and out in the neighborhoods talking to people. Give me your best estimate of where you were and when, and I'll match it to what Juana's tracker says."

"Can she take the tracker off?" Lauren asked.

"No, it's the same model that's used for Alzheimer's patients—a shoe insole that has the device embedded in it. They put it in her shoe after she went to bed last night, so she doesn't even know it's there. And just to be safe, they attached another under the seat of her tricycle."

"Will you let us know?" Harriet asked.

"I will when I can. Since I'm not officially on the case, I'll be getting it secondhand. Your aunt could call and ask tomorrow, and they might tell her. I'm going to go in now and talk to her, so I'll suggest she call." She disappeared through the door to the treatment area.

Harriet looked toward the vending machines and saw that James was on his phone. He noticed her watching, ended his phone call, and picked up the three bottles of water he'd purchased.

"Water anyone?"

Lauren took two and held one out to Harriet, and they both sat down.

"Let me check my phone first. I silenced it, but it's been buzzing in my pocket."

Lauren smiled.

"Probably all the Threads who weren't invited to the party."

Harriet tapped the unlock code into her phone and found texts from Carla, Robin and DeAnn asking for updates on Aunt Beth. There were three voicemail messages, all from Molly.

"Texts from the Threads, and voicemails from Molly."

"She sounds like she's getting to be a bit of a stalker," James said.

"Let's see what she has to say," Harriet put her phone on speaker and pressed the first message.

Harriet, I've got amazing news! Call me. Harriet erased it and started the next message. *Call me.* She deleted it as well and moved on to the last one. *I can't wait until you call back. I had a psychic come today, and she just told me how to find Amber's body. And Harriet—I remember. I'm going to go look.*

Detective Morse rushed out into the waiting room.

"Duty calls," she said as she hustled past James, Harriet and Lauren. She turned on her unmarked car's blue and red flashers and sped out of the unloading area.

Lauren leaned forward in her chair to watch until Morse's car disappeared from sight.

"I wonder what that was all about."

"Must be pretty serious if she put her lights on this soon," James observed. "I mean, there's a lot of highway between here and Foggy Point."

Harriet stared out the glass doors and sipped her water.

"It's especially curious since she works cold cases now. If they called her, it must be an all-hands-on-deck situation."

Lauren pulled out her phone.

"I'll text the group if you want to answer Molly's."

"Only because she's related to DeAnn am I going to do this. I don't want to be any more involved in Molly's delusions than I already am."

James's brow furrowed.

"Her message said 'how to find Amber', not 'where to find Amber', right? Doesn't it seem like if the person really had psychic powers, they could tell her where?"

"Good one, James," Lauren said. "We'll make a detective out of you yet."

"No, thanks, I'm but a humble cook. No detecting for this boy."

They laughed.

Harriet set her water bottle on the floor by her chair.

"Would you two hush so I can call her?"

Harriet tapped Molly's number into her phone. She was startled when a man answered.

"Who is this?" he said.

"Harriet Truman. Who's this?"

She held her phone out and pressed the speaker button.

"Detective Dane, Foggy Point Police."

"Why do you have Molly's phone?" Harriet's stomach clenched into a knot. She leaned forward in her chair.

"Are you a relative?"

"I'm a friend of her sister."

"What's her sister's name?"

Harriet told him and he thanked her and hung up.

The color drained from Lauren's already pale face.

"This can't be good."

Harriet stood up.

"I'm going to go tell Mavis. Can you call Robin? If this is what we think, DeAnn's going to want her."

Mavis had stepped out of the curtained ER room and was headed for the lobby when Harriet opened the door.

"I'm glad you're out here. Something weird just happened, and I'm afraid we're about to have some more bad news."

"Honey, you're not making sense."

"Walk with me, and I'll explain."

Mavis followed her into the lobby and over to where James and Lauren sat, and Harriet explained as they went. Mavis listened thoughtfully until Harriet had finished speaking.

"As you were talking, I was trying to come up with an innocent explanation for your facts, but nothing good comes to mind. If a police detective has Molly's phone and won't tell you why, it can't be as simple as her losing it."

Lauren tapped her phone off.

"I just spoke to Robin. She hasn't heard from DeAnn, but she'll call her and go wherever she is. I texted Carla with an update on all fronts."

"Did the doctor or anyone else come back to Aunt Beth and say anything about when she can leave?" Harriet asked Mavis.

"Jorge was helping her practice with that scooter thing. The nurse said when they all agreed she was okay with that contraption, she could go home."

"Maybe I should go back to your house and get my car to transport her in," Harriet said to James.

Mavis chewed on her lip.

"That might not be necessary. She and Jorge were talking about putting the scooter in the back of his truck. I think they may be planning on him driving her home."

"What!" Harriet all but shouted.

A trio of young women two chair rows over stopped talking and stared at her.

"Am I being replaced?" she said in a loud whisper.

Lauren laughed.

"You are. You are so being replaced by the dashing Jorge. Good for your aunt."

"I'm not sure how I feel about that," Harriet huffed.

"It may surprise you, but we old people have social lives, too. You aren't the only one who likes to go out to dinner with a handsome man once in a while," Mavis scolded.

"Do you have a boyfriend, too?" Lauren asked.

"After this reaction, I wouldn't tell you if I did." She narrowed her eyes and glared at James.

"Hey, what happens in my restaurant stays in my restaurant." He mimed zipping his lips. "My lips are sealed."

"You *do* have a boyfriend," Lauren chortled.

"This isn't about me, missy. We need to figure out what's going on with DeAnn as well as figure out who sabotaged Beth's car."

Lauren's face became serious.

"I'd almost forgotten about that part."

Harriet sipped from her water bottle.

"We'll have to wait for Morse to finish with whatever took her out of here so fast before she can check up on Juana. Then, I guess we'll have to make sure Aunt Beth isn't alone until we get to the bottom of this."

Lauren laughed again.

"With you and Jorge fighting over her here, and Connie waiting for her at home, you probably have more coverage than you need."

James twirled his empty water bottle between his palms.

"If you want, I can take you by your aunt's house when she's released and then back to my house for your car when she's settled. Or, if you want, my mom can help me bring your car to you."

Harriet sighed. "I don't think we need to bother your mom with this. It sounds like Connie and Jorge will be there with her. I would like to go by and make sure she has everything she needs, though."

"Rockin' Robin" sounded from Lauren's pants pocket. She pulled the phone out and tapped the answer button, stepped away from the group and covered her free ear with her hand while she listened. She spoke a few words, but Harriet couldn't hear what she was saying.

"That was Robin," she explained when she'd rejoined them.

"Yeah, we got that," Harriet said. "What did she have to say?"

"It is as bad as we feared. Molly's body was found in Fogg Park. Robin said DeAnn wasn't sure, but she thinks Molly was hit in the head. She was in the vicinity of where she was found when she was five."

Harriet looked up at the ceiling and sighed.

"I guess any hope we might have had that Amber's killer left the area was premature."

Lauren shook her head sadly.

"It's hard to believe there was anything Molly could find all these years later that would cause the killer to silence her."

Harriet looked at her.

"But she said she remembered. It's possible her so-called psychic really did say something that triggered her memory."

Lauren's eyes got wide, and her mouth turned down.

"Yeah. Molly was just the kind of person who would confront her killer by herself if she remembered."

No one could think of what to say after that, so the three women busied themselves texting the rest of the Threads while James gathered the empty water bottles and carried them to the recycling containers.

✂ --- ✂ --- ✂

Connie met Harriet and James when they arrived at Aunt Beth's front door.

"Where's Beth?" she asked and stepped aside so they could enter.

"Jorge is driving her. He's being a total mother hen. I don't think he's driving over ten miles an hour for fear of jostling her around."

Connie led the way to the TV room. As promised, the hide-a-bed was freshly made with extra pillows stacked in the side chair. Connie had placed a pile of new quilting magazines on a TV tray next to the bed, along with an insulated water bottle and the TV remote control.

Harriet fingered the magazine edges.

"Looks like you've thought of everything. We might need to move her chair in the living room back a little. They're sending her home with one of those knee scooters. She'll need a clear path to the bathroom. I suspect the wider the space the better."

James slid the chair back and moved the side table that went with it, too.

"The patient has arrived," Jorge announced as he pushed the door open with his foot and carried Aunt Beth over the threshold. Connie stood aside, and he carefully navigated the path to the TV room. Brownie barked and circled Jorge's feet until he had set Beth on the bed. The little dog jumped onto her as soon as Jorge let go and began licking her face.

"Enough, already," she said and pushed Brownie away with her good hand. "Now, tell me what's happened. Detective Morse went flying out of the hospital like her hair was on fire, and you've all been whispering and texting more than my situation warrants, so something else must have happened. I have a sprained ankle and a strained wrist, and you're all treating me like I'm on life support."

Lauren slid her phone into her pocket with a guilty look but deferred to Harriet.

Harriet cleared her throat.

"It seems Molly's been murdered. We don't know anything other than that. I tried to return voicemails she'd sent me, and a police detective answered her phone. Apparently they'd just found her body and were in the early stages of identifying her."

"That's terrible," Beth said. "Is Robin with DeAnn?"

"She was going to go find her," Harriet answered.

"We probably need a meeting of the Threads tomorrow," Connie said thoughtfully.

"I agree," Beth said. "It'll need to be here, of course."

Jorge stepped closer to the bed.

"I'm not sure that's a good idea. Your doctor said you would probably have neck pain in the morning when the morphine they gave you at the hospital wears off. He said he would arrange for you to see the physical therapist in the morning. He also suggested we see if a massage therapist could come here to see you since he thinks you clenched every muscle in your body."

Beth pressed her lips together and looked at him.

"You'd clench your muscles, too, if you went over a cliff."

Harriet waited to see if Jorge was going to continue the discussion, and when he didn't she took a step closer to the bed.

"He's right. You need to take care of yourself first. I'm sure we're going to need more than one meeting about this. We haven't figured out what happened to Amber yet. It's possible Molly's death doesn't have anything to do with Amber's, but that would be quite a coincidence if it wasn't related somehow."

Beth leaned back against her pillows.

"Okay, I suppose you're right, but you come over tomorrow afternoon and tell me everything you talk about. And don't forget to use the flip chart. It's in my kitchen utility closet."

"Will do," Harriet promised.

Lauren smiled.

"I'll go one better. I'll record it for you so you don't miss a word."

Beth visibly relaxed.

"Okay, then. If it's all right with you folks, I think I'd like to get in my nightgown."

Jorge and Connie both started for her bedroom while Harriet and Lauren looked at each other, wide-eyed.

"I got this," Connie told Jorge in her "don't argue with me" teacher voice.

Harriet and Lauren went back to the living room.

"Shall we meet at the Steaming Cup in the morning?" Lauren suggested.

"That works for me, although I don't think I'll be bringing our flip chart there."

"You can write up the chart after."

"I'm going to assume I still have to stitch the quilts for the fundraiser until someone tells me anything different. Given that, I need to work a good part of tomorrow."

"You're not the only one, but one thing at a time. I'll call Robin if you'll call Carla and Mavis."

"Deal." Harriet turned to James. "As soon as my aunt is settled, I think I'll be ready to go."

"Don't rush on my account. I've got culinary student interns right now, so I don't have to get up at the crack of dawn to prep food."

"Thank you, I owe you."

He smiled, and Harriet felt an unexpected warm glow in the center of her chest.

Chapter 13

It was foggy when Harriet opened the door the next morning. Scooter planted his feet and refused to move until she picked him up and carried him down the porch steps.

"Hey, you should be grateful you only have to go to the end of the street and back. I have to run three miles after you go back in." She tugged gently on his thin leash, and he finally gave up and started walking. "Be glad you don't belong to James. He'd be making you run races for publicity's sake."

Scooter began a slow trot as if to prove he could race if called upon to do so. Harriet laughed and wondered again how she'd survived for all those years without a dog.

They finished his walk and her run and shower in just over an hour. While she was running, she'd gone over in her mind all the stops she'd made the previous day and tried to remember where she'd parked at each place. If her memory was correct, she'd only been in secluded places twice. The first time was when she'd stopped at the dry cleaners—the shrubbery around the parking area would allow someone to approach the car without being seen, but she hadn't been in the shop very long; and besides, she'd driven the car all day after that without incident.

The second time someone might have tampered with the car was when she'd gone to the grocery store. The parking lot had been crowded, and the only spot she'd found was in the outer row of spaces that faced a thick laurel hedge. She'd made it easier for whomever had done it by backing into her space, something she routinely did when driving the Beetle, since the trunk was in the front. That had to be when it happened. She made a mental note to see if the grocery store had security cameras.

"You guys guard the fortress," she told her dog and cat as she dug in the kitchen closet for her purse then handed out a treat for each of them. "Be good," she admonished and headed for the door.

✂ --- ✂ --- ✂

Lauren pulled out the chair next to hers at the big table in the Steaming Cup.

"I saved you a seat."

Harriet looped her purse strap over the chair back and sat. She looked down the length of the empty table.

"Where is everyone?"

"Connie's going by to see your aunt, Robin had to go to her kids' school to deliver a forgotten lunch, and Carla just pulled into the parking lot. I don't know where Mavis is, but I'm guessing she's at your aunt's, too."

"I guess my suggestion to let her sleep late fell on deaf ears."

Their discussion was interrupted by the barista, delivering a large cup of hot cocoa to Harriet. As she sipped, the rest of the group arrived in rapid succession, including a member she hadn't seen in nearly six months—Jenny Logan.

"Hey," she said when Jenny came over with her cup of coffee. She stood up and leaned in for a hug. "I'm glad to see you back with the Threads."

"I thought it was time to rejoin polite society," she said and laughed. "I was visiting my son and daughter-in-law and the grand-prince last month, and when they asked me about my quilting and about all of you, I admitted I'd been staying home." She sipped her coffee.

"Mark took me by the shoulders, looked me in the eyes and said, 'Mom, the only one who cares about what happened when you were a teenager is you. Your friends have known you for years, and they miss the person they know and love.'"

Her eyes filled with tears. A quilt Jenny had made as a teenager had landed her in the middle of a murder investigation earlier in the year.

Harriet patted her on the back.

"He's right, you know. Everyone has a past. What we care about is now, and we've missed you."

Lauren pulled out the chair on the other side of her for Jenny.

"You don't even want to know what I've been hiding in *my* past." She looked at Harriet. "And no, I won't tell you, now or anytime soon."

"So, tell me what's happened since I went offline." Jenny looked at Harriet and then Lauren, who were staring at each other. Finally, they both laughed.

"Let's just catch you up on the current crisis," Harriet told her. "You probably read about the other stuff in the paper, and it would take our whole meeting time to explain." She then proceeded to do just that.

"Poor DeAnn. That's horrible, but I can't say it's a complete surprise. I got to know DeAnn's mother from when she worked at the video store —we were both on a downtown beautification project committee. I know she was very worried about Molly's obsession with Amber's disappearance. When she got involved in the missing-and-exploited children project, she was going to some pretty scary places trying to find out who was taking kids."

"We're making quilts to give to some of Molly's major donors at a fund-raiser she'd planned here in town," Harriet said.

Lauren stirred her caramel latte with a plastic stir-stick.

"Molly was pressuring Harriet and me and the rest of the Threads, too, to try to solve the mystery of Amber's disappearance. We tried to explain to her that we aren't private detectives or anything, but she wasn't hearing it."

Jenny looked thoughtful.

"Is it safe to assume that now you feel guilty and are trying to figure out what happened to Molly?"

Harriet's face turned pink.

"Something like that."

Jenny set her purse under her chair and looked at Robin, who had settled in a chair at the head of the table.

"You're still the group scribe?"

Robin smiled and pulled a yellow legal tablet and pen from her tote bag.

"Good to have you back, Jenny."

Connie hurried in the door and swept by the counter to pick up a drink she must have phone-ordered.

"Sorry I'm late. I had to stop by Beth's to drop off a clay ice pack I have. And before you all ask, she's sore and tired, but otherwise okay; and she hasn't heard anything from the police about who did this to her."

Harriet already knew this, since she'd called her aunt on her way to the coffee shop. Still, it was good to have someone report who had actually laid eyes on her, in spite of the fact they'd all disturbed her aunt's rest.

"We should get on with the matter at hand," she said. "We've got a lot of ground to cover."

"There's no shortage of suspects," Lauren said.

Robin drew a line across the top of the page.

"Who is our top suspect?"

Harriet propped both elbows on the table and clasped her hands.

"If you look only at her current situation and don't mix in her job or her past, I'd put Josh Phillips at the top of the list."

Lauren swept her long blond hair away from her face in a signature move.

"Well, playing by those rules, the new poet friend should go up there, too. You know how those crime shows always tell us our nearest and dearest are our greatest danger."

Connie pursed her lips.

"If you use that logic, we have to add DeAnn and her parents, and I don't think anyone wants to do that."

Carla's cheeks turned pink.

"You don't really think DeAnn would kill her sister, do you?"

Connie reached over and patted her hand.

"No, I don't. That family was more concerned with helping Molly than anything else."

Jenny cleared her throat.

"Are any of the people who were suspects when she was little still around?"

"Leo Tabor," Mavis offered.

Harriet and Lauren looked at each other.

"We talked to him," Harriet began. "And anything is possible, but I…" She glanced at Lauren again. "…we don't think he had anything to do with Amber Price's death. His only crime was trying to get her parents to keep better track of her."

"James's mother and her friend think a guy named Gary Alexander may have been involved in Amber's disappearance. He lived on the street and had gone to prison for domestic battery," Harriet said.

Robin wrote his name down.

"I'm not sure criminals switch their pattern like that, but violent is violent, I guess."

Carla tilted her head slightly and looked at Robin.

"Most people who commit crimes do the same crime," Robin explained, "or follow a progression of increasingly violent versions of the same thing. A kid who steals candy in grade school may shoplift candy bars in junior high school and then rob houses in high school, but he wouldn't shoplift and then molest children and then set fires. At least, not usually."

Harriet sat back in her chair and thought for a minute.

"What about the guy in the homeless camp who found Molly back then. I think he's still around. If he murdered Amber and hit Molly, and she went back to talk to him, maybe he finished what he started. It's possible he was in the process of killing Molly twenty years ago, and someone interrupted him. He could have said he found her when really he was the person who took her there in the first place."

"What's his name," Robin asked.

"Max," Harriet replied.

"I think a lot of people refer to him as Mad Max," Lauren added.

Robin added his name to the list.

"Do we know about her work?" Carla asked. "Maybe she found a missing child, and someone went to jail."

Lauren leaned forward so she could see Carla.

"Good point, Grasshopper. I can go to the local office of Molly's non-profit and see if I can sweet talk them into taking a look at her computer."

Carla's face turned a deeper shade of red.

"I'd like to have a chat with the psychic she contacted," Harriet said.

"The psychic wouldn't be in business long if he or she went around killing clients," Connie argued.

Harriet laughed.

"You're assuming she met with a real psychic. The killer could have offered his services as a psychic, and we all know Molly would have jumped at the chance."

Connie's shoulders sagged.

"You're right."

The group sat in silent thought. Robin set her pen down.

"This is off-topic, but have the police followed up on where Juana was when your aunt's car was tampered with?"

"I haven't heard anything," Harriet said and looked down the table to Connie and Mavis.

"Beth hadn't heard anything when I was there this morning," Mavis said. "And while we're off topic, how are we doing on the quilts for the benefit?"

Harriet blew a breath out and leaned back in her chair.

"I've got the one Mavis, Carla, Lauren and I did on the machine now. The Aunt Beth, Robin, DeAnn and Connie one is prepped and ready to go on the machine when the first one is finished. I'm still waiting on the third one."

Carla pulled a plastic bag with quilt squares in it from her purse.

"I've got my blocks done for that one."

"I'm finished with mine, too," Robin said. "And I'll go over and get whatever DeAnn's done from her and finish what I need to."

"We've got a few days for that one," Harriet looked up at the ceiling and calculated in her head. "Today is Tuesday. It'll take most of the week to finish the two I have. If the third one is ready to go on as soon as I finish, I can get it done by next Monday or Tuesday. That'll give us the rest of the week to bind them. And people can start binding the first two when they each come off the machine."

Jenny held up her hand as if asking permission to speak.

"Since I haven't done anything, I can finish DeAnn's blocks and sew it all together if you want. I can help bind, too."

"Thanks, that will help a lot," Robin said. "I picked up some extra yoga classes this week so one of my fellow teachers can go on a well-deserved vacation."

"No problem," Jenny said and smiled. "And while I'm catching up on things…" She wiggled her eyebrows up and down and looked at Harriet. "Is James, whose mother you quoted earlier, the hottie chef with the restaurant on the cove?"

Lauren sighed.

"One does need a scorecard to keep up with Harriet's love life."

Harriet blushed.

"I've been helping James with his racing wiener dog. I'm just subbing for his sister. Of course, it's given us a chance to get to know each other better."

"Yeah, like he's taken you home to meet the parents already," Lauren said.

"It was only his mother, and he knew I wanted to know what her friend Lois knew about Amber's disappearance. Lois lived on Amber's street back then."

Jenny smiled.

"It must be hard spending time with a good-looking guy who can cook."

Harriet sighed.

"He'd be the first one to tell you he doesn't have time for a relationship. He's married to the restaurant."

Everyone but Carla groaned and then smiled.

"That is such a line," Lauren finally said. "He's trying to get you to lower your guard so he can move in. He knows you're on the rebound from Aiden. Tom isn't as much of a threat as long as he's got geography problems. I don't see that changing as long as he's running his mother's art school and retreat center and still working his day job."

"You seem to know a lot about what's happening with Tom," Harriet countered.

"Ahh, you forget, my sibling works there," Lauren said smugly.

"No matter what you think, neither James nor I are looking for a relationship right now."

"The best relationships start that way," Connie whispered loudly to Mavis.

"I heard that," Harriet told them.

"Okay," Robin said. "I need to get going. Who's going to do what?"

Lauren took out her tablet and woke it up.

"I said I'd see what I can find out about any possible work problems Molly might have had." She tapped a note onto her calendar, reminding herself what she'd agreed to.

Connie gathered her empty cup and put her crumpled napkin into it.

"Mavis and I are scheduled to deliver food to the homeless camp tomorrow from the church pantry. We can talk to Joyce Elias and see what she knows about Max's whereabouts on the night in question."

Robin jotted down the assignments and then wrote her own name.

"I'll dig in the court records and see what I can find out about Gary Alexander. Anyone else?"

Carla coughed and cleared her throat.

"I could talk to the psychic."

"Oh, honey," Connie said. "That could be dangerous."

"When I was young, my mom dated a carny. We traveled with the carnival for a whole year. Madam Geni taught me some things about how to fake people out. She read fortunes, but it's the same idea."

Carla had probably been in more dangerous situations than the whole group together, Harriet thought.

"Look up the psychic on the Internet first. If he or she has a website or advertises their services, it should be okay," Harriet said and looked at Connie and Mavis for approval.

"I can agree to that," Mavis said.

"Since I've never seen the poet, I can go to the bookstore and ask after him. I will also go to his real job." Jenny looked at Harriet. "Didn't you say he worked at that convenience store out on the highway?"

"That's right. And while you all are doing your assignments, I'll see if I can track down Josh Phillips. I'd like to know if we can establish whether he was still in town last night. Molly's workplace may know, plus I can check at the motel."

Foggy Point only had one motel, so she didn't need to say anything more about it.

"I'm going to go by the police station and find out if Morse or anyone else will tell me if they were able to check Juana's tracker and see if she was near my aunt's car. If Morse is in, I'll ask if she knows anything she can share about Molly."

"Good idea," Lauren said.

Robin wrote the final assignments on her pad and stuffed it back into her purse with her pen.

"Shall we meet again on Thursday?" she asked.

"How about we meet at Jorge's for lunch on Thursday," Mavis suggested. She turned to Harriet. "You can bring the first quilt for us to start binding at the same time."

"Sounds like a plan. I'm going to swing by the PD on my way home, and then I need to get stitching. See you all Thursday."

Chapter 14

Detective Morse looked tired when she came to meet Harriet at the front counter of the Foggy Point Police Department. Her normally close-cropped hair was over her ears and showing signs of a long-overdue trip to the hairdresser, and the dark patches under her eyes were more pronounced.

"Let's put a visitor's tag on you, and we can go back to my desk."

Harriet wrote her name in the logbook and was given a stick-on badge by the desk sergeant. Morse buzzed the door open, and Harriet followed her through a warren of cubicles to the cold case squad section.

"Are you doing okay?" she asked.

Detective Morse rubbed her hand over her face and sighed.

"I'm fine. I've got some family drama going on. My mother can't live on her own anymore, and it's a battle royal among my siblings as to what we do next. Nothing that can't be solved—I'm just spending a lot of time on late-night phone calls from the warring factions."

Harriet's mouth tilted up on one side in a half-smile.

"I guess there are some benefits to being an only child."

Morse laughed.

"My sibs are a handful, but I'm glad I don't have to deal with my mother alone. Now, I'm sure you didn't come here to talk about my personal problems."

"I was hoping to find out if they've been able to track Juana's movements. And…" She watched for a reaction. "…I was hoping you could tell me something about what's going on about Molly Baker."

"Your pipeline will already have told you as much as I can. She's dead from a blow to the head, and one of the homeless camp residents found her. That's about as much as we know right now. Since she's connected to my cold case, I'm in on the investigation, so believe me when I tell you—we don't know anything yet. If you have any information for us, I'd like to hear it."

Harriet leaned back in her chair.

"You probably know I called Molly's phone, and it was answered by a detective. That was how I found out something was wrong."

Morse poured a paper cup full of water from a pitcher that sat on the tan file cabinet next to her desk. Harriet took it and sipped before continuing.

"I had three voice messages on my cell phone while I was at the hospital with my aunt."

Morse leaned forward but didn't say anything.

"The first two just said to call her."

"Did you save them?" Morse interrupted.

"No, I didn't know they would matter. Anyway, the third one said she'd spoken with a psychic and knew how to find Amber. And no, I didn't save that one, either. Molly had been pretty persistent in her demands for help finding out what had happened to Amber. I thought it was just one more of her crazy ideas."

"She said 'how' to find Amber? Not 'where' to find her?"

"We noticed that, too. It was definitely 'how.' It struck us all as odd."

"Anything else?"

"She said she 'remembered', whatever that means. Mostly my relationship with Molly was her asking me to help her find Amber and me saying if the police couldn't find her, I didn't know what she expected me to do."

"*Did* you do anything?"

"Only talk to Leo Tabor and his wife. Mavis and my aunt thought he might know something because he had taken Amber to the police when she was wandering the neighborhood."

"And because he was the number-one suspect back then?"

"Not really. Avanell Jalbert had told them he wasn't a molester or anything else. He had worked for her. They really thought he might know something. He was really nice, but all he knew was that Amber wandered the neighborhood unattended."

"You will let me know if you hear anything else, won't you?"

"You'll be the first to know."

Harriet felt only a little guilty that she hadn't mentioned the Loose Threads' plan to gather information. She was also sure Morse wasn't telling her everything the police knew.

"Let's go see if we can find out where Juana's been."

Morse led the way through the maze until they reached a police technician sitting in front of a computer screen.

"Have you been able to get the data from the GPS tracker on Juana Lopez-Montoya?"

The technician clicked a few keys and opened a new screen that showed a map on the top half and a list below it. He pointed to the map.

"This shows you where she went, and the list below tells you all the locations where she stopped for more than ninety seconds, and how long she was in those locations."

He clicked the keyboard again, and a new map was superimposed over Juana's trail.

"This is the map of where you said your aunt's car was." He pointed to first one then a second place on the map. "She was at or near the grocery store when you were there. And she was within a block of you when you went to the quilt store, but she was only there for four minutes, and it looks like she stayed at the corner. Was your car parked close to the intersection?"

Harriet shook her head.

"No, I was in the middle of the block."

The tech turned away from his computer and looked at Detective Morse.

"Someone needs to request the security footage from the grocery store. I can check it out if you get it."

"I'll tell the officers who are investigating the accident what you found. Thanks for rushing it."

The tech smiled.

"We aim to please."

He turned around and was clicking back to the screen he'd been working on when they interrupted him before they left his cubicle.

They started back toward the front desk. Morse stopped and turned to Harriet.

"I'll be surprised if Juana was able to work on your aunt's car in the grocery store parking lot without anyone interrupting her. This is a small town, and a lot of people know Juana. If she was messing with a car in broad daylight, I'd like to think someone would have come over to see what she was doing."

"If she didn't do it, then who did?"

Morse sighed.

✄ --- ✄ --- ✄

Harriet clicked her phone on to display the time and did a quick calculation. If she didn't linger long, she could swing by Aunt Beth's and see how she was doing. It might make her aunt feel better to know it probably wasn't Juana who'd tampered with her car.

She stopped at the florists and picked up an arrangement of lilies and roses and then drove out to the cottage on the strait.

"Hey, aren't you supposed to be in bed?" she asked when she'd let herself in.

Aunt Beth was propped in her recliner with a pillow under her feet. She clicked her television off with the remote.

"They just said I had to rest."

Harriet set the vase of flowers on the coffee table.

"I'm pretty sure when they said only get up to go to the bathroom they were thinking you'd be in bed the rest of the time."

"I'm fine here. If you must know, the doctor called this morning after Connie and Mavis left. He said the radiologist looked at my x-rays and decided I chipped my ankle bone. They don't do anything different for that, but it did give me the chance to ask if sitting in my recliner was okay; and he said if I put a pillow under my foot to help with the elevation, it was fine." She pressed her lips together and gave Harriet a smug look.

"Okay, fine, excuse me for trying to take care of you."

Aunt Beth's face softened.

"Oh, honey, I know you mean well, but you know how I hate daytime television. I'd go crazy laying in that hide-a-bed worrying about what sort of trouble you were getting yourself into.

"Can you sit a minute and tell me what happened at your meeting. And don't try to tell me you gals just talked about the quilts."

Harriet opened her mouth to speak, but the doorbell rang before she could get any words out.

"Are you expecting anyone?" she asked as she got up to answer the door.

"No one called ahead."

She opened the door and found DeAnn on the porch, a vase of purple and yellow wildflowers in hand.

"Is this a good time to visit? If it isn't, I can just drop these and go." She pulled a card from the side pocket of her purse.

Harriet swung the door wide to let her in.

"I think my aunt is up for a short visit." She took the flowers and set them on the bookcase."Would you like tea or anything?"

DeAnn set her purse down and perched on the corner of the sofa closest to Beth.

"How are you doing? Robin told me your car was tampered with?"

"It's nothing serious. I'm a little banged and bruised, but I'll be fine in a few days. Enough about me. I'm so sorry to hear about your sister. How are you holding up?"

DeAnn's shoulders sagged, and she looked first at Harriet and then Beth.

"This is going to sound terrible, and I am sad about my sister, but right now, what I feel most is relief. Am I a terrible person?" Her eyes swept from Harriet to Beth again, and a tear dribbled from her left eye.

Beth plucked a couple of tissues from the box on her side table and handed them to Harriet to pass to DeAnn.

"Honey, you are not a terrible person. Tell me what's going on."

DeAnn dabbed at her eyes with the tissue.

"I'm terrible to even say this, but Molly's obsession with finding out what happened to Amber and her was really disruptive. I know I should feel sorry for her, and I do…did…but her search dominated our family in more ways than one.

"My parents drained their savings account paying for her to go on one wild goose chase after another, to say nothing of the years of therapy they paid for. They put up the money for her to start her nonprofit, and I know it's a good cause. Who can argue with helping the families of missing and exploited children? But they can't retire now because they gave more than they really had.

"And then there were the 'crisis' calls. It didn't matter if it was their grandchild's birthday party, Mother's Day, Father's Day or any other holiday—if Molly called with a hot lead, or called because she'd followed a false lead one more time, they ran to her side, wherever she was, ruining whatever we had planned."

She dabbed her eyes again.

"I know I sound selfish, but how many times do you have to be taken advantage of by people trying to get your reward money for tips before you figure it out. There are no witnesses waiting to come forward. No one wants her to solve this. And now she's found out in a horrible way that whoever killed Amber and knocked her out doesn't want anyone to know what really happened."

She dropped her hands into her lap.

"Why couldn't she just be happy she'd survived?"

Harriet and Beth looked away while DeAnn sobbed. She wiped her eyes again and straightened her shoulders. She looked up at Beth.

"I'm sorry. I didn't mean to come over and dump on you two. I really did want to know how you were doing and say I hope you feel better."

"Honey, you come by anytime. You're in a real difficult situation, and I'm sure you're going to feel a lot of things when you think about your sister. It's okay, however you feel. And I'm sure there is a sense of relief when you consider your parents' situation. No matter how much you loved Molly and how hurt she was by what had happened to her, she wasn't seeing how she was causing problems for your parents. I'd be willing to bet you and your David have been thinking about how you were going to be able to support your parents when they can't work anymore. Now maybe they can save a little for the future."

DeAnn's face relaxed and her lips twitched into a half-smile.

"Thank you. Now, I really do need to go."

"You come back anytime, honey. And bring those cute kids by. Those boys are going to be in college before I see them again."

DeAnn laughed.

"It's not that bad. They're not out of grade school yet. I'll be sure and bring them by when all this…" She gestured to indicate everything that was going on. "…stuff, is over."

"You do that, and thank you for the beautiful flowers and card."

DeAnn picked up her purse and left.

Chapter 15

Aunt Beth picked up an appliqué flower block from the table beside her chair and began stitching the edge of a leaf with neat invisible stitches.

"So, tell me, what did you all figure out at the meeting this morning?"

Harriet recited the high points of the discussion.

"I've already done my first task, which was checking in with Detective Morse about Juana. I have to see if Josh Phillips was still in town. Carla is checking on the psychic Molly went to, Lauren is going to research Molly's work background to see if there's anyone else who had a grudge against her. Robin is checking court records to see what Gary Alexander is up to." She explained about James's mother and her neighbor. "On a happier note, Jenny came to coffee, and she looked really good."

"That's good," Aunt Beth interrupted.

"Yes, it is. Anyway, she's going to the bookstore and that convenience store out by the highway to see if we can figure out where Molly's new boyfriend was during the critical time. And I don't know if you've talked to Connie or Mavis yet, but they're going out to the homeless camp to see what Joyce and her crew know."

"Is anyone going to go talk to Sandra Price? She must have a theory about what happened to her daughter."

"Hmmm, we didn't talk about that. We were more focused on Molly and who would have wanted her dead."

"If it was related to what happened before, she might have some ideas." Aunt Beth squirmed in her chair and repositioned her foot.

"Is your foot hurting? Is it time for a pain pill?"

Aunt Beth gave her a weak smile.

"I haven't been taking them. I hate how that stuff makes me feel."

"You mean free of pain?"

"You stop your sassing and get me a glass of water to take it with."

Harriet laughed as she went into the kitchen to do as she was told.

"Do any of the Threads have a relationship with Sandra Price?" she asked when she'd returned and handed her aunt the water.

Aunt Beth took her pill then rubbed her chin with her hand.

"I think Connie had her son in school. She's probably your best bet. Of course, DeAnn's family knows her—they had a lot of contact when the little girl disappeared. But they've got enough on their plate right now. I'm going to snooze a while, and then I'll call Connie and see if she can talk to Sandra. *You* need to go get stitching on those quilts."

"Let me know what she says, and you call me if you need anything."

Beth closed her eyes.

"A little peace and quiet might be nice," Harriet heard her murmur as she made her way out.

✂ --- ✂ --- ✂

Harriet was doing the yoga stretches Robin had taught her when Carla knocked on her studio door several hours later.

"I'm sorry to interrupt," she said and hesitated on the porch when Harriet opened the door wide.

"Come on in. I've been working on this quilt for hours. I was just stretching before I take Scooter out and fix something to drink. Can you stay and have a snack?"

Carla looked at her shoes.

"I don't have to pick Wendy up from playgroup for…" She looked at her phone. "…forty-five minutes.

"Can you go in and pour us some lemonade while I take the little prince out?" Harriet's dog was lying in his bed, his snout over the edge, looking from Harriet to Carla and back to see if anyone was really going to make him get up.

"So, did you find the psychic?" Harriet asked a few minutes later when the two were seated at the kitchen table, lemonade and chocolate chip cookies in front of them.

Carla shredded the edge of her napkin.

"I met her at her…I don't know what you call her place. It was all draped with silk scarves, and there were real crystal balls on metal stands and other kinds of crystals. And there was a lot of incense burning. There weren't any real chairs, just big pillows all over the place."

"You're sure this is the one Molly met with?"

Carla didn't answer the question. "She said she'd asked Molly for an object of hers to hold on to, and Molly gave her a keychain. She showed it to me—it was from her missing-person place."

"Did she offer to read your palm?"

Carla blushed.

"She did. And I couldn't stop her. She grabbed my hand and started apologizing for what a bad upbringing I'd had. She was just like a carnival palm reader. I don't think she was a real psychic. Anyone could look at me and guess I'd not had a normal childhood."

"I don't think that's true, but I think you're right—she sounds like a fake. Are you sure this is the person Molly visited? I know she had the keychain, but half of Foggy Point has those."

"I called Molly's office and asked the secretary to look at her calendar. There was an appointment with Madame Lenormand last Friday, so that's who I went to see."

"Wait, did you say Lenormand? That's the name of a famous Parisian fortune teller in the late eighteenth, early nineteenth century. She supposedly was a confidant of the Empress Josephine as well as others." Harriet stopped talking for a moment. "Sorry. I did a boarding school stint in a French convent, and she had lived there. I don't know much about psychics, but when you combine the theatrical setting with the name, I'm even more sure Madame isn't genuine." She looked at Carla. "Whatever that is. Besides, I think Molly would have called me sooner if she'd gotten anything on Friday."

"Let's check with the secretary and see who Molly met with in the last few days then look each of the names up and see if any are psychics."

"I should have thought of that," Carla said and sipped her lemonade. "Molly's secretary is one of the moms from the single-parents group at church. They're all upset about her being killed, so I'm pretty sure she'll tell me."

Harriet chewed a bite of cookie.

"I'd have gone to that lady first, too, if I didn't recognize the name. How were you to know? In the meantime, when we're finished, would you take a look at the first of our quilts and tell me if you think I've done enough quilting on it?"

Carla smiled and nodded.

✂ --- ✂ --- ✂

Scooter ran into Harriet's studio barking, followed closely by Fred. They jumped into the wing-back chair closest to the bay window and did their own special harmony that consisted of barking and yowling. She looked up to see James's van parked in her driveway and the chef himself walking Cyrano on a leash in her yard.

"You two hush," she scolded as she opened the door. The sun had gone down while she was stitching, and she hadn't noticed she'd been so intent on watching the quilt under her needle. The ceiling lights in her studio were the natural-sunlight variety, and she kept them on all the time when she was working so the thread color would be true.

"Hey," she called.

"Hi, I hope you don't mind me stopping by. I'll just put Cyrano back in the van and get the snack I made."

"He can come in with you and your snack. These two are all bark and no bite, and they're used to being around my aunt's dog so I don't think they'll be a problem."

James grinned, and Harriet smiled back, considering not for the first time that he really was a good-looking guy. She'd always chalked it up to the fact that he usually was handing her chocolate or some other amazing treat when he smiled at her, but tonight she realized it was more than that.

He reached into his van and pulled out an insulated carrier and a plastic container.

"I figured you would be working day and night on those quilts you have to make for that benefit, and I was hungry, so I decided to take a chance. I threw together a pizza. I hope you like artichokes."

Harriet took the carrier from him.

"I could eat cardboard I'm so hungry."

"You're easy," he said. His face turned red. "I didn't mean…I'm glad you like…"

Harriet put her hand on his arm.

"James, stop. I know what you meant, and anyway, sometimes I *am* easy," she said and, with a wicked grin, led the way back into the house.

He followed her into the kitchen and busied himself removing the pizza from its container. Harriet prepared bowls of food for Scooter and Fred on the other side of the kitchen bar.

"Can Cyrano have a little snack?"

"I'd like that…I mean, he'd like that…I mean, he hasn't eaten yet, and now I won't have to rush off to feed him. I'm not inviting myself to dinner, I really did bring this just for you."

Harriet laughed.

"James. Stop. Of course you're staying for dinner and after, too, if you want."

"I'd like that. I mean, I'd like to stay if you'd like me to stay. I'm sorry, you must think I'm an idiot."

Harriet walked around the bar, took the pizza from him, and set it on the counter. She pulled him into her arms and planted a kiss on him before he could react. He put his arms around her and leaned into the kiss, prolonging it, his hands sliding down her back and grasping her bottom.

She opened her eyes and gazed into his, which were dreamy and half-closed. The thought that she might be ruining a great friendship flashed through her mind as she parted her lips slightly, and he kissed her again. His teeth toyed with her lower lip, and he gave her a quick last kiss and stepped back.

Her face was warm as she smiled at him; he seemed to be shocked speechless. She set the animal food dishes on the floor and stood back up to face him.

"I thought we should get that out of the way so we could enjoy our pizza. I know you said you aren't looking for a relationship because of the restaurant, and I've been in a very messy relationship. I'm not trying to compete with the restaurant, but…"

He put his finger on her lips.

"Stop. I'm committed to my restaurant, but I'm not dead. I know you're in a bad situation, and I've been trying to respect that, but I think we can agree, I wouldn't be coming around if I wasn't interested in you. I'd like to think you keep letting me in for more than my food, fantastic though it is. What if we agree that for now we'll be friends with just a few benefits and see what happens? I don't know about you, but I get tired of spending my evenings talking to a dog."

Harriet kissed his finger, and he pulled her into another brief kiss then leaned back to look at her.

"Do we have a deal?"

"I think an uncomplicated relationship sounds great. And you're right —I'm getting tired of spending every night alone with these two."

"Okay, then, let's eat—I'm starving."

Harriet felt warm all over as she reached into the cupboard and got two plates out. She wasn't sure if she was doing the right thing, but for the first time in months, she felt good.

Chapter 16

Foggy Point was thick with its namesake weather the next morning, and Harriet was thoroughly chilled even after her post-run shower. She fed her pets and grabbed a thermal mug from her cupboard, intending to get a mocha to go.

Her plans changed when she noticed Lauren's, Connie's and Mavis's cars in the Steaming Cup parking lot.

"Am I crashing a party?" she asked when she'd gotten her drink and come over to the large rectangular table in the middle of the room.

Connie looked up at her.

"Mavis and I went over to keep your aunt company, but we drove by and her lights weren't on, so we figured we'd let her sleep a while longer."

Lauren keyed her laptop computer off and closed the top.

"I'm just here working."

"Have you learned anything useful about Molly's work background?" Harriet asked her.

"I might be on to something. Molly testified against a guy named De-Shaun Smith. He apparently had a big-time prostitution ring going and beat one of his girls to within an inch of her life. He was sentenced to twenty-five years, but he was released last year on a technicality. I found an address in Seattle."

Harriet sipped her mocha then set her cup on the table and sat down.

"Sounds like a road trip is in order."

"After the quilts are finished," Connie reminded her.

"I know. I'm coming right along. The first one is off the machine, and I've got a couple of hours into the second one."

93

Lauren leaned back in her chair and sipped her coffee.

"Have you had a chance to check with Detective Morse yet?"

Harriet took a deep breath and blew it out.

"I did. We talked to the technician who is monitoring Juana's tracking chip, and it doesn't look like she could have sabotaged Aunt Beth's car."

Connie visibly relaxed.

"I'm so relieved. I've been so angry about someone hurting Beth that I could strangle them with my bare hands, but at the same time, I've felt terrible guilt for wanting to harm a developmentally challenged person."

Lauren patted her on the back and laughed.

"I'm so glad you're going to be able to strangle a fully able person."

The thought of Connie, all four-foot-eleven and ninety pounds of her, strangling anyone made Harriet laugh out loud.

Connie blushed.

"I'm not going to hurt anyone, but it makes me so mad. Beth never hurt anyone, and in fact, she does more good in this community than any of us."

"And now we're back to square one," Harriet said. "I haven't checked on Josh Phillips yet. I figured I'd better work on the quilts."

"Good decision," Mavis told her.

"Carla came by yesterday. She'd checked out the psychic who was listed in Molly's calendar, but she turned out to be a fake."

"Aren't they all?" Lauren said.

Connie reached out and patted her on the arm.

"You hush now and let Harriet speak."

Harriet nodded at Connie and smirked at Lauren.

"Thank you. As I was saying, Carla didn't get anywhere on the first go-round, but she has a friend in Molly's office. She's going to get the names of the people Molly had appointments with for the last few days…"

"You're assuming she had an appointment with this person," Lauren interrupted. "What if she saw a sign from the road and pulled in for a five-dollar palm reading?"

Mavis set her hand-piecing block on the table in front of her.

"Whoever Molly saw was credible enough that it jogged her mind into remembering everything. That's what she said, right?"

Harriet nodded and picked up her drink.

"That doesn't sound like a five-dollar palm reader. A credible psychic would have a more businesslike arrangement. I think Carla will find the name on Molly's schedule."

Connie sipped her tea.

"Let's hope you're right."

Harriet gathered her purse and cup and stood up.

"When you go see Aunt Beth, would you please encourage her to take her pain medication? When I saw her yesterday, she was obviously uncomfortable and confessed she hadn't taken any of her pain pills. I got her to take one, and she was asleep before I left her driveway. She needs to rest if she's going to get better."

Lauren made a mock salute.

"I'm going to go talk to Sandra Price later this afternoon," Connie said and looked at Harriet. "Do you want to come with me?"

"Sure. If I stitch on the quilt from now until then I should be in good shape. Call me when you're on your way over so I can get to a good stopping place."

Mavis packed her sewing project and drained her coffee cup.

"Connie and I better get going, too. We need to pick up sandwiches to take to the homeless camp."

Lauren turned her computer off.

"I feel like a slacker. I've just got to work all day for paying customers."

Harriet laughed.

"I can almost remember what that's like."

The group broke up after Harriet promised to fill Lauren in on whatever was learned from the day's activities.

✂ --- ✂ --- ✂

"Come on, Scooter," Harriet called. "Aunt Connie is coming, and you need to walk before that."

Scooter stretched as he crawled out of his bed. Harriet had been stitching for four hours straight, and neither of her pets was amused. Fred had woven through her legs and meowed, but when the only action he could get was an ear scratch, he went off in a huff and flopped down in the wing-back chair closest to the window. She'd finally put a dog DVD on her computer for Scooter to distract him from taking up Fred's post at her feet. After thirty minutes of whining and barking along to his show, he retreated to his bed under her desk.

They'd just returned to the house when Connie pulled into the circular driveway.

"How was the trip to the homeless camp?" she asked when Connie was out of her car.

"It's always nice to visit with Joyce, but that's about as far as it went. They didn't really know anything. It seems the newspapers made more of their involvement than was actually supported by facts. Molly was dropped in the woods near one of the main trails. Max was the one who found her, but anyone could have been the one. Joyce said she and Max had just come back from a walk into town, so she'd been with him for the three or four hours before he found Molly, and he was only out of her sight for a few minutes before he came back to get her help. They said she was right in plain sight, so the park security guard would have found her at closing time if one of them hadn't come across her earlier."

Harriet led the way back inside to get Scooter settled. She refreshed his water and fluffed his bed.

"You behave while I'm gone," she said and turned to Connie. "Does Sandra know we're coming?"

"I called and asked her if we could come by. She agreed, but she didn't seem very enthused."

"I'll be curious to hear what the police told her back then. They must have had some idea as to what happened, even if they couldn't prove it."

Connie pulled her keys from her purse.

"I'll drive," she volunteered.

✄ --- ✄ --- ✄

A laurel hedge partially blocked the view of the Price house from the street. It was untrimmed and had big sections missing, probably from past storm damage. Moss crusted the roof of the house, and a large tree leaned ominously in the direction of the second-story gable. Someone had made a half-hearted attempt at painting the house but had failed to sand the peeling previous coating.

Connie parked on the street.

"Are you sure this is it?" Harriet asked her.

She looked at the address she'd written on a piece of paper.

"This is the address she gave me when I called." She looped her purse strap over her arm. "Come on, let's get this over with."

Sandra Price met them at the door and ushered them into the kitchen eating area. She was a small, thin woman with blond hair and the kind of tan that made you think tanning bed, not sunny beaches.

"I'm Sandra," she said to Harriet. "Connie tells me you're Beth Carlson's niece. Would you like some coffee?" She pulled out a chair for Connie.

"No, thank you," Connie said as she sat down in the offered chair.

Harriet held her hand in front of her.

"None for me either, thanks."

Sandra nodded toward the chair opposite Connie, and Harriet circled the table and sat down as well. Sandra sat at the end of the table between them. Before sitting, she pulled a small box of mints from her pocket, opened the lid and held it out.

"None for me, thanks," Harriet told her.

Connie declined, too, then clasped her hands on the edge of the table. "How are you doing? I'm sure this business with Molly Baker has stirred up some bad memories for you."

While Connie was sympathizing with Sandra, Harriet took the opportunity to look around the house. The counters were clean, if dated. The linoleum was worn but shiny with wax. A bowl of fresh fruit sat in the center of the table. Pictures covered the front of the refrigerator, all of recent vintage. The beige carpet in the living room was free of stain or wear patterns, and the brocade drapes free of dust. Not at all what she'd expected when they'd pulled up.

"I'm sure you all didn't come by just to see how I was doing," Sandra said. She reached over and patted Connie's hand. "I do appreciate your sympathy, but how can I help you?"

Harriet cleared her throat.

"Molly is, or was, the half-sister of one of the women in our quilt group. When she came back to town in advance of a benefit her organization is putting on, she stopped by and talked to us about helping her figure out what happened to her all those years ago."

Sandra looked down and shook her head.

"I don't want to speak ill of the dead, but that girl has plagued my life for the last ten years or more. As soon as she reached her teens, she started coming around here, asking if we could tell her anything about the time when she was kidnapped. Losing a child is the worst thing that can happen in this life, and then having to relive it year after year has been almost unbearable. At one point, I even talked to the police. I didn't want to have to take a restraining order out on her, but she was upsetting my other kids."

"Did she come here in the last couple of weeks?" Connie asked.

"She did. She'd left us alone for probably six months, but she came back…" She thought for a moment. "…Tuesday of last week, maybe. It might have been Monday. She wanted to know if I'd remembered anything new. Seriously, my daughter disappeared twenty years ago. I've wracked my brain for anything the police could use to help figure out what happened to Amber. If I knew anything I'd have told them then."

She blew her breath out. "If I'd known she was going to be taken, maybe I'd have been able to remember better, but honestly, it was just a day like any other. I remember I was doing laundry, but I did laundry every day. I was in the basement folding clothes. Amber and Molly had been watching a cartoon on TV. I didn't let my kids watch a lot of TV, so I'd set the timer and she would stay right there until the bell went off.

"Anyway, as I said, I was working downstairs, and I guess I didn't realize that Amber hadn't come down—when her timer would go off, she'd usually come to wherever I was and try to talk me into another show. I figured she and Molly were playing."

Sandra got up and got a tissue from a box in a crocheted cover. She dabbed at her eyes then returned to her seat.

"I don't know how long I was down there before I noticed she hadn't come. I feel so guilty. If I'd just gone upstairs and checked on them, Amber might still be here."

"I'm sorry we're bringing this all back up again," Connie said and looked at Harriet.

"Molly had asked us to try to figure out what happened to her back then, and now she's dead, so we're hoping to find some answers for her sister. What we wondered is if you could tell us what the police thought happened twenty years ago. I know lots of times the police have an idea what happened in a crime, but they can't get enough evidence to prosecute anyone."

"Honestly, they told us they thought she had been taken by a man who took several children in the Puget Sound area in that same time period. A man named Joe Kondro. They never found Amber." She sobbed a little. "They put him in jail for killing a couple of other children. He died in prison in twenty-twelve. I have to tell you—for me and my sons, it's over. I'll always feel guilty about leaving Amber and Molly upstairs alone, but I believe that man killed her, and now he's dead."

"Did they say back then what they thought happened to Molly?" Harriet asked her.

Sandra shook her head.

"They said she was a lucky girl, that she somehow escaped whoever took them. Or maybe the killer had a plan that involved only one girl. Molly didn't fit his pattern. God works in mysterious ways. Apparently, though, he wasn't done with her." She shook her head. "I tried to tell her she was the lucky one, but she didn't believe me. My therapist said she had survivor's guilt."

"*Diós mio*. That poor girl suffered her whole life because she was the one who lived." Connie pressed her lips together and shook her head, unconsciously mimicking Sandra.

Harriet stood up.

"Thanks for taking the time to talk to us. We'll pass on what you told us to Molly's family. I think it'll help them."

"I hope so. It's time for all of us to stop living in the past."

"Thanks again," Harriet said.

She and Connie didn't speak until they were in the car and driving away.

"So, what did you think?" she asked.

"I feel so sorry for that woman and her family. I can't imagine losing a child."

"That's what I was thinking. And then to have Molly wanting to talk about it all the time must have made it worse than it already was."

"Funny, Molly never mentioned the serial killer explanation."

Harriet looked down at her hands.

"It's terrible to say, but if Molly accepted it was a serial killer that would mean it was random, and she'd have to move on with her life. She wasn't ready to do that."

"It makes you wonder what happened in her head that she got stuck at that time and place in her life."

"What it makes me wonder is who killed Molly if it wasn't related to what happened when she was five."

"We still have the abusive ex to track down, and we've got to see what Lauren's found in her search of Molly's past work situations."

"Do you have time to drive us to Molly's office? That's our first stop in tracking Josh Phillips."

"This is more important; what I need to do can wait," Connie said. She turned left at the next corner and headed them toward the offices of the local missing children's organization.

Harriet's heart made an involuntary lurch when she saw a familiar vintage black Bronco in the parking lot of The Carey Bates Missing and Exploited Children Organization. Connie looked at her and reached a hand out to pat hers as she drove in and parked.

"Honey, it's not Aiden."

Harriet stiffened at the touch.

"I didn't think it was."

"Aiden asked Carla to drive each of the cars in the garage once in a while."

A closer looked showed Wendy's car seat in the back.

Connie turned to Harriet.

"I know this has been hard on you, but it's been hard on Aiden, too. He's still trying to figure out what it all means."

"Avanell was your friend, and I understand that you and Aunt Beth and Mavis feel like you have to rally around Aiden in his time of trouble. The part I'm having trouble with is being cut out of the whole process. He's all but stopped calling me, and when he does, we don't have anything to talk about. There hasn't been the slightest suggestion about the future. He talks about his work in Africa and how exciting it is and how it helps him forget what happened here. There hasn't been any talk about us. None."

Harriet had spent more than a few sleepless nights trying to convince herself that Aiden's escape to Africa and his lack of communication since was understandable, given his mother's death and then his sister's betrayal. But even with all of the tragedy he'd had to deal with, if he loved her the way he'd said he did, why did he insist on shutting her out? More important, did they have a future as a couple if he wasn't willing to talk?

A tear slid down Harriet's face and dripped down onto her folded hands.

"Oh, honey, I'm so sorry. You didn't do anything to deserve this, and we care about and support you, too. None of us is enjoying seeing you hurting."

She handed Harriet a tissue from a box on the car's center console.

Another tear followed the first down Harriet's cheek, and she dabbed at it with the now wadded-up tissue.

"What if he never comes home?" she said her voice bleak.

"You will be just fine. You have me and your aunt and the rest of the Threads. Besides, I think you need to think more about what you're going to do when he *does* come home."

Harriet looked stricken.

Connie handed her another tissue.

"Come on, dry your eyes. This isn't the time for this discussion. We can talk it out later when your aunt and Mavis are there. We need to find out about Josh and see what Carla has learned."

The workers in the office were all wearing their own personal version of mourning. A girl who looked like she was still in her teens had on an orange tunic with black trim over black-and-white striped leggings. An older woman wore a plain white sari over salwar kameez, the pants and shirt often seen under a sari, although her skin was so pale it was hard to imagine her as East Indian.

A blonde in a gray linen suit came out to greet them.

"How may I help you?" she said automatically and then recognized Harriet. "I'm sorry, you're Molly's friend. She showed us your picture on the Internet from when you helped with a local murder."

"Which one?" Connie muttered so only Harriet could hear. Harriet elbowed her.

Since Harriet didn't respond immediately, the woman continued.

"We're all so sorry about Molly's death. Her organization has helped us so much. We were just a small local effort until Molly asked us to join her group. She connected us to national databases we didn't even know existed. And she held meetings with other groups like us so we could pool our resources when an event happened. We've recovered four girls since we came under her parent organization." She looked at the woman in the sari. "I hope someone continues her work."

She paused a moment. It seemed like it was the first time she'd thought about the broader implications of Molly's passing.

"She told us you were helping her find out what happened to her when she was young," the woman finished, "and also helping to figure out what happened to little Amber Price."

Harriet took a deep breath and let it out slowly.

"I'm afraid Molly greatly exaggerated our crime-solving abilities. Our quilt group has been involved in a few local crimes, but only when it impacted us somehow. We're not detectives, we're quilters."

"So, if you're not here to investigate what happened to Molly, how can I help you?"

Harriet looked at Connie for help.

"We came to see if you know how to get in touch with Josh Phillips. As you know, we're making quilts for the three major donors at your fundraiser. We planned the quilts when it was just the two that were going to women. We were thinking we maybe should check with Josh to see if our color selections were going to be okay for him. If he's keeping it, he might want a more masculine choice."

Harriet kept her face carefully neutral and watched the blonde. She knew there wasn't a chance on earth they would start over on Josh's quilt. He was getting lavender and green whether he liked it or not.

"I don't know if he's still in town, but as of Monday he was. He came by in the morning to talk about the arrangements for wiring his donation to our account."

"Do you know how to get in touch with him?" Harriet asked.

"He's staying at the motel downtown. At least that's what he said."

Carla came in from an interior hallway. She looked at the girl in the orange tunic.

"Thanks, Sadie," she said and paused only briefly to say bye to Connie and Harriet before hustling out the door.

"We'd better get going, too," Harriet said and followed Carla before the blond woman could ask the questions that were clearly occurring to her, judging by the look on her face.

"Thanks," Connie said over her shoulder as they exited.

Carla was standing beside Connie's car when they were all clear of the building.

"Nice save," Harriet told Connie as they walked up to the car. She filled Carla in on the deception.

"I was worried when I saw you in the reception area," Carla said. "Sadie told her boss that I wanted to consult the psychic Molly had gone to, and that she'd let me check her calendar."

Harriet smiled.

"Good going. Will your friend be in trouble for helping you?"

Carla's mouth curled up on one side.

"No, the office manager is her aunt. She gets away with murder." She paused, and her face turned pink. "I didn't mean…"

Connie patted her arm.

"We know what you mean. Now, did you find a name?"

"I did." She held out a piece of paper with a name and number on it. Harriet looked at the paper then folded it and put it in her purse.

"If it's okay with you, I'll give her a call and see if she can meet with us tomorrow. Did you see anything else while you were in Molly's office?"

"I wasn't sure what might be important." Carla pulled her smartphone from her pocket and tapped several buttons on its screen.

"I took pictures of her calendar on the computer and the paper appointment book on her desk."

Harriet patted her on the back.

"Good going. You may have a future as a real detective."

Connie looked back toward the office building.

"We should go. I don't want that woman seeing we're still here and coming out here to ask more questions."

Chapter 17

$\mathcal{H}$arriet checked her phone as Scooter sniffed at every blade of grass along the side of her driveway. She realized she'd silenced it before she and Connie went into Molly's office and had forgotten to wake it up when they left. Jorge had left a voice message. She pressed the speaker button then activated the message.

"I'm making tacos al pastor for your aunt tonight. There will be plenty for you to join us, and bring Blondie, if you want." said the disembodied voice. "No need to call, just come around six."

Harriet looked at the time. She could stitch for thirty minutes or so and still make it in plenty of time.

"Want to go see your friend Brownie?" she asked her dog. He looked up at her briefly and went back to sniffing.

She called Lauren, and they arranged to meet at her aunt's house in an hour.

✂ --- ✂ --- ✂

They arrived at Beth's house at the same time.

"Are you sure your aunt is up for this party?" Lauren asked as they started for the front door.

"I called her before I left home, and she specifically said to bring our dogs. She said Brownie is going stir crazy having to stay home and wanted company of the canine variety."

"I think we know who's the one going stir crazy," Lauren said and tapped on the door before opening it.

"How are you feeling," Harriet asked when she'd unleashed her dog and put her purse in the front closet.

103

Beth was sitting in her leather recliner, her foot elevated.

Harriet removed her shoes without thinking. The chair sat on a large hand-braided wool rug her aunt had spent years making. Beth didn't care if shoes touched her rug, but Harriet knew how much work had gone into the gathering, cutting and dying of all the wool coats that went into the rug and didn't want to chance soiling it.

"I'm fine. I've been trying to tell everyone I'm fine. You don't have to keep treating me like an invalid."

"Until your doctor decides you're good enough to start physical therapy, we're going to make sure you follow his orders and keep your foot elevated and rest," Harriet told her.

Aunt Beth pressed her lips together but didn't say anything. Harriet guessed she'd lost this argument more than once in the last two days.

Jorge carried in a tray with an artfully arranged plate of meat, tortillas and vegetables and set it across Beth's lap.

"I'm going to weigh a thousand pounds if you keep feeding me like this." She smiled up at him.

"I trust you ladies can help yourselves in the kitchen," he said without looking at them.

In the kitchen, Lauren handed Harriet an empty plate from a stack Jorge had set up on the counter and took one for herself.

"That Jorge's a clever one."

Harriet scooped meat onto her plate and picked two soft corn tortillas from a Styrofoam holder.

"You mean the way he lured us over here to entertain my aunt? I'm willing to do his bidding as long as he throws in a meal like this."

They carried their loaded plates back to the living room and sat on the sofa.

"Eat your dinner, and then you can fill me in on what I've missed," Beth instructed them.

"We haven't learned much since we last saw you," Harriet said when her plate was empty.

"Actually, we've learned a lot. It just isn't very useful," Lauren corrected.

"We met Sandra Price," Harriet began. "Two things came of that. First, she was getting tired of Molly constantly reminding her of her loss. Second, there was a serial killer who was active in the area and specialized in small children. He was captured and subsequently died in jail. The police at the time told her that, while they had no physical evidence in Amber's case, she fit the profile of the three other victims."

Beth straightened in her chair.

104

"That's interesting. It doesn't tell us anything about Molly's death, but it's curious she didn't tell us about it. And she must have known, as often as she says she checked in with the police."

"If we assume the police were right, that gets us back to Josh Phillips as our prime suspect. We haven't confirmed his whereabouts, but it's looking possible he's still in town," Harriet said.

Lauren set her plate on the coffee table.

"Not so fast there, pardner. There's another suspect. That guy Molly helped put in jail when she first got out of college. He was tried as an adult in an underage prostitution operation run by his older brother. He was let out of jail two months ago."

"Where does he live?" Harriet asked.

"Near Seattle."

Beth looked at Lauren, then Harriet.

"I think you need to go check him out. I mean, you don't need to meet him in a dark alley—after all, he might be dangerous; but maybe you could go see where he works and find out if anyone saw him on Monday evening. Or can you find that out on the computer? And also, can you find out if he's on some sort of post-jail supervision?"

"I think when his conviction was overturned, he was set free. This wasn't one of those 'we reserve the right to retry him' situations. If I understand what I read, he shouldn't have been put in an adult jail, but he was while awaiting trial and, while there, was assaulted by adult inmates. After several years of litigation, they concluded he shouldn't have been tried at all. He was a victim of his brother, not an accomplice."

"That's terrible," Beth said. "That's all the more reason for him to be angry with Molly, if she was instrumental in putting him in prison in the first place."

"I read the court findings, and I think Molly might have been the one who testified that he was a pimp. However, it turned out his brother used him as bait against his will. The brother had assumed custody of him when his mom went to jail on drug charges," Lauren said. "And I know already he works for the Archdiocese of Seattle—their main office is the employer listed. That means he could actually be anywhere in the western part of the state. And we don't know what his role is. He could be a janitor or a gardener or anything else. I'm guessing they have some sort of jobs program for people who need a little help rejoining the work force."

"All the more reason to go look," Beth said. "And I mean *look*. Not speak to, not meet with, just ask for him at headquarters and see what you can find out and see if you can lay eyes on him. We can decide what to do from there, depending on what you find out."

"Couldn't they do that by phone?" Jorge asked. "You know if these two go to Seattle, they aren't going to just look."

Harriet and Lauren stared at each other. He was right. If they went that far, they weren't coming home until they'd spoken to DeShaun Smith. Harriet wasn't going to say that in front of her aunt, though, and she was pretty sure Lauren wouldn't, either.

Aunt Beth ignored his warning, and Harriet wondered why her aunt was mixing her message. She had to know they were going to interview the guy.

"They could, but I'm thinking Molly wasn't a petite girl. If this Mr. Smith is a smaller man, he would drop down the suspect list."

"I've got to finish the second quilt before I go anywhere," Harriet said.

Aunt Beth leaned back in her chair as Jorge took her tray back to the kitchen.

"What else?"

Harriet took Lauren's plate and stacked it with hers.

"Carla is working on the psychic angle. Molly seems to have gone to more than one. The first was a bust, but she's got another name, and I was going to go with her to that one."

"Are you taking over a task you gave to Carla?" Beth asked.

Harriet blushed at the rebuke.

"I am, but hear me out. The first one she went to was clearly a fake. Carla could see that, but if the next fake is a little more subtle, she might fool her. I was thinking if two of us went, we might be able to get a better idea if we're dealing with the real deal."

"If there is such a thing," Lauren muttered.

Harriet turned to her.

"Let's not forget that someone Molly talked to caused her to at least think she'd remembered what happened."

"How about the new boyfriend?" Beth interrupted.

"Jenny is checking on him," Harriet looked at Lauren. "Have you heard anything?"

Lauren shook her head.

"Since I'm still grounded for another couple of days, why don't you let me sew the binding on the first quilt? I know the group was going to work on it tomorrow, but you all have a lot of other things you could be doing. The group can work on the second one. Didn't you say you're almost done with it?"

Harriet stood up and took the dishes she was holding to the kitchen.

"If I go home pretty soon, I can finish the second quilt." she called. "I can drop it off at the Threads meeting, and if Lauren is free, we could drive to Seattle tomorrow afternoon and see what we can find out about Mr. Smith. That means we'll have to put off meeting with the second psychic, but I think that's okay."

"I have to do some work with an East Coast client early tomorrow, but if we leave from the Threads meeting, I can do it," Lauren said.

"I need to arrange a babysitter for Scooter. I'll see if Mavis can take him. If that works, then I think we have a plan."

✂ --- ✂ --- ✂

Harriet carried the two disappearing nine-patch quilts into the larger class room at the back of Pins and Needles the next morning. Connie was already there, arranging a tray of mugs.

"*Diós mio*, are you finished with both quilts already?" She left the tray and helped Harriet spread the quilts out on the large table.

"Lauren and I are going to Seattle after the meeting, so I stayed up late last night to get number two finished. Aunt Beth volunteered to do the hand stitching on the first quilt's binding, so I went ahead and applied that, too. I'm hoping someone can drop it off at her place after the meeting. I figured the rest of you could work on the second one at the meeting and then tomorrow I can stitch the third quilt."

"I wouldn't waste too much time doing anything fancy on that one. That man only wanted to get a quilt so he could stay connected to Molly. Now that she's gone, who knows what he'll do with the quilt."

"I agree with the sentiment, but my name is going to be on the machine quilting, and he may give his quilt to someone who's a quilter. I don't want the ultimate recipient to find my stitching lacking."

"I can see that. You're right, we don't know who will end up with the quilt, and it will have a label, listing us as the makers. It just galls me that we've been manipulated into making a quilt for Molly's abuser."

The rest of the Loose Threads trickled into the room, each in turn coming to the table to admire Harriet's stitching job.

"This looks really nice," Robin said as she ran her hand over the stitched surface.

"I'm just glad they're done. One more, and my life can hopefully return to normal. I've been stitching night and day for a few weeks, now."

Connie patted her on the back.

"We appreciate the work you've done on this project. The quilts are beautiful."

Harriet smiled.

"I wasn't fishing for compliments, but I'll take it.

Robin picked a mug off the tray and carried it into the small kitchen to fill it with coffee.

"We should get started if you and Lauren have to go to Seattle," she said when she returned.

Jenny came in as everyone else was getting seated.

"Sorry I'm late. I had one more cafe that holds an open-mic night to check up on."

"Tea or coffee?" Harriet asked her.

"Coffee, please," she said.

Carla went to the kitchen to get her drink, and Harriet pulled out the chair next to hers.

"Were you able to pin down where he was on Monday?" she asked.

"Unfortunately, what I discovered is there aren't any open-mic sessions for poetry on Mondays at any of the cafes or coffee houses in a forty-mile area from here." She looked up and smiled as Carla set her coffee in front of her. "He wasn't on duty at the Penny Mart either. My research was a total bust."

Robin made a note on her yellow tablet.

"That's useful information. It means we can't eliminate him from our suspect list."

Lauren laughed.

"That's great. So far, we've eliminated one suspect—Leo Tabor—but we added DeShaun Smith, so we're even with those two. Now we've looked at Molly's former boyfriend and current boyfriend and can't tell where either of them was at the critical time."

Harriet chuckled and picked up a mug from the tray.

"Don't forget, Morse and company pretty much eliminated our only suspect in Aunt Beth's problems, too."

She got up and took her mug to the kitchen.

Robin tapped her pen on her tablet.

"I'm not sure this is worth writing down, but I checked out the court records of Gary Alexander, the Price's neighbor who is also a convicted domestic abuser. He did, indeed, do jail time for battery, but he's back with the wife, and they live in an apartment on Miller Hill. He may have killed Amber, but frankly, I think it's a reach. All we have are the suspicions of the neighbors. Like I said before, from what I've seen in the courts, criminals tend to stick to type."

Lauren tilted back in her chair.

"So, another non-starter, is what you're saying."

Mavis stared at her teacup.

"Maybe the time has come for us to hang up our imagined detective badges and let the real police handle this."

Robin pressed her lips together.

"DeAnn is my friend, and I want to find out what happened to her sister. Having said that, I'm with Mavis. We are not equipped to investigate something like this and according to DeAnn, the police are working it hard."

Lauren looked around the table.

"Does everyone else feel that way? Should we cancel our trip to Seattle?"

"I can't believe I'm saying this," Harriet said and sat back down with her cup of tea. "I'd like to go check out DeShaun Smith, because…" She smiled. "…I've already got a dog sitter, and I could use a break from my machine."

Connie laughed.

"Oh, honey, have we been working you too hard?"

"Yes, no…I'm okay. I just was looking forward to a break. I agree with everyone, though. I feel bad for DeAnn—I mean, Molly was her half-sister, but…"

"I know," Mavis said. "We all feel bad for DeAnn. I'm just not sure us getting involved in trying to solve Molly's murder is the right way to honor her memory."

Lauren drained her cup and set it on the table.

"If we're going to go, we need to get this show on the road."

Harriet stood up.

"Can someone take the first quilt to Aunt Beth so she can bind it?"

"I'll go by," Connie said. "I need to check on her, anyway."

"If we're all going to be working on binding, why don't we move the meeting to Beth's house—if she feels like it, of course," Mavis suggested.

Robin made the call, and Beth was thrilled. The group had packed their stitching bags before Harriet and Lauren finished clearing their cups and gathering their purses.

Chapter 18

Harriet sat opposite Lauren at Greenleaf Vietnamese Restaurant a few blocks from the Catholic Center in downtown Seattle.

"This pho chin is fabulous," she said.

Lauren dipped the salad roll made of fresh vegetables in a soft rice wrapper into peanut sauce. She chewed slowly, a look of sheer bliss on her face.

"These aren't half-bad, either."

Harriet looked around the restaurant.

"Finding this place made it worth the trip, even if our mission was a bust."

"It wasn't a bust. It's just like with Leo. Eliminating people as suspects is useful."

"I'm not sure either man was really a suspect." Harriet took another spoonful of her soup."Now that we've decided to drop our efforts to find Molly's killer, I'll admit it. I think we were out in left field with all our suspects."

"It's true there isn't a shred of evidence to suggest anyone on our list could or would have killed her."

"The best we've got is a few people with a lack of alibi for the time she was murdered."

Lauren laughed.

"And we seem to be going in the wrong direction. I mean, I could believe her abusive boyfriend is a possible, but DeShaun Smith? Working for the archdiocese should have been a hint, along with his complete exoneration from all charges against him, but even I didn't expect him to be a seminarian."

Harriet smiled.

"I could imagine him holding a grudge against her for testifying against him, although there were many people who were more directly responsible for him going to jail. If he was an angry young man, I'd think the DA or judge or the detectives who arrested him would be riper targets. Him being at Bishop White Seminary in Spokane not only makes it unlikely he's feeling vengeful but it puts him around four hundred miles from Foggy Point."

Lauren, finished eating, crumpled her napkin and put it on the table.

"I don't know about you, but I think we're done with DeShaun. If someone wants to drive to Spokane, more power to them."

"I agree. I think it would be a big waste of time." Harriet picked up her water glass and took a sip. "While we're in Seattle and finished with our business ahead of time…" She looked at Lauren to gauge her reaction so far. "…I was thinking we should go by Stitches fabric store on Pike Street. One of my customers told me they carry Charley Harper print fabric, and I'd really like to get some to make pillows for my TV room."

"Isn't he a little contemporary for your house?"

"I know my aunt went with Victorian decor inside and out, but I'm slowly adding in a few pieces of my own style. I'm not changing anything big. Just a few pillows."

"It's a slippery slope, that's all I'm going to say on that. But, since Charley Harper is my style, too, yeah, I'd like to go look." She glanced at her phone. "And we do have plenty of time."

Harriet picked up the check the server had quietly slid onto the edge of their table while they were talking.

"Since you drove, lunch is on me," she said and headed for the cash register.

✂ --- ✂ --- ✂

It was later than either of them had expected when Lauren guided her car onto the Bainbridge Island Ferry.

"I don't care that we had to wait for a second ferry—this beats driving the extra thirty-five minutes it would have been on the freeway."

Harriet unlatched her seatbelt, Lauren locked the car when they were both out, and Harriet led the way up to the observation deck. She glanced back at the Seattle skyline as the ferry moved away from the pier, then turned her attention to the open water in front of the boat.

"Don't forget the part about getting to whale watch on the way back when you're comparing this route with the all-freeway option," she commented.

"It's not whale season, and it's almost dark, but okay."

Harriet looked at her.

"It's always whale season here. The orcas don't migrate. Only the gray whales migrate, and they're mainly out in the Pacific."

"Aren't we just Jacques Cousteau Junior?"

"I brought Steve to meet Aunt Beth when we got engaged, and we went whale watching while we were here." Her eyes unfocused as she gazed out over the water. "It was the only time he ever came here."

"Did you see any whales?"

Harriet smiled.

"We did."

"Do you realize this is the first time you've told me anything about your marriage that wasn't you being angry or him having lied about something?"

Harriet turned and looked at her friend.

"Maybe I'm finally ready to stop being mad at him for dying."

"Wow. I'm glad. Really. I do have to wonder—why now?"

"I think it's a combination of things." Harriet leaned on the deck railing. "During the crazy-quilt retreat, I spent a fair amount of time reminiscing with my roommate about shared times we'd had in the Bay Area. It was all when my husband was still alive. I finally realized that, yes, he lied about his health, and I never became close with his childhood friends; but when you set that aside, we had a lot of great times in the five years we were married.

"If I'm going to be honest, it also has to do with Aiden's departure. I've had time to reflect, and I keep coming back to the fact that when something happened in my life, Aiden was right there to support me and help me heal, sometimes literally."

"That's a good thing, isn't it?"

"It would be if he'd let me reciprocate, yes. But whenever anything happened in *his* life—and we both know he had some whoppers in the last year —he pulled away. His being gone now is a perfect example. He decided to leave without us even talking about it. He didn't ask me if I wanted to run away with him."

"Would you have?"

"No, but he could have asked. And there was always the chance he could change my mind."

"What are you going to do when he comes home?"

"I'm living my life in the here and now, and if or when he comes home, we'll see where we both are. Since his calls are few and far between, and the last few were reduced to talk about the weather, I'm not sure it's going to be an issue.

"Anyway, it made me realize that, apart from his condition, Steve and I talked about everything. And after giving it a lot of thought, I think he was in such denial about his health that he didn't think his not telling me was ever going to be a problem. I think he thought he was going to outlive his disease."

The two women were silent until the horn sounded, letting everyone know it was time to return to their cars.

✂ --- ✂ --- ✂

Night had fallen by the time Lauren turned onto Harriet's hill.

"Did you see that?" She pointed out the windshield. "Blue flashing lights. Looks like they're on your street."

Harriet craned her neck to see up the hill from the side window, but they'd reached a section of the road that had mature trees and shrubs on both sides, obscuring the view.

"Something's going on at your house," Lauren said as she slowed to make the turn into the driveway.

She pointed, and Harriet could now clearly see two Foggy Point police cars parked behind a red fire truck. She threw her door open and jumped out before Lauren had fully stopped, causing her to slam on the brakes, and began running toward the house. She stopped when James grabbed her around the waist.

"Let me go," she shouted.

"You can't go up there right now. The fire is out, but they have to check before anyone is allowed back in."

"Fire? My house was on fire?" She slumped, and he held her tighter, preventing her from falling to her knees.

"Fred is fine—he's locked in my van. It's okay," he told her. "I got here just after the fire started, and I called nine-one-one and then got my car's fire extinguisher out. I would have broken a window to get in, but the door was open. When I had the fire out, I looked for the dog, grabbed the cat and waited for the fire truck. Your dog is with you, right?"

Harriet took a deep breath.

"He's with Mavis. What happened? Was it an electrical fire? Did I leave an iron on? I haven't ironed anything today. Oh, no, Fred! Is he really okay?"

"Fred is fine. I'm no vet, but he was upstairs the whole time. I don't think he even knows there was a fire."

Tears streamed down her face.

"I want to see it."

James handed her a kitchen towel, and she dabbed at her eyes.

"I don't think they're going to let you in yet. Let's go sit in the van, and I'll tell you what I know." He led her to his catering vehicle and opened the side door. "Here, sit."

He grabbed another towel and spread it out on the floor edge for her to sit on then dug around in a cooler behind her and came out with three chocolate brownies. Lauren joined them, and he scooted closer to Harriet to make a place for her to sit. When she was settled, he handed each of them a brownie before speaking.

"We'll have to wait and see what the firemen say about what started the fire, but what I saw was a wastebasket sitting next to your big quilting machine with flames coming from it. I think there's no doubt it was arson." He looked down at his brownie.

"What aren't you telling me?" Harriet asked. Fred came out from behind one of the big catering coolers that were permanent fixtures in the van; he head-butted her, and she set her brownie down and swept him into her arms, burying her face in his fur.

James hesitated before reaching behind her. He dug two bottles of water from a case and handed one to Lauren and another to Harriet before speaking.

"What aren't you telling us," she pressed.

"Someone did a number on your quilting machine. I don't know how badly it's hurt, but it looks like someone took a sledgehammer to it. The fire seemed like an afterthought, maybe an attempt to obscure evidence. The only thing the wastebasket was close to was the metal framework of your machine, and that was never going to catch on fire."

She stood up, and he grabbed at her and she danced out of his reach.

"I have to go see how bad my machine is."

Just then, Mavis drove up; Harriet waited as she got out and hurried over to them.

"Oh, honey, are you okay? Lauren called me, and I came as quickly as I could." She pulled Harriet into a hug.

Lauren went over to the police car, chatted with the patrolman and came back.

"They called Darcy and the rest of her bunch to come process the scene." Darcy Lewis was a quilter and sometime Loose Thread who worked for a tri-county criminalist team.

Mavis loosened her hug but kept an arm around Harriet. She looked at Lauren.

"So they've determined the fire was arson?"

James repeated what he'd seen.

"I asked the officer when you can get into your house," Lauren continued, "and he said it wouldn't be any time soon. He also said he could call you on your cell when they're ready to talk to you."

"In that case, I think we should go to Beth's house and tell her what's going on," Mavis decided. "You know Jorge has a police scanner, and he'll tell her, and she'll be in a state until she sees for herself that you're okay."

Harriet turned to James.

"Can you come to my aunt's? Fred's not a great traveler, and I think he'll do better if he can stay in the dark back of your van for the trip over there."

"I'd be happy to be the kitty transport."

Harriet gave him a weak smile and got into the passenger seat of the van while Lauren and Mavis returned to their own vehicles, and they all drove to Beth's cottage.

✂ --- ✂ --- ✂

The door to the cottage opened, and Jorge pulled Harriet inside.

"I thought I'd have to tie your aunt down to keep her from racing to your place the minute we heard on the scanner about the fire."

"What happened?" Beth demanded when Harriet reached her recliner. "Is the house still standing? Are Fred and Scooter okay?" She started to get up, but Harriet kneeled beside the chair and took her hand.

"Scooter is at Mavis's house, and Fred is outside in James's van, and everyone is fine." She turned her head to look for James, who was coming through the door behind Lauren. "James came by my house right after someone set a wastebasket on fire. He had an extinguisher in his van and was able to put the fire out."

"It was pure luck," James added. "I went by Harriet's to drop off another round of test truffles…" He trailed off.

"Sounds like it was a good thing you did," Jorge said.

Mavis shrugged her coat off and dropped it on the back of the sofa. "Shall I make tea?"

"I've got the kettle on already," Jorge told her. "Here, sit down."

He stood and pointed to the seat next to Beth he'd just vacated. Mavis smiled at him gratefully and sat down.

"Why would someone want to destroy Harriet's quilting machine?" Lauren said thoughtfully as she joined Mavis.

"Do you really have to ask that question?" Jorge said from the kitchen.

"Wait a minute," Beth said. "What happened to the quilt machine?"

"We'd already decided to stop investigating," Harriet protested.

115

"What about the machine," Beth demanded.

Harriet looked at her aunt.

"I haven't seen it yet, but James has, and he said it's destroyed."

Lauren leaned back on the sofa.

"And yet there we were in Seattle," Lauren continued the first discussion. "The casual observer would think we were still on the case."

"So, somehow our seminary student was threatened by us going to Seattle and teleported from Spokane to burn my studio?" Harriet smirked. "I'd sooner believe a rival wanted to put me out of business."

"Have you got a better explanation for someone breaking in and trying to destroy the place?"

"Blondie has a point," Jorge said as he carried in a tray of teacups and set it on the coffee table. "No one knew you were bowing out of the mystery of Molly but yourselves."

Aunt Beth smiled at him.

"He's right. Our group hasn't advertised the fact we were trying to help Molly, but we *have* been making inquiries. More important, Molly was so obsessed with her past she probably told anyone who would listen."

James came to Harriet and took her free hand.

"Come, sit down."

She got up, and he led her to the sofa then made her a cup of tea and handed it to her, wrapping his hands around hers briefly as he gave it to her. She took a sip, and he settled on the floor next to the her.

"Is there any possibility this isn't related to Molly at all?" he asked. "I mean, the whole group has been looking into Molly's past and now her murder, but only Beth and Harriet have been targeted. It doesn't seem possible the two incidents aren't related. Is it possible this is about something else and not about Molly at all?"

Harriet pressed her lips together, considering that thought. Beth started to speak then stopped and looked at her.

"I can't imagine a reason anyone would have to target us," she finally said. "I suppose it could have something to do with your parents given their stature as international scientists. It's hard to believe bothering us would accomplish anything. They certainly wouldn't come here to check on us if that's what someone was hoping."

That was an understatement, Harriet thought. If they hadn't sent her to stay with Aunt Beth in between boarding schools when she was young, she'd have never known either one of them even knew Foggy Point existed. In fact, she wasn't sure her father had ever been here. Her mother had left when she started college at the age of sixteen and had never looked back and never mentioned it.

"That would also mean there was a much larger conspiracy going on and I don't believe that's true. Unless something has changed, my parents aren't involved in anything that would create that sort of enemies."

Jorge set a steaming cup of tea on the table beside Beth's chair.

"The boy has a point, though. It is odd that no one else has been harmed. Blondie has been with Harriet when she's been talking to people, and she's not been targeted."

James turned to look up at Harriet.

"How rich are your parents? Didn't you say they'd invented something that had commercial value?" He continued. "Maybe there is a financial motive for someone to get at them through you two?"

Lauren smiled.

"Don't you think they would kidnap them and hold them for ransom, if that were the case?"

"Maybe." One corner of his mouth curled into a half-smile. "What if they don't know how to find, or get in touch with the wealthy parents? When your mother didn't come after Beth was injured, they upped the ante by trying to burn the house down."

Harriet looked at her aunt and laughed. Beth tried to remain serious, but then she laughed, too.

"Anyone who knows anything about my sister and her husband would realize that nothing, and I mean nothing, would bring them back here."

"They'd send their representative, a very scary woman who acts as secretary, travel agent and all-around girl Friday," Harriet said, still chuckling.

Mavis cleared her throat.

"I don't mean to take attention away from a serious situation, but it occurs to me we still have another quilt to finish before the benefit, and without your machine, we need to come up with a plan."

Beth put her hand over her mouth.

"I didn't even think of that."

"Of course—you were worried about Harriet, but I've been thinking. It's hard to stitch a quilt of that size on a home sewing machine, but the church has a quilting frame in their storage area. I know we only have a few days, but if everyone available could take shifts hand-quilting, I think we could get it done."

"It could work," Beth said. "I can help stitch. I'm sure we can figure out how to keep my foot up once I get there."

"I'll text the team," Lauren told them and began tapping on her phone.

Chapter 19

Once the rest of the Threads had been notified of the change in plan, Jorge got up to refill cups. Harriet leaned her head against the back of the sofa, lost in thought, while Lauren stared at her phone, willing the absentee Threads to reply to her texts. Beth and Mavis had each pulled hand-piecing projects from their ever-present canvas quilting bags and were stitching quietly.

James smiled at Harriet.

A loud knock on the front door startled them and set Beth's dog to barking.

"Everyone, stay where you are," Jorge boomed from the kitchen. "I'll get it."

He wiped his hands on the dish towel he was carrying and took a moment to look through the peephole before opening the door.

"Detective Morse, come in," he said and held the door open. He continued holding it open, blocking Brownie with his foot. "Connie is coming," he explained.

"This isn't a good time to talk about Amber's disappearance," Beth said to Morse.

"I'm not here about that. There was some sort of gang shooting down at the docks tonight, so the on-call detectives are all down there. I was called in to come interview you-all about the break-in and fire at Harriet's."

Harriet looked at her hopefully.

"Have you been to my house?"

"I did swing by and take a look."

Connie came in, dropped her purse and jacket and crossed the room to pull Harriet into an awkward hug.

"*Diós mio!* Are you all right?"

"I'm fine," Harriet said in a voice muffled by the fact her face was buried in Connie's shoulder.

Connie released her grip and studied her closely.

"You weren't hurt by the fire?"

"It was just a wastebasket," Morse answered for her. "Harriet wasn't home, and her friend James seems to have arrived right after it was set." Morse looked at James, with one eyebrow raised in a questioning arch.

"I was bringing truffles," he stammered. "And the door was open." His face turned red.

"Lauren and I were just getting home from Seattle…" Harriet volunteered then paused. "Wait a minute." She looked at James. "You said my door was open? How did someone get past my burglar alarm?"

He shrugged. "It was open, and the alarm wasn't going off when I got there."

Jorge brought in a cup of tea for Morse. He took her jacket and hung it on the coat closet doorknob and handed her a napkin. He carefully set it on the coffee table then went to the dining area and brought chairs for Morse and Connie; everyone sat down.

Morse sipped her tea.

"This is wonderful," she told Jorge then returned her attention to Harriet. "I haven't talked to Darcy and her crew yet, but I noticed one of them was taking pictures of your security system keypad. Some of the keys had black powder on them. This is just a guess, but I think whoever broke in sprayed your keypad with graphite or some other fine dark powder to see which four keys had fingerprints on them. No one ever touches the keys that aren't part of their code," she explained.

"The bad guys rapidly cycle through all the combinations using those four keys," she continued. "They may even have some info as to the most frequently used four-digit codes as a starting point. At any rate, most systems give you at least a minute to enter the code, and you can enter a lot of combinations in that amount of time."

Harriet ran her hand through her hair.

"What I don't get is why damage my machine? If they're trying to run me out of town, the arson attempt sort of makes sense, but why attack the machine?"

Morse leaned back in her chair.

"I think the whole machine/fire thing was an afterthought."

"What do you mean?" Harriet asked.

"When they let you back in your house, you can check around your desk, but I think your office area was the real target. Someone dug in your files and left some on the floor, and the hard drive on your computer is missing."

Lauren looked at Harriet.

"You signed up for the back-up service I recommended, right?"

"I did."

"Whew." Lauren blew her breath out in a rush. "All you need is a new drive, and we can call all your information back, good as new."

"I'd like to have a look when you do that. If you don't mind, that is," Morse said.

"I hope they're ready to be disappointed," Harriet said with a grim smile. "I didn't have anything related to Molly's issues on my computer."

Lauren laughed.

"Little did they know, they should have purse-snatched Robin's bag."

Morse looked at her, confused.

"She makes notes on legal tablets at our meetings," Harriet explained. Connie sipped her tea.

"Do you think we need to warn Robin that something might happen?"

Morse pulled a small notebook and pen from her pocket and made a note.

"I doubt most people know who is in your group, and even then, they wouldn't know who takes notes. Just in case, though, I think I'll ask for increased patrols in all of your neighborhoods."

Jorge reappeared from the kitchen with the tea kettle.

"Anyone need a refill?"

Beth smiled up at him, and he topped off her cup.

"Are you sure this has to do with Molly?" he asked when he got to Morse.

"I don't think we're sure of anything, but I don't happen to believe in coincidence. Molly comes to town and asks Harriet and the rest of the Loose Threads to help her solve her mystery from twenty years ago, and then she gets murdered." Morse raised her eyebrows. "If Beth's accident and Harriet's break-in aren't a result of that, I'll be amazed. No, I'll be shocked. Both of those events are related to Molly now and Amber Price in the past. We just don't know how yet."

Connie stiffened her back.

"So, what are we supposed to do?"

Morse laughed.

"I feel like a broken record. You all need to do nothing. Finish your quilts, go to the benefit, and let us take care of the bad guys."

"What if we're making a quilt for the bad guy?" Lauren asked.

"Just stay away from him and everyone else related to this case. We'll have plainclothes policemen at the award ceremony, just in case."

Harriet sighed.

"Can I go home?"

Morse sipped her tea, and then pressed her lips together firmly.

"You should plan on staying somewhere else tonight," she finally said. "The fire department has an arson investigation crew there along with the usual criminalist team. You can call the PD in the morning to be sure they've released the scene before you go home."

Harriet's shoulders sagged.

"You can come stay with me," Mavis offered. "Your dog is already there, and I have a kitty pan and litter from when I took care of Fred when you and Beth went to that quilt show in Arizona."

"Thanks, that would be great," Harriet agreed.

Connie stood up and started gathering her things.

"Shall we meet for coffee in the morning before we go to the church to get the quilt frame out and set up?"

Lauren slipped her messenger bag over her shoulder.

"Sounds good to me. And, Harriet…" She leaned forward to make eye contact. "I have a couple of spare new hard drives on my shelf. I can bring you one and install it whenever you get your house back. The police probably won't take your computer, since it's the hard drive that's missing."

"That would be great."

"No problem. I also keep spare power supplies, if that ever comes up."

"Good to know," Mavis said.

James stood and held out a hand to help Harriet.

"We should get going, too."

Her mouth twitched into a weak smile as she took his hand and rose.

"I guess we're lucky Jenny still has the third quilt top." She looked around for her purse, but James found it first and handed it to her. "I'll see you all in the morning."

"I can call Jenny and Carla," Aunt Beth said.

Jorge started gathering cups and napkins from the table.

"You all go on ahead, I can get this."

Beth smiled at him in gratitude as the rest left.

James turned to Harriet when they were both settled in the van's front seat.

"Do we need to stop at the store before I take you on to Mavis's house?"

Harriet tried to smile but failed.

"Sadly, I have toiletries at her house left over from the last time I had to stay someplace that wasn't my own home."

"You'll have to tell me that story later." He reached to pull her across the bench seat, scooping her into his arms. "Are you okay?"

She leaned her head against his chest.

"No, I'm not. I've had enough of Foggy Point. I've lived here a little over a year, and in that time, I've been whacked in the head, the leg and had my arm burned. My house has been broken into twice, and all my friends cars were bombed in my driveway. I'm done. As I was sitting there in my aunt's house looking at her with her bum foot and injured arm, I realized this isn't working for me. I may not have been completely happy in California, but never once was my physical being attacked, and my aunt was safe and sound."

James hugged her closer and kissed the top of her head.

"You don't know that your aunt's trouble has anything to do with you, and, do you really think the rest of your friends wouldn't be checking out Molly's death if you weren't here?"

"Lauren wasn't involved in this sort of stuff until I came along, and the others might talk about it, but I'm the one who always takes action for the group."

"But look how many people are in jail because you took action. What if they investigated without you, and they weren't as good at it, and the criminals prevailed? What then? Your friends could be in worse trouble."

"I know you're trying to help, but I'm seriously thinking I need to leave town. My machine getting damaged is a sign. And now that I've made peace with Steve's friends in California, there's nothing to stop me. I could restart my long-arm quilting business there."

James dropped his head.

"Just when we were getting to know each other. Can you at least stay until the police catch Molly's killer? I don't want to have to worry about whoever it is following you to California. Besides, maybe if we have more time to make out in your kitchen, you'll change your mind and stay."

"This isn't a joke."

"Who's joking?"

James turned her in his arms and lowered his mouth to hers. He kissed away the protest she'd been going to make and slowly massaged her back with his hands.

"I'm not leaving until my aunt's back on her feet, at any rate," Harriet said with a sigh when they'd separated.

James kissed her again—one last, quick brush of lips together—and settled her in the seat beside him, reaching across her to pull down the center seat belt. Harriet smelled his unique blend of soap and lemon disinfectant and sighed. Things had been so clear when she was in her aunt's house, staring at her aunt's injury and trying to figure out if she needed to call her insurance man or a quilt machine rep. Besides, she reminded herself, she was done arranging her life around a man.

She watched him as he checked the mirrors and pulled out onto the road. He seemed so open—*seemed* being the operative word. One conclusion she'd come to during her late-night, sleepless self-analysis sessions was that the last two men she'd loved hadn't liked to share the important issues in their lives. Choosing two in a row with the same characteristic wasn't a conscious choice on her part, but it was definitely something she needed to be aware of; and she wasn't sure what it said about her. Until she figured that out, she wasn't ready to get involved with anyone.

James looked at her and smiled, testing her resolve.

Harriet sighed again and smiled back.

✂ --- ✂ --- ✂

Mavis had arrived first and had the dogs out in her yard when Harriet and James got there. Harriet opened the side door on the van and crawled inside to find Fred.

"I'll bet you're ready to go inside," she said when she'd pulled him from behind the big cooler.

"I'll get your purse and coat," James told her as she passed him with her armload of cat.

Mavis herded the dogs toward the door.

"Make sure the gate latch catches," she instructed James before she followed Harriet indoors. "I'm warming milk for hot cocoa. You looked like you could use a little chocolate."

Harriet gave her grateful glance.

"I could use something, that's for sure."

James set Harriet's purse and fleece jacket on the kitchen table.

"I'm going to take off. I'm sure Cyrano's wondering where his dinner is."

Harriet walked him to the door.

"Thank you for everything. I can't tell you how grateful I am that you came to my house when you did."

"If I'd gotten there sooner, maybe you'd still have a working machine."

"And you might have gotten hurt by whoever broke in. I'm just glad you got there in time to put out the fire before it had a chance to spread."

She started toward the kitchen where Mavis was rattling cups. Then, she spun back and pulled James into a quick embrace, kissing him before she stepped away. She listened to make sure she could still hear her friend working safely out of view.

"I mean it—thank you."

James grinned.

"I like it when you're grateful. We'll have to continue exploring your gratitude when we're alone."

Harriet couldn't help smiling back.

"We might just have to do that."

He turned and went out the door.

"If you're done mooning over your new friend, I've got cocoa ready," Mavis called from the kitchen.

Harriet chuckled, reminded once again that nothing got past the Loose Threads.

Chapter 20

Harriet was surprised by how well she slept in Mavis's guest room. Scooter was curled up in the space created by her bent knees as she lay on her side. Fred stretched out next to her, his head on her pillow, a position that never failed to make her smile.

"This is great, guys, but we have to get up. We have things to do, places to go, people to see."

Scooter raised his head and looked at her before putting it back down on his front paws. Fred ignored her completely until she sat up, jostling him off the pillow. She grabbed the cotton robe Mavis had loaned her and put it on before leaving her sleeping pets.

"I'll have your tea steeping," Mavis called as Harriet made her way to the bathroom.

She had freshly buttered toast on a plate beside a steaming cup of tea when Harriet returned a few minutes later and sat down at the kitchen table.

"Did you sleep all right?"

Harriet sipped her Earl Grey.

"I slept like a log, which is surprising, given my two little bed buddies."

"I got a new mattress for that bed. It's a combination of memory foam and inner springs."

"It was great. I just wish I hadn't had to impose on you."

"Oh, honey, it isn't an imposition. And until they figure out who broke into your house, I feel better knowing you're here and safe. I know you're aunt feels that way, too."

"What if whoever did it discovers I'm here and tries to burn *your* house down?"

"We'll call nine-one-one, and if we aren't here, my house is insured."

"You can't mean that," Harriet said.

"I do, but I also don't believe anyone will come here. What would be the point? I don't have anything anyone would want, or want to destroy, for that matter. I don't really think they were trying to burn your house down, either. A child could have done a better job of it, according to James." Mavis shook her head. "Whatever mischief they were up to, I don't believe destroying your house was part of it."

Harriet chewed her toast thoughtfully.

"You may be right. Maybe someone found whatever they were looking for in my files and burned it in the wastebasket." She set the toast down on the saucer. "I can't imagine what that would be. My paper records are mostly receipts I keep for tax purposes. I also have copies of the work orders from customers. Again, it's hard to believe any of that is threatening."

Mavis reached across the table and patted her hand.

"Try not to dwell on it. We can't solve anything until you can get back into your house and see if anything's missing. In the meantime, we need to be thinking about the pattern for our hand-quilting project."

Harriet leaned back in her chair.

"You're right. The pattern I'd been planning is way too dense to hand-stitch in the time we have available. I'd planned an all-over, continuous-line flower pattern." She thought for a moment. "Maybe we could still do flowers, but just spread them out a little more."

"That might work. I was thinking of doing something simpler than that. I thought we could stitch around each square in the pattern, a quarter of an inch inside each seam."

"That *would* save us a step. We wouldn't have to mark a pattern if we use the seam lines as a guide."

Mavis stood and picked up the empty cup and saucer.

"Let's get dressed and go see what the rest of the group has in mind. The bottom drawer of the dresser in the guest room has clean clothes I picked up at the thrift store in various sizes for when my kids and their kids come visiting and forget stuff—and they always forget something. Help yourself."

"Thank you, I can't tell you how much I appreciate everything you've done for me."

Mavis's normally ruddy cheeks turned redder.

"Oh, honey."

✂ --- ✂ --- ✂

Mavis was rinsing their breakfast dishes and putting them on the drying mat when Harriet came out of the bathroom, dressed in her own jeans with a long-sleeved pink tee-shirt and matching pink cotton socks from the community drawer.

"That looks very nice. You should wear pink more often."

Harriet looked down at the shirt and shook her head.

"If you say so."

"You ready to head over to meet the group? I walked the dogs while you were getting ready."

Harriet thanked her and went to the guest room to get her purse and coat.

"Do you think it's a sign? You know, my house being broken into and my machine destroyed?" she asked when she'd returned to the kitchen.

"What do you mean, 'a sign'?" Mavis led the way out the door and into the garage.

"A sign that I should give up on Foggy Point and go back to California. Aiden's gone, my livelihood is in jeopardy, maybe the universe is telling me I've worn out my welcome here."

"I don't know about it being a sign. I do know bad luck can happen to anyone, and running away from whatever's going on won't solve anything." She got in and unlocked the passenger door. "I can't believe you'd run out on your aunt when she's hurt, either. You don't know what happened to her was because of you. What if she has trouble all on her own? Are you just going to leave her to it?"

Harriet slid into the passenger seat and strapped on her seatbelt. She hung her head.

"Of course I won't leave until we know who slashed her tires and sabotaged her car. I'm just tired of having my person and my things attacked by crazy people. That never happened when I was in California."

"Were you engaged in your life down there after your husband died, or were you just hiding at home passing time? Being truly alive involves risk." Mavis looked at her to make sure she was hearing what was being said. "I'm not saying we all couldn't be more careful—Jane Morse may be right about that. You just can't be so careful you forget to live."

Harriet looked out the window as they backed out onto the driveway.

"I suppose," she finally said.

"Oh, honey," Mavis said, reaching over to pat Harriet's leg. "Just promise me you'll think about what I said before you make any decisions."

"I can't make any promise except that I'll wait until Aunt Beth is better before I do anything."

Mavis shook her head and sighed.

"I guess that'll have to do."

Connie and Carla were sitting at the large table at The Steaming Cup when Mavis and Harriet arrived.

"Get your drinks then come give us your opinion about quilt batting."

The new arrivals did as instructed and returned a few minutes later, their mugs filled with their hot liquid of choice. Harriet sat down next to Carla and hung her purse on the back of her chair.

"Are you thinking we need to change the batting to make it easier to hand-quilt?" she asked Connie.

Connie set down her half-empty mug.

"I was just explaining to Carla the difference between cotton and wool and silk when it comes to hand-quilting. Given our time limits, I think we need to go with something other than cotton."

Mavis settled in her chair, pulling her hand piecing project from her purse.

"As my granddaughter would say, it chaps my hide to spend the extra money to buy silk batting for that jerk."

Arriving just then, Lauren laughed as she set her messenger bag on the table and sat beside Harriet.

"Tell us how you really feel, Mavis."

"I'm sorry, it just doesn't seem right that we're having to spend extra time and money to make a quilt for an abusive man who only donated the money so he could maintain some sort of contact with Molly in violation of her restraining order."

"Don't forget he could also be her killer," Connie reminded her.

"I'm willing to pay the extra money for silk batting," Lauren told them. "We aren't buying it for him, we're buying it for us and the health of our own hands. We're all going to have to do a lot of hours of stitching, and silk will be a lot easier to work on."

Mavis pressed her lips together.

"It's still not right."

Robin and Jenny came in together from the parking lot.

"We were just talking about the batting," Jenny said.

Lauren laughed.

"So were we. We've established we'll change to silk, and I'll pay for it because Mavis doesn't want us to spend another cent on the jerk of a recipient."

Robin slid her jacket off and draped it over the back of her chair.

"We didn't discuss our distaste for Josh Phillips, but Jenny also volunteered to buy silk batting to save our hands."

Lauren looked across the table at Jenny.

"Want to split it?"

Jenny nodded.

"Sure. Have you-all talked about our schedule yet?"

Harriet sipped her cocoa.

"No, we just got here ourselves."

Robin went to order her tea and returned to the big table.

"Did I hear someone say schedule?" She pulled a handful of papers from her shoulder bag. "I took the liberty of making a spreadsheet. I set up two-hour blocks that people can sign up for. I stuck to the hours the church office is usually open. I thought we could see how it goes the first day, and then, if it's obvious we need more time, we can ask to have access to the church during off-hours, too."

Stewart Jones entered and approached the group before anyone could comment on the schedule. His hair was dyed a hard black and styled into a faux-hawk. Harriet watched Robin scoop the papers back into her bag in a practiced move before he could see what was written on them.

"Thank heaven I found you ladies. Are you going to Molly's funeral?"

Harriet looked at Robin.

"Why do you ask?" Robin queried in her cold professional voice.

"I wrote a poem. For Molly." He pulled a folded paper from his pocket.

No one said anything, so he continued.

"I haven't known Molly for very long, and I didn't want to intrude on her family, but I wrote a poem, and I think they might want to use it at her service." He looked around the table and was met with stone-faced silence. "I can see I've made a mistake asking you. I'm sorry."

He started to turn away.

"Give it to me," Robin said and held her hand out. "I'll read it, and if I think it's appropriate, I'll pass it on to her mother."

Stewart's face turned a hot, angry red.

"I don't need your approval of my poetry, and I think I know what's appropriate."

Robin dropped her hand and turned her attention away from him.

"Wait. I'm sorry, this isn't about my ego."

He held the paper out. She took it and put it in her bag.

"Aren't you going to read it?"

"Not now. We're having a meeting."

Stewart stood, unmoving.

"Was there something else?" Robin asked.

"Can you at least tell me if or when you pass it on? I don't even know when the funeral is. I know you don't like me and that I only knew Molly a matter of days, but she and I had something real."

A tear slid down his cheek, and he swiped at it with his balled fist. He hesitated then turned on his heel and swept out of the coffee shop.

Harriet leaned back in her chair and followed him with her eyes until he was out the door.

"Is it just me, or was that weird?"

Carla made eye contact with her.

"Was he wearing *eyeliner*?"

"And eye shadow," Lauren answered before Harriet could. "He was rocking the tragic poet look."

"Be nice," Connie scolded her. "That might be his work outfit if he's doing a poetry reading."

Lauren glanced at the time display on her phone.

"Pretty early for a poetry reading."

"Maybe he's still up from last night," Carla suggested.

Harriet once again wondered what Carla's childhood had been like that made staying up all night in your party clothes seem such an easy explanation. She drained her mug and set it down, then looked around the table at her friends.

"Everyone ready to head over to the church?"

Mavis slid her project back into her bag.

"The sooner we start, the sooner we finish," she announced and stood up.

"You can leave your cups," the young man behind the counter called to them. "I'll get them."

Everyone thanked him, and they all went to their respective cars and left.

✂ --- ✂ --- ✂

Aunt Beth was already in the church basement sitting beside the quilting frame when the group arrived. Her foot was propped up on a pillow that was held to her knee scooter with a bungee cord. Marjorie came in carrying a pillow-shaped bag of quilt batting.

"Lauren called and asked if I could make an emergency delivery."

She opened the package and gently pulled out the large folded quilt bat.

"How do we do this?" Carla asked.

Jenny had the folded quilt top inside a pillowcase. She pulled another folded piece of fabric from the case.

"I hope no one minds that I went ahead and bought some extra-wide backing fabric. I thought it would be easier than piecing the back—and that was before we decided to hand-quilt."

"Thank you for that," Aunt Beth said. "I was wondering what we were going to do. I had Jorge bring my portable sewing machine and some muslin, but this will be much easier."

Harriet and Lauren pushed several of the large cafeteria tables together, and Jenny laid her piece of backing fabric down. Marjorie added the batting and Jenny carefully unfolded the quilt top onto the two layers.

Mavis handed Carla a spool of thread and a needle.

"First thing we need to do is baste the quilt sandwich together, just like when you're going to quilt on your sewing machine."

Harriet and Lauren threaded needles with the pink basting thread when Carla was ready.

"Smooth the layers as flat and wrinkle-free as you can with your hand and then start basting, starting in the middle," Mavis continued and then stopped. They all heard someone clattering down the steps to the basement.

Harriet stopped what she was doing as well and stared at the open door that led to the stairs. Josh Phillips rushed in and strode over to them.

"Oh, good—I found you in time."

"And you are?" Connie demanded as she joined the others by the table.

"Meet Josh Phillips," Harriet told her. "Molly's ex-boyfriend."

Josh turned to face her.

"And you are?"

"Never mind who I am. We're busy. What do you want?"

"Now that Molly's dead, I want to cancel my quilt order."

"Your *what?*" Harriet, Mavis and Connie all said at the same time.

Lauren smirked.

"This day just keeps getting better."

"I think you're confusing us with the other quilt group in town," Mavis said. "We aren't doing a commission quilt. This quilt is a thank-you for your donation."

"I'm not confused. This is the quilt I paid ten thousand dollars for. I don't want it anymore. Since you haven't made it yet, I'm canceling my order. Now, is anyone from the missing children place here? I went by the offices, but I couldn't find anyone. I stopped at the quilt store and they said you were here. And luckily I found you before you finished my quilt."

"You didn't *order* a quilt." Harriet told him, her voice rising.

"Call it what you want, I'm withdrawing my donation. If you want to thank me with a quilt, feel free. I'm going back to Seattle. When you talk to the missing children people, tell them now that Molly's gone, so is my money."

The big blond man pivoted and left the way he'd come in.

"Can he do that?" Lauren asked Robin.

"It depends. A pledge is a legally enforceable contract, but in Washington, it needs to be in writing. If he's given them the money already, and he signed a pledge contract, he's out of luck. He's beyond any conceivable buyer's remorse period. I don't think that would apply, anyway.

"If he hasn't actually transferred the money yet, it's a different story. They'd have to sue him to get it. Most nonprofits are afraid they'll scare off future donors and seem greedy if they take a donor to court, so they just accept the loss."

Harriet pulled a chair out from the table and sat down.

"So, where does that leave us and our quilt?"

"Since we don't know which of those we're dealing with, I think we need to forge ahead with it," Mavis advised.

Connie picked up a box of thumbtacks and went around to the end of the quilt frame.

"I agree with Mavis. Until the people at the nonprofit tell us otherwise, we need to have three quilts ready for their fundraiser, and this one isn't going to stitch itself."

Lauren shook her head.

"This day just keeps on getting weirder."

Carla raised her hand.

"Oh, honey, you don't need to do that when you want to speak," Mavis scolded her gently.

The young woman's cheeks turned pink as she spoke.

"What are the thumbtacks for?"

The group spent the next half-hour showing Carla how the thumbtacks were used to hold the quilt sandwich to the wooden quilt frame.

✂ --- ✂ --- ✂

Harriet stood up several hours later, grasping the back of her chair and bending back at the waist to stretch.

"Do we have a lunch plan?"

"We haven't done Chinese in a while," Lauren suggested.

Robin stabbed her needle into the quilt top.

"Sounds good to me. And while we're at lunch, I thought I'd call the missing children center and see if our reluctant philanthropist Josh has approached them about retracting his pledge."

Carla looked at Harriet.

132

"Should we call the second psychic?"

Harriet studied the ceiling.

"I'm torn. I had decided I was out of the investigating business. Now, with my machine and my house under attack, I'm not so sure."

Connie slid her chair back from the quilt frame.

"We can't give up now. What will we tell DeAnn? And what about Beth? Can you let it go, not knowing who hurt her?"

Mavis stood up and stretched as well.

"I don't want to see any of us put ourselves in harm's way unnecessarily, but what if whoever sabotaged Beth's car and broke into your house isn't done? If we do nothing, and another one of us suffers some sort of harm, we'll feel terrible."

Lauren set her needle down on the quilt surface.

"Besides all that, don't you want revenge for your machine?"

"Lauren, it's just a machine. An insured one, at that," Beth said.

Harriet looked at her friend. Her eyes narrowed.

"You're right. It *was* my machine."

"Hold on a minute," Beth cautioned. "Maybe we should consider the possibility that anything else we do could cause whoever is responsible for my car and Harriet's house and machine to do something worse."

"That could happen anyway," Lauren countered.

Robin paced the length of the quilt frame and turned to face the group.

"I don't advocate taking the law into our own hands. It never ends well when citizens try to do the job of the police. That being said, I do think DeAnn's family deserve answers. Molly may have been obsessed with the disappearance of Amber Price, but that doesn't mean she was wrong to try to find out what happened.

"The police have had twenty years to come up with something, and they haven't. We need to be careful, but if we can figure out what happened to Amber, it might go a long way toward explaining what happened to Molly."

Mavis and Beth exchanged a look.

"Robin, are you sure you're thinking straight?" Mavis asked her gently. "DeAnn is your best friend and that may be clouding your judgment."

"I'm not suggesting we do anything wild, but following up with Molly's psychic shouldn't step on anyone's toes."

"How do you feel about us talking to Molly's co-workers again?" Harriet asked. "We need to discuss this quilt with them, anyway. Maybe if we get them going they'll reveal something they didn't think of when we were there before."

Robin thought for a moment.

"That should be okay, too, as long as you're really subtle. Let them do all the talking."

Lauren slung her messenger bag over her shoulder.

"Now that we've sorted that, can we go to lunch? I'm starving."

Chapter 21

Harriet slid her phone into her pocket as she returned from the foyer to the round table in the back of the Chinese restaurant.

"We can't see the psychic until tomorrow at ten o'clock. Does anyone mind if I take a few minutes to drive over to the missing children center on the way back to quilting?"

"As long as you don't go alone, I think that would be okay," Aunt Beth answered for the group.

Lauren waved her hand.

"I'll go. She needs a driver, anyway, if I'm not mistaken."

Harriet laughed.

"Oh, yeah, I forgot that little detail."

Robin wiped her mouth and set her napkin on the table beside her plate.

"Until Molly's killer is caught, I think we'd all be wise to travel in pairs."

"Does Wendy count?" Carla asked.

Connie straightened her spine and pressed her lips together and Harriet knew she was transforming into teacher mode.

"Hey! Not one of us has thought about Carla and Wendy during all this." She glanced at Harriet but continued speaking. "With Aiden out of town, they're alone in that big house. And if I'm not mistaken, Terry won't be back for another two weeks."

Terry, Carla's boyfriend, was in the Navy Criminal Investigation Service, based out of Naval Base Kitsop Bangor in Silverdale. His schedule was unpredictable, but they were making their relationship work.

Mavis sucked her breath in.

"Oh, honey, I'm so sorry we've been neglecting you."

135

Carla looked from Mavis to Beth and then Harriet to Lauren.

"Don't *you* all live alone?"

Harriet had to admit the girl had a point. She might be young, but with the upbringing she'd had, she was likely better equipped to deal with trouble than most of the Threads.

"None of them live in such an isolated location," Connie said. "It's true Harriet's house sits off the street, but Aiden's is also surrounded by hedges and woods and is much farther from the road."

Carla slipped into her jacket.

"I can bring the dog into the house. She barks at everything."

"That will help," Connie told her. "But maybe you and Wendy should sleep at my house until this is all over."

Harriet opened her wallet and counted bills out then set them on the plastic dish beside her plate. She looked at Robin.

"Do you really think the situation warrants disrupting Carla and Wendy's lives like that?"

Robin sighed.

"I don't know. Without knowing if Beth's car sabotage and your break-in are connected, and whether they're related to Molly's murder, it's hard to say if we're overreacting. But, if there's a chance at all it's the same person or persons, we'd be wise to take every precaution we can."

Connie smiled at Carla.

"I'll call Grandpa Rod and tell him to prepare for company."

✂ --- ✂ --- ✂

"Do we know the name of the office manager?" Harriet asked Lauren as they pulled in to The Carey Bates Organization. This time there were no other cars in the parking lot.

"No, we don't, but I'm sure Mr. Google can tell us."

Harriet pulled her phone from her pocket and tapped the organization name into the search engine.

"The office manager is one Nancy Finley. I think she was the one in the gray linen suit when we were here before. Carla said her young friend's name is Sadie. The only other name listed as staff is Patrice Orson."

"I guess she was the one in the sari. I may be wrong, but from what you told me about your last visit, I think she's the one we want to talk to. We can ask the manager, but she might not be inclined to talk about a situation that could end up in court."

"I agree. What if you ask her about Molly's files on Amber Price's disappearance? Tell her you just want to read them. And it isn't a lie. I do want to know what Molly had, just in case she made any notes about her psychic visit and what it was that triggered her memory. It's probably too much to hope that she actually documented her recovered memory.

"Anyway, I'm hoping Nancy'll take you to her office or to the space Molly was using. I'll hang around in the waiting area and see if I can get Patrice talking."

✂ --- ✂ --- ✂

Harriet accepted a cup of coffee from Patrice as she sat in an overstuffed chair that had seen better days in the reception area. She was amazed at how easily Lauren had convinced Nancy of her need to read Molly's file on Amber.

"Can I get you anything else?" Patrice asked her.

Harriet shook her head.

"I can't believe Molly's gone."

Patrice slid into the mismatched chair opposite her.

"I can't, either. We've been having trouble concentrating on work, knowing her killer is still out there. I mean, what if it was retaliation for one of the cases she worked on? Everyone knew she was helping us, and since we joined her, we not only brought four kids home but we also were instrumental in putting three people in jail. Each of them was a low-level operator in a bigger enterprise."

"If they were low level, their bosses probably wouldn't want to draw attention to themselves by seeking revenge. I wonder about her boyfriend. He came by the Methodist Church where we're quilting. He's a real piece of work."

"That cute poet? I thought he seemed nice, in a dark and tortured sort of way."

"Oh, no. I meant her *ex*-boyfriend. Josh Phillips. He was ranting about not wanting our quilt any more."

"I'm sorry he pestered you like that. We do appreciate all the hard work you're doing making those quilts."

"Do you think he'll follow through with his threat to withdraw his pledge?" Harriet tried to infuse her comment with concern.

Patrice's laugh came out more like a bark.

"He can try, but Nancy's a sharp one. Molly wasn't here when he came in to donate, so she wrote the paper on his pledge. He signed a contract, and not only that, she made him write a check for half the amount on the spot."

"That's a relief. No matter what, you'll have five thousand dollars."

"We've been burned before. It's a real problem when people pledge money to us, and we get grants that depend on matching funds, and the pledge

137

falls through, dragging the grant money with it. Nancy consulted a lawyer to figure out how to protect against it. Now, she insists on an upfront partial payment and a binding contract, including a clause agreeing that they will pay the legal fees if we have to collect our money in court."

"Wow, that sounds thorough."

"Well, that's our Nancy. Josh Phillips has no idea."

"I need to get going. We're hand-quilting that third quilt. Could you possibly check on my friend?"

"Sure, you finish your coffee, and I'll see if I can shake her loose."

She returned followed by Nancy and Lauren.

"I'm sorry we took your time without calling ahead," Lauren told Nancy.

Nancy's brows drew together.

"It's no problem. Until someone figures out what happened to Molly, we find ourselves paralyzed. We don't know if our efforts contributed to her murder. If so, we don't know which of our cases were involved. The number of missing children in our area is staggering. On any given day, we're actively following up on half a dozen local kids who are missing.

"Lately, because of Molly's organization, we've been networking with more than a dozen other missing persons groups. Those groups have asked us to research an increasing number of missing people who were last seen in our general area. It could be any of them."

Harriet stood up.

"So, how long have you been working with Molly?"

Nancy looked up and put her hand on the side of her face.

"Seems like a long time, but I guess, in reality, it's only been a few months." She looked at Patrice. "Do you remember when we started working with her?"

"It was right after Christmas. Remember? We were making our resolutions for the new year, and Molly came in and changed everything."

"You're right. It was six months ago."

Lauren slid her tablet computer from her bag and tapped it awake before typing herself a note and then putting it back to sleep.

"If you'll email a list of names of the external cases you've been working on," she offered. "I'll see what I can find out. I may have a few resources that are different from the ones you've already pursued."

Nancy looked at her but didn't say anything.

"Any help you can give us would be great," Patrice said. "Even if you can just clear one or two names, that would allow us to return to work. As you might guess, we've told the police all this information, and they've been less than willing to share anything they know with us."

"As I said, I'll see what I can do. We have a little experience with the Foggy Point PD and their level of cooperation with interested lay people."

Harriet started for the door, and then turned back.

"Speaking of the Foggy Point PD and their communication skills, did Molly have anything in her Amber file about the serial killer theory?"

Nancy gave her a blank look.

"I don't know what you're talking about."

"We heard a man was arrested in Longview, Washington, in nineteen ninety-nine and successfully prosecuted for two child murders. One of them took place in 'eighty-five and the second one ten or twelve years later. It was commonly believed he'd killed more—those were just the ones they had enough evidence to prosecute. Amber Price fit his victim profile and the time frame."

"Did Molly know that?" Nancy asked.

"Maybe, maybe not. You knew Molly. Would she have failed to make a record of information that didn't fit her theory of what happened to Amber?"

"Never," Patrice snapped. "Molly always encouraged us to follow the facts wherever they took us. One of our missing-child cases turned out to be a case of filicide. The grieving parents had killed their own child. We were giving the parents a lot of latitude, but Molly said to leave no stone unturned. She would never leave out that sort of information."

"It's possible Molly didn't know," Harriet said. "Amber was the victim, so it makes sense that her mother was told. The police might not have seen a reason to tell Molly's family, and the family did leave town for a while. By the time Molly was doing her own investigation, things were tense with Amber's parents. They felt Molly was harassing them, so they may not have told her anything."

"We better get going," Lauren said. "We're going in circles and we've got a quilt waiting to be stitched.

Harriet reached out and shook hands with Nancy and then Patrice and Lauren did the same.

"I'll let you know if I find anything," Lauren told Nancy.

She guided her car out of the parking lot and was on the road back to the Methodist church before either of them spoke. Then, Harriet looked out the side window and sighed.

"I guess we're not getting out of finishing Josh's quilt."

"Nancy is nothing, if not thorough," Lauren agreed.

"If she's right about Molly not knowing about the serial killer possibility, and if he really did kill Amber, we're back to Molly being killed because of something she was currently working on."

"If that's the case, it's not something we're going to be able to figure out. I mean, if she connected our local missing children group with a dozen or so out-of-area cases, and she was working with who knows how many other groups like this one, there could be a lot of people who wanted to put her out of business, especially if she was starting to have some success. I could research on the computer full time and never get through all of them. And we both know I don't have time to do this full time."

"Some nebulous child-smuggling ring coming after Molly because she's had a small amount of success in recovering missing children just doesn't feel right to me. If it was a professional hit, why do it in Foggy Point? She would have been returning to Seattle in a few weeks, and there would be many more anonymous places to kill her and leave her body."

"Good point."

"Besides, I can't imagine any professional criminal enterprise breaking into my house or messing with Aunt Beth's car."

"We still don't know if those two—or three, really—crimes are connected."

"Oh, come on, Lauren. You think someone randomly burgled my house and business and some unrelated person messed with my aunt?"

It was Lauren's turn to sigh.

"You're right. If I had to bet money, I'd go with they're connected."

"So, that leaves us with—what, now?"

"Now, we go stitch and put it in front of the group. Maybe one of the Threads will have an idea."

Harriet and Lauren returned to their spots around the quilt frame and explained what they'd learned at the Center. Connie stopped stitching and stretched.

"So, what you're telling us is we don't have enough information to solve this one."

Harriet looked at Lauren before answering.

"I got nothing," Lauren told her.

"All we've established about Molly's death is we have no idea. We're not even very clear on what the motive is. Could be her work, could be her investigation of Amber's death, including whatever it is she remembered. It would help if we knew whether she told anyone about remembering something."

Mavis set her needle down and looked across the quilt at Harriet.

"Yet, here Beth sits with her wrapped-up foot and bum wrist, and you're camping out at my house. I'd say we've whacked a hornet's nest some-

140

where. We need to figure out which of the people you've talked to and eliminated should be put back on the list."

Robin sighed.

"Good point. I just can't see what we've missed."

"Maybe we should give it a rest for a while," Beth suggested. "We're chasing our tails."

"I think that's a good idea," Detective Morse said as she came into the room. "I came by to let Harriet know she can have her house back, and to see if I could help stitch for an hour or so."

"We can use any help we can get," Connie told her.

Robin stood up.

"Here, you can have my spot, I've got to go pick kids up."

Morse came around the frame to Robin's place.

"Will my stab-stitching mess anyone up?"

Most quilters make their quilt stitches by rocking the needle in and out of the fabric at an angle, loading several stitches on the needle before pulling it through the quilt sandwich. Stab stitchers make their stitches one at a time, putting the needle straight down into the fabric and then coming straight up a short distance away.

"As long as your stitches are uniform, we don't care what technique you use," Mavis answered her. "I brought several types of needles, if you want to use something different than what Robin left there."

Morse got up and went to Mavis, selecting a shorter needle before returning to her place and starting to quilt.

"Before anyone asks, I haven't heard anything about what happened at Harriet's. The criminalists didn't find anything immediately remarkable, but they have fingerprints to process and with that other shooting I told you about, it may be a few days."

Mavis caught Harriet's attention.

"I think you should continue staying at my house until this is sorted out."

"I'll have to think about that. What if they never catch anyone? Do I abandon my house?"

"You should reprogram your alarm when you get home and maybe upgrade the locks on all your doors," Morse suggested. "It looks like your door lock was picked."

Lauren paused her needle mid-stitch.

"One of my clients is working on a flexible key lock. They claim it's unpickable. I can probably get you a couple of prototypes."

"Thanks."

Harriet looked down at her hands as she stitched.

"It occurs to me that California might be a safer option for me right now."

Beth dropped her needle.

"Oh, honey, you can't be serious."

Harriet felt her cheeks turn red.

"I'm just tired of all this."

"This isn't the time to make that sort of decision," Mavis said and gave her a stern look.

Harriet didn't say anything else.

"I'd like to see all of you be a little more careful until our current situation is resolved," Morse said.

Connie paused her rhythmic stitching and glanced over at Morse.

"Rod and I have invited Carla and Wendy to stay with us for a few days."

"That's a good idea. I don't think Lauren has to worry because of her apartment's location. Between the bars and restaurants being open till all hours, and the store under her opening early, I think she's good.

"Jorge is at Beth's so much I think she'll be okay, and, Harriet, if you'll stay with Mavis that should cover everyone who lives alone. We're probably being overly cautious, but I'd rather that than someone running into whoever these yahoos are."

Harriet sighed.

"I'd like to at least go clean up my place and get the insurance adjuster out to look at my machine."

"Just don't go alone," Morse cautioned. "Also, I need all of you to stop by the department and have your fingerprints taken for elimination purposes. And before you ask, we won't have the results for a while; all that stuff you see on TV is not real. We'll have technicians with a magnifying glass looking at all of them."

"Okay, got it," Harriet agreed.

Beth and Mavis exchanged a look with Connie and turned the conversation to the results of the quilt show they'd gone to in Bothell the previous week.

Chapter 22

Harriet felt her phone buzz in her pocket. She pulled it out and saw it was a text from James. Aunt Beth had just invited her and Mavis to dinner at Jorge's, but she tapped her phone open and read the message.

Emergency race meet. Can U come?

Harriet looked up.

"James just texted that there's an emergency dog-race meeting. I'm sorry, I have to go. I'll have him drop me off at Mavis's when it's over."

She texted James, asking him to pick her up at the church.

"Around the corner, come out when ready," he texted back.

"He'll pick me up here," she told the group.

"Should I come get you tomorrow morning?" Carla asked.

"Sure. If you can pick me up at nine-thirty that will give us plenty of time to get to the psychic's by ten."

She stuck her needle into the border of the quilt near where she'd been working, picked up her purse and looked at Mavis.

"I'll be back whenever the meeting is done."

Aunt Beth straightened in her chair.

"I hope your chef will take you to dinner after dragging you away with no notice."

Harriet laughed.

"I have no doubt he has enough food to feed the whole town in the back of his van, if nothing else." She checked the time on her phone. "I better get going—he should be getting here soon."

"I'm free for dinner," Lauren said to the group in general.

"Oh, honey, you don't need an invitation to join us at Jorge's," Beth said with a smile.

"What happened?" Harriet asked James as she slid into the passenger seat of his brown BMW SUV. "I thought everything was set for the next race at the last meeting."

James tilted his head down and gave her a sheepish grin, looking up at her through his impossibly long lashes.

"I might have fibbed a little."

Harriet turned in her seat.

"What's going on?"

"Don't be mad, but I was thinking about what you said last night about leaving the area. I figured it must be hard, sitting with your aunt and your good friends all day, trying to think about your options but not able to. At least, I think you weren't able to discuss options with them."

"I did tell them I was thinking I should leave."

"Yeah, but did they believe it?"

Harriet smiled. He was right. Nobody sitting around the quilt would think she was seriously thinking about leaving.

"So, what is this?" She gestured.

James pulled away from the curb.

"This is me taking you out to dinner. Anywhere you want. Not my place, of course, since the chef is out on a date."

Harriet laughed.

"What would you have done if I'd said no?"

"I didn't start the car rolling until I was sure you weren't going to jump out." He watched for her reaction. When she didn't show signs of physical violence, he continued. "Seriously, I would have taken you to Mavis's or wherever you wanted to be."

"As it happens, you were right." She watched as a broad smile creased his face. "I'm still not sure what I'm going to do, but tonight, I can use a break."

James visibly relaxed.

"Whew!" He mimed wiping his brow. "I took the liberty of making us reservations at Cafe Garden in Port Angeles."

"I've never heard of it."

"They've been around for about twenty-five years. They were actually one of the reasons I became a chef. I went there with my parents when I was in grade school, and I immediately thought, *I* want to do this."

"Sounds good."

"Seriously, if I'm being too pushy, say the word, and I'll turn the car around."

She reached over and put her hand on his arm.

"This is exactly what I need. I'm sick of talking about Molly and Amber and all the people who might or might not be involved in their murder and disappearance. I know it's selfish and insensitive of me, but I just want my machine to be fixed and my life to return to normal."

"That's not selfish. We all agree Molly's death is tragic, but it's not your job to solve every crime that happens in Foggy Point."

"If I don't do anything, I feel like I'm letting DeAnn down. Molly *was* her half-sister."

James didn't say anything.

"You're right. You're offering me a night off, and I need it. I'm not going to spoil it by talking about Molly anymore."

He smiled.

"Let me tell you about the menu at Cafe Garden."

He proceeded to talk about food for the duration of the twenty-minute drive to Port Angeles.

Harriet slid a forkful of warm blackberry cobbler into her mouth and closed her eyes.

"Mmmmm, this is so delicious." She slowly opened her eyes. "Not as good as yours, I'm sure, but delicious, nonetheless."

James took a bite from their shared dish. He chewed slowly and swallowed.

"I have to admit, I can't think of anything I'd do differently."

"Thank you for bringing me here. It's just what I needed. And the seafood was fabulous."

James reached across the table and twined his fingers in hers.

"I have ulterior motives—I like your smile."

"I bet you say that to all the girls."

"You mock me," he said with feigned injury.

"Seriously, thank you."

"Judging from your tone, I'm guessing it's time to return to the real world."

"Sadly, it is. And if you wouldn't mind, could you take me to my house so I can get my car? Detective Morse said the police are done with my house, so I can get in the garage now."

"You're not planning on staying there, are you?"

"No, Detective Morse doesn't want any of us to stay alone until they sort this out. If I go home, it leaves Mavis alone, and after what happened to my aunt, none of us want that."

"Would you mind if I come in the house with you? I don't like the idea of leaving you there by yourself."

"Sure. I'd like to think I'm not afraid of my own house, but I think I'd like some company tonight."

"Really?" he said and raised his eyebrows.

She laughed.

"Since I'm sleeping at Mavis's, I think she might take issue with that sort of company."

"A boy can dream."

James was making hot cocoa in the kitchen when Harriet came in to get a broom and dustpan.

"Okay, I think we've got the bulk of the mess cleaned up. I found my customer order book, and thankfully it appears to be undamaged. I'm just going to sweep the floor and call it good for now. I can call my current customers tomorrow after I talk to the insurance people and then the machine people."

James stirred the warming milk with a whisk.

"Do you have a sense of how long the repair might take?"

"Not really. If they have parts on the shelf or a loaner system, I might be up and running within the week. If they have to order parts, it's anyone's guess."

He stirred cocoa powder into the milk as he spoke.

"Do you have any heavy cream I could whip?"

Harriet laughed.

"My whipped cream's in the fridge."

James opened her refrigerator and pulled out a can of Reddi-Wip.

"Surely, you jest," he said in a stricken voice.

"It's that or nothing."

He gasped.

"I guess it'll have to do. The cocoa's almost ready; if you sweep fast, it'll still be hot when you finish."

She returned to the studio and began sweeping, starting at the wastebasket where the fire had been set. Flakes of paper ash had settled around the area. From the partially burned papers, it looked like whoever had broken in had grabbed a handful of pages from the paper recycling bin and held a lighter or match to the corner of them before tossing them into the wastebasket. There were footprints in the ash, but it was impossible to tell if they were from James, the police, or whoever had set the fire.

She stooped to take a closer look and noticed white powder in one of the footprint ridges. It was thicker than the ash, and she poked her finger in the small pile then put her finger to her nose. The predominant odor was ash, but with a slight trace of mint. She supposed it was some sort of forensic material and made a mental note to ask Detective Morse if the criminalists had taken shoe prints from the fire debris and if anything had come from it.

Just in case, she pulled her phone from her pocket and took several pictures of the partial footprint before sweeping it into the dustpan and dumping it into the scorched wastebasket. The paint was blistered on its metal surface. She was sure Aunt Beth would expect her to sand and repaint it, but she made a mental note to buy a new one when she had a chance.

She stood up as James pushed the door open.

"Cocoa's ready."

She abandoned her broom and joined him in the kitchen.

"I'm going to have to up the mileage on my morning run if I keep hanging out with you." She sipped from the mug he handed her. "This is so much better than what I make."

"Thank you, I think. It's not too hard to beat powder-in-a-bag."

"So we're not all gourmet chefs like you are." She smiled as she reached across the kitchen table and took his hand.

They sat like that for a few minutes, enjoying their chocolate and each other's company.

"What's on your agenda for tomorrow?" he finally asked her.

"Quilting, quilting, and more quilting. Oh, and Carla and I are going to go talk to the psychic Molly visited not long before she died. Remember the messages she left on my voicemail? The ones I listened to at the hospital? She said she'd talked to a psychic, and something that they talked about caused her to remember what had happened twenty years ago.

"What we don't know is if the memory came back while she was still with the psychic, in which case the woman might know what she remembered. If it happened after she left, the psychic might be able to tell us what triggered the memory. If we know that, it might give us a direction to explore. Right now, we've got nothing."

"First, are you sure you *want* a direction? I thought you were done with detecting. Second, if the person Molly went to is a real psychic, won't she know everything? I mean, can't you just ask her what happened to Amber and Molly?"

"I'm not sure how it works. To be truthful, I'm not sure it works at all."

"You're a skeptic?"

Harriet put her head in her hands, then ran her fingers through her hair.

"I don't know what I think. I do know there are a lot of charlatans out there."

James scooted his chair around to her side of the table and put his arm around her shoulders.

"I'm sorry I asked. Let's not think about tomorrow until tomorrow. Are you ready to go back to Mavis's place?"

Harriet leaned into his embrace.

"That would be great," she finally said.

"Let me clean up my mess, and we'll get going."

Harriet went upstairs and packed some clean clothes and some toiletries into a blue duffel bag.

"I took the liberty of grabbing your box of test truffles," he told her when she'd returned. "You can share them with Mavis. Just be sure to note her impressions on the paper I gave you."

She smiled at him.

"You're pretty cute, you know that?"

"Hey, I'm serious about my truffles."

She laughed and took the box from him.

"I can see that."

✂ --- ✂ --- ✂

She and Mavis pulled up in front of the cottage at the same time.

"Did James let you drive home all by yourself?" Mavis asked as Harriet got out of her car.

"I told him he didn't need to follow me all the way out here. I locked my door and promised I'd call as soon as I arrived." She held her cell phone up. "I'm texting him now."

"I don't know how I feel about him letting you drive home alone."

"Mavis, it isn't even all the way dark yet."

"Well, you can't be too careful."

✂ --- ✂ --- ✂

Carla and Harriet met at the Methodist Church the following morning since they were going to be stitching after their appointment. Aunt Beth was sitting in her own chair, one Jorge had brought from her house after he deemed the church's folding chairs not stable enough. Her foot was propped on a pillow on an ottoman he'd brought from his own living room.

148

"You're looking very queenly," Harriet told her when she entered the basement.

"Jorge is a very attentive nurse. And speaking of him, he's preparing lunch for us so we can get more done. Will you and Carla stop by his place to pick it up on your way here from your meeting?"

"We'd be happy to. I could eat his cooking every day and never get tired of it."

"Me, too." Aunt Beth blushed. "He does have a way with a tortilla."

"Or something," Harriet teased.

Carla came in and set her quilting bag next to the chair she'd been using the day before.

"Is it okay if I leave my bag here while we're gone?"

Beth smiled at her.

"Of course it is, honey."

"We better get going if we're going to be there by ten," Harriet said.

"Do you have a paper and a pen with you?" Beth asked. "You probably should write down everything she says so you'll have it straight; it might be important."

Harriet laughed.

"Have I ever given you bad info?"

"This is different. This is a psychic. Exactly what she said to Molly might be critical."

"Assuming she *remembers* 'exactly what she said to Molly.' Besides, just because she's a psychic doesn't make her words magic. She's no different than any other suspect we've talked to."

Carla quietly headed to the stairs.

"We'll see you at lunchtime." Harriet said and followed her out.

✂ --- ✂ --- ✂

The first surprising thing about the psychic—that is, the first surprising thing besides her name, which was Martha Gray—was the absolutely ordinary home office she ushered them into. The room was divided into two spaces. Half was devoted to a desk and file cabinets with the other half containing a beige overstuffed sofa with two matching side chairs organized around a gas fireplace set into the end wall of the room. Two large plants flanked the window on the front wall. It could have been the office of an accountant or an architect. Harriet wasn't sure what she'd expected, but it wasn't this light and airy room.

"I'm Martha," said the attractive middle-aged woman who had answered the door and ushered them into the sitting area. She was wearing a rose-colored plaid wool skirt and pale pink silk blouse.

149

"Before you tell me anything, I'd like to tell *you* a few things. I find people sometimes come in and tell me the answer they're seeking and then suggest that I'm not actually reading for them. I find if we start with me talking and you listening, we save a little time.

"If I'm tuning in to you, I should be able to tell you ten things and have eight of them be correct. If I can't do that, I'm not connecting, and you can leave. I realize you didn't come for a reading, and to be clear, there is no charge for me answering a few questions about Molly Baker. I'd just like to get past the whole skeptic thing before we talk.

"And if you're agreeable, I'll record our talk and give you the recording to take home with you. I find people often have questions after they go home and think about what we've discussed. If you have the recording you can replay it as many times as you want."

Harriet looked at Carla, who nodded slightly.

"That sounds reasonable to us."

"First of all, you're both skeptics. That fact doesn't require my abilities. Most people are skeptics. You…" She looked at Harriet. "…have an interesting background. You didn't go to school in the United States, you are fluent in a lot of languages, and you developed a love of horses and riding at your boarding school."

Carla looked at Harriet with a raised eyebrow. Harriet smiled. Not many people knew about her equestrian background.

"You…" Martha turned to Carla. "…are the opposite of your friend. You grew up in the Northwest, but not always Washington. You moved with your mother frequently and spent more time taking care of her than she did caring for you." She paused for a moment. "You also love horses, but your riding was on a ranch."

"Okay, you got me," Harriet told her and looked to Carla.

"Me, too," Carla agreed.

"Now, let me just say. I can tune into some things and some people, but I don't know everything about everybody at all times. No one can hold that much information in their head. I also can only know what's true at the time I talk to you. The future is not fixed. I can tell you some of the pitfalls on the path ahead of you and you can choose to take it or not. There are many variables and if any one of them changes, it can change the future.

"And you may know this already, but psychic ability is not a circus trick. I can't tell you how many fingers you're holding behind your back or what your mother's birthday is. I can sometimes tap into a person's energy and emotion. No guarantees. If, knowing all that, you still want me to give you a reading, we can proceed."

Harriet looked at Carla.

"Are you good with going ahead?"

"I think we have to."

They both looked at Martha.

"Okay, what is it that's troubling you."

"Our friend's half-sister, Molly Baker, was murdered earlier this week. She has been investigating a missing-persons case she was a part of when she was five years old. Some would say she was obsessed with it. My friends and I believe she was killed because of something she learned or remembered.

"The thing is, she called me not long after she visited you. Something you told her caused her to, in her words, 'remember everything'. What we'd like to know is if you're able to tell us what you told her that triggered her memory. If she remembered everything while she was here, did she tell you what it was she remembered?"

Martha clasped her hands and sat silently for a moment.

"If she were alive, I wouldn't be able to tell you anything that happened during her session. Likewise, if she'd signed a confidentiality agreement it would still be binding. In this case, she didn't. I wouldn't tell you anything that was harmful to her surviving relatives, but I don't think that will be an issue.

"Regarding what she asked me about. As I'm sure you already know, she asked me about the incident that happened to Amber Price and her when they were children and resulted in Amber's disappearance."

She stood up and went to a side table that held a pitcher of water and glasses.

"Water?" she asked and held up a glass.

Harriet and Carla shook their heads. She poured herself a glass and returned to the chair opposite the other two, who were sitting on the sofa.

"I can tell you the first thing I told Molly, and that is that I believe Amber is no longer living. I feel sure of that, but doing a reading when children are involved is always difficult. Time also presents issues. Do you have anything that Amber had contact with? Touching something the person has had contact with helps focus my search."

"I don't," Harriet answered.

"Molly didn't, either. Given the amount of time that's passed, I'm not surprised."

Martha sat back in her chair, closed her eyes and thought for a few moments. She finally shook her head and opened them again.

"The trouble with young children is that their thought processes are immature. At five years old, we don't have a clear sense of what is fact and what is fantasy. Monsters seem as real as does Santa Claus and the Tooth Fairy, and they all bring out strong emotion.

151

"Amber was taken from behind. The 'monster' grabbed her from behind and covered her face. She woke up in a dark place but then everything went dark again. From there, it got confusing. She definitely believed she was underground, but then I got a strong impression she was in water. Deep water. And they weren't the same place. Like she was somewhere, and then was moved, possibly. But it could be that her understanding of where she was changed."

Harriet leaned forward.

"And that's what you told Molly?"

"That's what I told her about Amber. As for her, I also feel like she was grabbed from behind. I get the feeling something was put over her mouth. Maybe someone had a cloth with chloroform or something like that. She was in a dark space. And I mean physically, not just emotionally."

Martha hunched her shoulders.

"She was also in a tight place. Something was pressing on her shoulders; something cold. Metal, maybe? In her mind, she went into a rabbit hole and became small. Her impressions start to track *Alice in Wonderland*, so it's hard to make sense of it. I don't know where the truth ends, and her imagination took over."

"Could she have been given a psychedelic drug like LSD or something?" Harriet asked.

"Possibly. That might explain her fragmented memories."

Harriet thought for a minute.

"Did she remember any of this?"

"Not while she was here. And believe me, she tried."

Carla leaned forward and made eye contact with Martha.

"Do you know who killed her?"

Martha smiled.

"I wish it were that simple. My impression is, Molly was walking, and she felt as though she was being followed. She started to turn her head to look…" Here, Martha put her hand to the base of her neck. "But she felt a terrible pain in the back of her head, and then she crossed over. She was in a forest, but I think you know that, since that's where she was found."

"Can't you just ask her what happened, like that guy on TV?" Carla pressed.

"I'm afraid it doesn't work that way. There are many types of psychics, and then there are mediums. Mediums are the people who say they communicate with the dead. I can't tell you if they do or they don't. All I can speak to is my own impressions about people.

"Some psychics are able to jump from the victim to the perpetrator of a crime at will. That's not me, either. I'm just a plain vanilla psychic. I can only tell you what the person I'm connected with was seeing or feeling."

Harriet chewed on her bottom lip.

"I have a question that may or may not be related to Molly. If you want to charge me a session fee, I understand."

"I don't think that will be necessary. What's your question?"

"My aunt's car was tampered with a few days ago, and she was injured as a result. My quilting studio was broken into, and my machine was damaged. Was this just our bad luck, or are our incidents related to Molly's murder?"

"I can't tell you who the person is who is causing these events, but I have no doubt the events you've described are related. And make no mistake—you have a very powerful and dangerous enemy. Be careful." Martha got up and turned her recorder off. She removed the tape and handed it to Harriet. "I hope you have a cassette player. I haven't upgraded my technology in a while."

"Thank you for agreeing to meet with us. And yes, we can come up with a cassette player."

"I wish I could have been more helpful. Let me know if you have any more questions after you've reviewed the session tape with your friends. I'll try to answer anything I can. I can't emphasize enough, you're dealing with someone very dangerous."

Harriet stashed the cassette tape in her purse.

"Do you see something else happening?"

Martha thought a moment before answering.

"I do. I don't think it happens directly to either one of you, but someone close to you. I wish I could tell you more. Right now, all I have is a feeling. If it becomes clearer, I'll call you immediately."

Carla's face lost all its color.

"Wendy," she said softly.

"We will not let anything happen to Wendy. Rod and Connie won't let anyone near her."

Harriet turned back to Martha and reached her hand out.

"Thank you for your time. We've certainly got a lot to think about."

The psychic took the hand in both of hers.

"Be careful."

✂ --- ✂ --- ✂

"That was spooky," Carla said when they'd returned to the car.

"I was hoping she could tell us a little more."

"She told us we're in danger."

"Carla, we knew that already. I did, anyway. My aunt got hurt, and my house got violated. I was pretty sure whoever is doing this is dangerous."

153

Carla shrank back in her seat.

Harriet sighed, realizing she'd spoken more sharply than she'd intended.

"I'm sorry. I'm just frustrated. I'm not sure I even believe in psychic powers, but at the same time, I was hoping she was going to be able to tell us who killed Molly."

"So did I."

"What she said about the difficulty in reading children makes sense, though."

Carla stared out her window.

"I guess," she finally said.

Chapter 23

Harriet carried a large thermal bag full of the lunch she'd picked up at Jorge's restaurant in one hand. In the other hand, she held a gallon jug of iced tea. Carla followed with a shopping bag filled with paper plates, cups, plastic utensils wrapped in napkins, and containers of salsa, guacamole and sour cream, along with a big bag of tortilla chips.

Harriet set her bag down on one of the eight-foot cafeteria tables in the food service area of the church basement.

"Jorge said to tell you he made quesadillas for us." She opened the bag and began unloading as the group around the quilt frame stabbed their needles into the fabric and joined her. Robin wasn't stitching today, so Jorge hadn't had to include her usual "healthy" meal, which was usually some sort of salad. Jenny had once again taken her place at the quilt.

"We have fajita beef, chicken or plain cheese," Harriet continued. "Jorge said to tell everyone he pre-cut them so we can mix and match if we want, and he included three more quesadillas then we have people to allow for meat preferences."

Connie took the plates and started setting them out on the table.

"He does think of everything."

Harriet looked over Connie's head to her aunt.

"Do you need help?"

Beth was gliding along the cement floor on her knee scooter.

"No, I'm good. I'm getting pretty handy with this thing."

Mavis sat down at the table and began unwrapping her eating utensils.

"Are you going to keep us in suspense while you talk about food? Or are you going to give us a report?"

"I'll do better than a report. The psychic tapes everyone's session and gives them the tape when they leave. Even though we weren't clients, she taped our talk and gave it to us. Carla and I stopped by the church office and borrowed their cassette player, so as soon as everyone gets their food and is settled, we'll play it for you."

Carla brought the player around to where Harriet was sitting and put it on the table. Harriet popped the compartment open and inserted the tape. When everyone had their food and was settled, she pushed the on button.

Mavis wiped her mouth on her napkin as the tape finished.

"Well, that's as clear as mud. She has no idea who did anything?"

Harriet grimaced.

"Apparently, if we believe any of this at all, psychics are not all-seeing and all-knowing. And it sort of made sense, if she can only know what the victim knows. The hard part is figuring what, if anything, of what she got from Molly was real and what was fantasy."

Lauren slid her tablet computer from her messenger bag and woke it up.

"Let's think a minute. What are all the possible underground options? She could have been in a sewer pipe, or a basement."

Carla's face brightened, and she started to raise her hand, but dropped it back into her lap and spoke instead.

"She could have been buried in a box underground with an air pipe. My mom lived with a man from Mexico who was laying low here after he'd kidnapped some bigwig from a company down there and kept him in a box until his insurance paid the ransom."

Her face turned pink as the quilters seated around the table fell silent and stared at her.

"I was in the closet and was supposed to be asleep when he was telling her about it one night."

Lauren started tapping notes into her tablet.

"Okay, we'll add coffin-like box to the list. What else?"

"Does anyone around here have bomb shelters?" Harriet asked.

Aunt Beth pressed her lips together.

"I'd say yes...probably. I'm not sure how you can find that out."

"Lots of people built them in the fifties," Mavis added. "People were very paranoid during the Cold War."

Lauren looked down at her tablet screen.

"So far, I'm not finding any sort of listing of privately-owned bomb shelters. If a home was sold and listed that as a feature, I might be able to find it but it will take a while."

"I'm not sure I'd spend a lot of time on that," Harriet said. "Suppose they *were* held in a bomb shelter. It could have belonged to any random stranger. I'm not sure we can even establish if that serial killer guy had access to a bomb shelter. If a lot of them are abandoned, Amber's killer might have been using one anywhere, and it could have no relationship to him."

Lauren clicked her tablet off and leaned back.

"You're right, but at least it's something. I'm pretty sure the serial killer didn't come back from the dead and kill Molly. We haven't been able to rule the boyfriend in or out yet, so I think we should keep an open mind about all possibilities."

Harriet picked up a tortilla chip and scooped it into the guacamole before popping it into her mouth. She chewed thoughtfully then wiped her mouth with her napkin.

"Maybe we should hang up our detective creds. We haven't figured out anything about this situation; and if the psychic is right, and my studio and Aunt Beth's troubles are all connected, we're going in the wrong direction, big time."

"Morse has been telling us we shouldn't stick our noses in police business," Connie pointed out.

Lauren twirled her plastic fork in her fingers.

"Can you sit back and wait to see what's going to happen next?"

Harriet tried to keep her face serious but finally gave up and smiled.

"No, I can't. Now that we've poked the hornet's nest, I don't think we can un-poke it."

Beth got up and mounted her knee scooter.

"I think we can and should let Morse do her job. We've got enough on our plate with this quilt to stitch."

She wheeled over to the frame and sat down at her position, ending any further discussion.

✂ --- ✂ --- ✂

It was two o'clock on Sunday afternoon before the quilters were able to remove the protective bed sheet they'd stretched over their quilt frame. The church served a meal after the main Sunday service, and it took a while for the last stragglers to leave.

Mavis put her pillow onto the seat of her chair and sat down.

"I'm glad we went to the early service."

Harriet sat down beside her and arranged her purse and quilt bag underneath out of the way of her feet.

"I am, too. It gave me time to do my laundry. I was going to be out of clean socks."

"Heaven forbid. We can't have you sockless," Mavis said and laughed.

"Glad you have time to do laundry," Lauren said as she came over to the quilt frame. "I got up at six and worked all morning."

157

Mavis raised her eyebrows but didn't say anything.

"Hey, some of us have to work for a living, and if I've got to be here for the rest of the day quilting, I have to get stuff done at non-standard times."

Harriet located the spot she'd stopped at the day before and began stitching.

"I had another thought."

Lauren looked at her, grateful for the change of topic.

"What if the underground location is a cave?" Harriet continued. "Aren't there some caves on the hill below Sarah's cabin?"

Mavis began stitching.

"My boys used to play in some caves that were in the public land off Hewitt Road." She pulled her cell phone from her pocket. "Let me call Peter."

"If there are caves, it wouldn't hurt to go have a quick look," Harriet said in a low voice.

"Works for me," Lauren whispered.

Mavis ended her call and turned back to the quilt frame.

"Pete says there are two caves. He said to park by the sign to the hiking trail—it's just past the three-mile marker on Hewitt Road. Go down the trail for half a mile and then take a smaller path to the left, behind a large oak tree. He said you'll see a large rock formation. The entrance is to the right side of the rocks."

Lauren tapped notes into her phone as Harriet kept stitching.

"We need to wait and see how many people show up to quilt before we go anywhere," Harriet said. "If we don't get at least six, we need to stay and stitch."

"You're the boss," Lauren told her.

Mavis bent down and rummaged in her bag. She raised her hand triumphantly, an automatic needle threader clutched in her fingers.

"I know Carla isn't coming—she said she needs to spend time with Wendy. Robin has to be home with her kids, too."

"I'm here," Connie announced as she came down the stairs. "And Beth and Jorge pulled up as I was coming in."

"Four down, two to go," Lauren counted.

Harried looked up a few minutes later and saw Marjorie Swain coming down the stairs.

"I heard you ladies could use some help."

"I thought you were keeping the store open on Sundays," Harriet said and resumed stitching.

Beth smiled.

"What my niece meant to say was, yes, we can use all the help we can get. Especially from a prize-winning hand-quilter."

158

Harriet's cheeks pinked.

"That's what I meant to say. Here, let me get you a chair." She got up and went to the rack that sat against the wall to select a folding chair for Marjorie.

"I plan on opening on Sundays once school gets out and the tourists start coming to town, but for now the doors are still closed. I love to hand-quilt, so I'm happy to be here, but the word on the street is the guy who's getting this quilt doesn't even want it."

"Yeah, the ingrate," Lauren said.

Harriet looked at Marjorie.

"Wow, word travels fast. It's complicated. Josh Phillips is Molly Baker's ex, and she had a restraining order against him. He donated ten K so they would have to let him attend the fundraiser and donor thank-you event, and he'd be able to see Molly. Now that she's passed, he wants his money back and doesn't want the quilt. Unfortunately for him, that's not going to happen. He signed a pledge agreement, which is a contract, and he already gave them at least part of the money."

"I figured it was something like that. Patrice Orson came in for some buttons yesterday. She was trying to be coy."

"She probably thought she was being professional," Lauren interrupted-ed.

"Well, whatever she was being, she pretty much told me the whole story. She said the unnamed donor was hopping mad. He wanted his money back, and he has no use for a quilt. I already knew who he was and how mad, since he'd come by my shop to find out how much a quilt like the one he was getting would sell for. I tried to be generous, but I think he already knew it wasn't worth ten thousand dollars. He was like a three-year-old who'd had his lollipop taken away. For a minute, I thought I was going to have to get him an ambulance, his face turned so red."

Mavis handed her a spool of thread and a packet of needles.

"I'm sorry you had to deal with our 'friend'. And I'm glad you're here to help. Getting enough stitches in this quilt before Saturday is going to be touch-and-go."

Beth looked over at Harriet and Lauren.

"The task is made all the more difficult by our resident investigators and their frequent fact-finding sojourns."

Harriet stopped stitching.

"Hey, I was ready to give up."

"Yeah, like that was going to happen," Lauren muttered.

Jenny came down the stairs and hurried over to her place at the frame.

"Sorry I'm late. My husband took my car to the car wash and didn't pay attention to the time."

"You're here now, that's what matters," Beth told her.

Lauren stood up.

"And with that we have a quorum." She picked up her messenger bag and looked at Harriet. "Are we ready?"

Harriet rose and followed her up the stairs and out.

✂ --- ✂ --- ✂

Lauren drove, since Harriet had come to the church with Mavis. She was quiet, which was out of character. Harriet watched the small muscle in her jaw twitch.

"What are you not telling me?"

Lauren glanced at her.

"What do you mean?"

"You obviously want to say something to me, but you're holding back, for some reason."

Lauren's eyes narrowed. She refused to make eye contact.

"I know you've had a lot going on lately, I get that having your livelihood threatened is a big deal, even though we both know you don't really depend on your long-arm quilting to pay the bills, but we'll pretend you do. It probably worried you a little when your aunt got hurt. I get that, too."

"Thanks for that," Harriet interrupted.

"Let me finish. I know you've had some real stuff going on, but I'm getting whiplash here with all the flip-flopping. One minute you're Nancy Drew, girl detective, ready to go cave-hunting and doing anything to solve the crime, but then the next you're Princess Buttercup—life is too difficult in Foggy Point, and you're going to turn in your detective license and run home to California.

"And don't even get me started on the romance thing. First you're so depressed because Aiden dumped you that all you can do is work, and next time the group sees you, you're playing footsie with the cute chef. And still you feel sorry for yourself. Lots of us would be happy to find *one* good guy. You've got three, and still you're not happy."

Harriet was quiet for a moment. She slumped in her seat.

"Wow, I didn't realize I was such a burden."

"Come on, you know that's not what I mean. I'm just saying, you've taken a leadership role in our group, especially as it relates to some of the situations we've gotten into in the last year. In that role, you don't have the luxury of being wishy-washy.

"And don't forget, all of us have had a hard time this last year. I was suspected of killing someone. Mavis had that business with her husband,

160

and then there was Jenny and poor Sarah. And DeAnn went through that whole adoption thing, and now her sister is dead. Imagine how she feels."

Lauren reached over and put her hand on Harriet's arm.

"I know you're not being a drama queen on purpose, but it's time to buck up."

"Have the other people in the group been saying things?"

"Not to me, but I *have* seen a few looks exchanged."

Harriet turned and stared sightlessly out the window.

"Hey, I'm not trying to minimize what you've gone through. I know it's been rough. I've been with you for most of it. I think you need to think a little about the rest of the group, that's all. Every one of us has had stuff happen. I'm sure Carla would like to get off the merry-go-round sometimes, too, but she doesn't have the luxury of pulling up stakes and leaving. She's got a child and has to work to support her."

"Enough. I get it. I'm an insensitive ingrate."

"That's not what I'm saying at all. And if you really think going to California is the best move for you, just go. Stop with all the drama. If you're going to stay and help figure out what happened to Molly, then do that and stop threatening to leave all the time."

"It's hardly been all the time, but I get it. You're right. I have been feeling sorry for myself."

"In reality, if you hadn't spent weeks working night and day and barely eating while you worked on those quilts for that lady, you probably would have been better able to cope with all this mess, but that isn't how things happened, and as they say, life is messy."

"Well, thanks, I guess."

Lauren laughed.

"That's what friends are for. And hey, maybe I'm off-base. Talk to your aunt or Mavis; see what they think."

"I don't need to talk to anyone, I may not agree with everything you said, but you made your point. I *have* been self-indulgent lately. You're right about being tired, too. Between the client quilts and then these three for Molly's benefit, I haven't been getting enough rest, and the business with Aiden hasn't helped my sleep. I have to say, the 'cute chef' is helping on that score, so don't knock him."

Lauren rolled her eyes.

"Is that the trail sign?" she asked and pointed out the windshield as she slowed the car and pulled off the road.

"Looks like it."

Harriet retied her tennis shoes and got out of the car while Lauren popped the trunk then fished out two bottles of water and handed her one. Lauren picked up a flashlight and slid it into her messenger bag.

"Now, we walk," Harriet said.

* * *

The trail was rocky and steep, so it took almost an hour to reach the smaller trail Pete had described.

"This has to be the rock formation," Harriet said when they reached the end of the path. "It's the only one." She walked to the right for the third time and poked into the brush along the rock face with a stick. On her second poke, her stick slid in without resistance.

"I think I found something," she called.

Lauren, who had backed up the trail to take a broader look, returned; and both women began pulling branches away from the rock.

"Interesting that none of these bushes are rooted," Harriet commented. "It's like someone piled them here." She rubbed her fingers on one of the leaves. "These feel like someone spray-painted them green." She picked up a bush. "I think these are permanent set pieces."

Finally, between the two of them, they moved enough of the dry brush to reveal an opening about the size of a washing machine.

"Uhh…" Lauren said and backed up.

"Yeah, me, too. I was expecting something a little bigger."

"If the whole cave is this big, I can't do it. I'm sorry, I'm claustrophobic."

Harriet squatted down and bent her head to look.

"We've come this far. I have to at least try, especially after your pep talk."

"I was talking about being decisive, not being a risk taker."

"Hand me the flashlight. I'll go in a little way and see if it opens out or stays small."

Lauren handed her the light, and she turned it on and disappeared into the dark hole.

"Hey," Lauren called almost immediately. "I thought you weren't going in too far."

"Come on in," Harriet answered. "It's huge once you get past the first six feet or so."

She heard Lauren suck in her breath and then the scraping sounds of someone crawling.

"See, that wasn't so bad." She helped Lauren brush the dirt off her jeans as she stood up.

"That was the longest hundred feet of my life."

"Lauren, if you lay down you can almost reach the outside from in here."

Harriet turned and flashed the light around the large cavern. Against one wall were two cots with sleeping bags on them, a lantern, and a jug of water. A few feet away sat a large trunk. She walked to the trunk and swept it with the light. A combination lock secured a central hasp on the front.

Lauren came over and rapped her knuckles on the top of the trunk. A dull thud sounded.

"Sounds like it's full of something."

"It looks like someone could have been held here, but something's off. First, don't you think the opening would be more secure?"

"Not if the prisoner was secured inside."

"But there aren't any bolts in the wall or anything else I can see that would allow you to shackle someone inside here."

Lauren looked around.

"You're right."

"It's also pretty clean in here. Doesn't it seem like if Mavis's son and his friends came here when they were young there'd be at least a little litter? Kids aren't that conscientious, are they?"

"You're asking me?"

She shone the light on the dirt floor and leaned down to get a better look.

"It looks like it's been swept."

Lauren came closer and looked.

"Someone's been using this cave for something."

"Yeah. Unfortunately, there isn't anything to suggest it has anything to do with Molly's death. And if this was the place Amber was held, it's been too long ago for there to be any evidence of it. Let's see if we can find the second cave Pete told Mavis about."

Harriet crawled out into the daylight and was searching the rock face for another opening when Lauren made her way out, white-faced and shaky.

"Maybe you should sit down for a minute."

"Look," Lauren said and pointed. "There's a path."

She did and could barely make out a faint trail. She followed it around the rock formation.

"Found it."

She was facing a wide, low opening that led into a shallow chamber. A quick look showed that this was the place where the local kids hung out. There were cigarette butts, candy wrappers and beer cans littering the dirt floor. A tattered blanket was rolled up against the wall. Like the first cave, there was no other opening leading out of the main chamber.

"There's nothing here." She called back to Lauren.

"Good, 'cause I don't have another small closed space in me today."

Harriet emerged and went over to where Lauren was now sitting on a big rock.

"Come on, give me the keys," she said. "I'll drive."

Chapter 24

J ane, you're just the person I wanted to see," Harriet said as she took her place at the quilting frame.

The detective sat across from her. She stopped mid-stitch.

"What's on your mind?"

"Carla and I went to see the psychic Molly had gone to right before she died. The one who she said triggered her memory."

"Did Molly tell her what she remembered?"

"No, unfortunately. She had no idea what, if anything, had caused Molly to remember."

"She was so young when whatever happened to her and Amber happened, I'd be surprised if she truly remembered it."

"That's sort of what the psychic said. She told us kids that age have trouble distinguishing fantasy from reality, and her perception of what Molly knew back then was heavily colored by fantasy."

Harriet picked up her needle and made a few stitches.

"What the psychic did say was in regard to Amber. She had a feeling she had been underground."

"That would make sense if she was buried." Morse said.

"She said Amber thought she was underground and later thought she was in deep water. Anyway, we were brainstorming about what that might mean, and we thought maybe they'd been held in a cave."

Harriet looked to Mavis.

"I called my son," Mavis said, taking up the story. "He and his friends used to play in some caves off Hewitt Road. I called him, and he told me how to find them. I told Harriet and Lauren, and they just came back from exploring them."

Lauren grimaced.

"Something I'm never doing again."

Beth reached over and patted her hand.

Harriet sighed.

"Someone could have mentioned their claustrophobia before we left."

"I didn't think we were going to have to crawl on our bellies to get into it," Lauren said.

Morse cleared her throat.

"Your question?"

"The bigger cave was hard to find. Someone had put some effort into concealing the opening behind fake bushes. As Lauren said, the opening was small and led into a larger chamber that had a locked trunk, a couple of cots and a lantern. As near as we could tell, someone had gone to some trouble cleaning the place up, too. It looked like the floor had been swept."

Morse put her needle down and took a small notebook and a pen from her purse. She wrote a few notes and returned them to her bag.

"I'll ask around and find out if anyone has permission to use the cave for some legitimate purpose. It's possible Fish and Wildlife cleared some bats out or something. If not, I'll see if I can send someone from the crime lab to check it out. It's pretty thin, but frankly, we've got nothing else going on where Molly's concerned."

Lauren clipped the end of her thread and rubbed her finger over the spot where she'd buried her knot.

"Our only other thought about underground places was the bomb shelter idea. I'm not saying we're buying into the whole psychic thing—at least, I'm not. But we've got nothing else, either. And we have to face DeAnn."

Beth stabbed her needle into the quilt.

"Plus we don't feel very safe the way things stand."

Morse looked down at her work.

"I wish I could tell you we knew what was going on, but we don't. We've been through all the evidence more than once. The chief is going to put out a Crimestoppers bulletin on Monday to see if we can get someone to call us with a tip."

"Back to the bomb shelter idea," Lauren said. "What if the underground place was a bomb shelter? Do the police have a record of bomb shelters in this area?"

Morse stopped stitching and thought for a moment.

"I don't think we do, but the city might. I can ask. I don't know if they had to have permits or be inspected."

Mavis laughed.

"Good luck with that. Building permits are a fairly recent invention in Foggy Point."

Morse made another note in her little pad.

"At least it's something to do. I'll let you know what I find out."

✂ --- ✂ --- ✂

"Anyone want to go get something to eat?" Mavis asked at seven o'clock that evening.

Harriet put her needle into the edge of the quilt.

"I'm with you."

Mavis smiled.

"Thank you, sweetie, but I assumed since I drove us that *you* were with me." She looked around the women seated at the frame. "Anyone else like to join us?"

Marjory stretched her back.

"Sounds good. I don't feel like cooking, that's for sure."

Jenny took her cell phone from her purse and called home.

"Count me in. My husband is going to his friend's house to help him set up a model train."

One by one, the group parked their needles, picked up their bags and headed for the parking lot. Harriet's phone buzzed as Mavis guided her car out of the parking lot. She read the message on the screen.

"James just texted to see if I want to go to dinner. Do you think anyone would mind if I invited him along?"

"I'm sure Jorge will be with your aunt. He'd probably appreciate another male being there, especially one who cooks."

Harriet tapped a quick message into her phone and, a moment later, received a reply.

"He says he'll meet us there."

"So, what's going on with you and James?"

"We're…friends. Okay, I know everyone says that, but we've decided to spend some time together without any strings and with no pressure to be anything else for now. He's busy with his restaurant, and I guess the people he's dated lately want more than he can give. After this last year with Aiden, I'm not in a position to get involved with anyone else.

"So, James and I were talking the other night, and we acknowledged the fact that, while we're not in a place to be in a committed relationship, we'd like to have someone to go to dinner with or watch a movie with. For me at least, that's enough."

"Tell yourselves whatever you need to for it to work, but I've got eyes, and you mark my words—that boy is falling for you."

Connie and her husband Rod were sitting at a large table in Mama Theresa's Pizza with Carla and Wendy when Mavis and Harriet arrived.

166

"How's the quilting going?" Rod asked.

The women at the table looked at each other and laughed.

"Is that a good laugh or a bad laugh?" he asked.

Harriet sat down across from him.

"Hand-quilting is a daunting project under any circumstance, but in this case, the intended recipient first sort of forced us to make him a quilt; and now that Molly is dead, he's trying to withdraw his donation and, therefore, his qualification as a quilt receiver."

"At least it's a pretty quilt," Connie mused. "It could be worse. They might have let the donors pick their own fabric or pattern."

"True," Harriet agreed.

James came in and sat beside her.

"Have you ordered yet?"

"We just got here ourselves," Mavis told him.

He set a piece of paper on the table in front of her and Harriet.

"Here's something for you quilters to consider while we're waiting for everyone to get here."

Harriet took the paper and read out loud.

"'Appliqué At Galveston Bay—A Retreat. June twenty to twenty-five.'"

"That's not too far off," Mavis said.

"I heard it wasn't full up yet," James said. "I'm going to a cooking class, and as part of the class, we're presenting the banquet dinner at this event."

Harriet looked at him.

"I thought you already knew how to cook."

"You can never know enough about food. We covered Southern cooking in school, but this will be with working chefs and will focus on regional ingredients. I'm stoked. One of the days we cook alligator all day."

Lauren slid her bag off her shoulder and settled into a chair across from Harriet.

"Sounds hideous. I only heard the tail end of that. Why are you cooking alligator all day?"

"I'm going to Galveston, Texas, to get up-close-and-personal with East Texas cuisine."

Harriet slid the paper across to her.

"James is suggesting we go to an appliqué retreat that takes place at the same time as his class. His bunch is going to be serving the banquet dinner one night."

"After all the work you've been doing on that donor quilt, I thought you all might want to get away for a while."

Lauren read the details on the paper.

"It actually sounds kind of fun. My appliqué skills *could* use some help. It says here you get to choose two different classes."

"Is it expensive?" Connie asked.

"Not really, considering it covers the hotel, the class, breakfast all week and the banquet."

Lauren handed the paper to Connie. She read the flyer and handed it to Rod.

"Sounds okay to me," Rod said. "If you want to go, I can hold down the fort here."

Lauren consulted her calendar on her phone.

"I'm in."

Beth rolled in on her knee scooter, followed by Jorge, and a brief pizza discussion resulted in James and Jorge going to the counter to place the group's order. Harriet handed Beth the flyer about the retreat, and she read it and laid it back on the table.

"I think it would be a great get-away—for you. I'm going to be doing physical therapy for at least a month, according to my doctor. I think I need to stay here and concentrate on getting mobility back in my ankle. Before you ask, I'd be happy to take care of your pets while you're gone."

Harriet made eye contact.

"Are you sure?"

Beth nodded.

"Count me in, too, then." Harriet said. "I'll call them in the morning and see if they have room for us. If anyone else wants to go, let me know early. Has anyone here ever been to Galveston?"

It turned out everyone except her and Lauren had been there at least once, and the rest of the dinner was spent with each person in turn describing their memories of the place.

An hour later, Harriet crumpled her napkin and tossed it on the table.

"I can't eat another bite." She looked at Mavis. "What do you think? Should we head out?"

"We all need to rest," Beth said. "We need to bear down if we're going to get that quilt finished and bound by Saturday."

Chapter 25

The next few days passed in a blur of hand-quilting, meals out and precious little sleep, but by Friday, the end was in sight. Harriet finished the last small square of her last "daughter block" of the disappearing nine-patch in front of her. She sat back to admire her work.

"Done with my last one," she announced.

Aunt Beth stabbed her needle into the block in front of her.

"I've got a few more stitches to go, and then I'm done, too."

Connie and Carla were working at a card table they'd set up to hold Connie's small portable sewing machine and a square ironing pad and an iron. They had cut the quilt binding in the morning and were in the process of sewing the segments together and pressing them.

"We're almost done with the binding," Connie told them. "Carla is going to roll it onto an empty tissue roll so it will stay nice until we're ready to start sewing it on. I was thinking I'd move my machine to one of the big lunchroom tables to do that part so the quilt won't touch the floor while I'm working on it."

"Sounds good," Beth said. She looked over at Harriet and Lauren. "You girls can take a break, if you want. Mavis and I can finish up the quilting and clip any loose threads, and then there's nothing else to do until Connie gets the binding on."

Mavis stood up and moved around the quilt frame to another spot where a square waited to be finished.

"We'll probably get a bite to eat after we finish this part," she said. "Then, if everyone comes back around two, we can lay the quilt on one of those big tables, and each of us can take a section to bind. It'll take no time at all with all of us working."

Lauren stood up, stretching her arms in the air before she stepped away from the quilt.

"You don't have to ask me twice. I'm out of here." She looked at Harriet. "Want to go get a rice bowl?"

"I do, but I want to stop by the Carey Bates Center on our way."

"What for?"

"I had an idea—"

"Always a scary thought," Lauren interrupted.

Harriet glared at her, but continued.

"As I said, I had an idea while we were sitting here stitching. Bear with me, 'cause it's a little out there.

"First, we know Molly was found both times in Fogg Park. Martha Gray sensed she was underground, and that she thought the space was metal."

"Go on."

"What if she crawled into a vent?"

"What would it be venting?"

"Maybe a bomb shelter, or maybe Carla's box in the ground. But I was thinking. What if the vent came out in Fogg Park."

"Fogg Park is a big place."

"We could look where they found Molly the first time."

"Where does the Carey Bates Center come into it?"

"When Molly was first asking for help, I think she mentioned them having a metal detector."

"Are we looking for a vent pipe? Don't you think a vent big enough for a five-year-old to crawl into would be easy to spot?"

"I'm thinking it might be grown over by now. Plus, it might cover some amount of distance. Whatever the vent is connected to, it isn't likely that space is in Fogg Park. I'm thinking it's somewhere nearby, but the vent pipe is still going to be pretty long."

"You've had some wild ideas in the past, but this one takes the cake. On the other hand, I've got nothing else to do for the next couple of hours."

"I don't think I like this plan," Aunt Beth said.

Lauren looked at her.

"Believe me, this is likely a wild goose chase. We'll go, we'll run the metal detector until our arms get tired of holding it up, we won't find anything, and we'll grab lunch and be back in time to help bind."

Aunt Beth shook her head and turned back to the quilt.

Harriet grabbed her purse and headed up the stairs, followed by Lauren.

"Hey, glad I caught you," Detective Morse said as she came in through the main entrance doors. "I just got the report from the criminalists about the cave."

Harriet stopped at the top of the stairs.

"Did they find something?"

Morse's lips pressed into a thin line.

"No...and yes. That is, it was so clean it's suspicious because of what wasn't there."

Lauren pushed past Harriet and stood facing Detective Morse.

"Explain."

"That cave is so clean you could almost do surgery in it. There isn't dust anywhere but the dirt floor, there are no spiders and, unlike the other cave, there are no empty cans or bottles, no candy wrappers, nothing."

Harriet came up the final stair step and stood beside Lauren.

"What was in the trunk?"

"Tarps, flashlights, and freeze-dried meals, all without a single fingerprint or any other biological fluid we could test."

Harriet looked at Lauren, but for once her friend had no comment.

"Well, that's weird, isn't it?"

"Clearly, someone's been doing something in there they don't want anyone to know about. Could be drugs, could be a temporary stash for stolen goods, could be anything. We'll have patrol keep an eye out and see if they can catch anyone coming or going. I've put in a requisition to get video surveillance set up, too, but I don't know if that will happen."

Harriet hesitated. "So, I can imagine Molly coming across someone doing something in the cave, and someone killing her and tossing her in the park to keep their secret. But the psychic said *Amber* was underground, not Molly. She said Molly was in a narrow metal space."

Morse shook her head.

"I can't speak to what a psychic did or didn't say or see. All I can tell you is that cave is suspicious. Something's happening there, but whether it has anything to do with Molly's death, it's too soon to tell."

Harriet made a move toward the door.

"You ladies look like you're on a mission," Morse called after her. "Anything I should know about?"

Lauren followed Harriet.

"Probably not," she answered over her shoulder and went out the door.

✂ --- ✂ --- ✂

Harriet pulled into the parking lot of the Carey Bates Missing and Exploited Children offices and parked in front of the door in one of the visitor spaces.

"Looks like there's someone in the waiting room," Lauren commented. "What do you think they're doing?"

"Given the center looks for missing kids and uses volunteers, I'd guess it's either someone who lost someone or someone who's helping find someone. Or, if they're lucky, it's someone donating money."

Lauren strained to see through the sheer curtain that obscured her view into the building.

"Please let it be a donor, I'm not sure I'm up for any more drama than we already have."

"I haven't heard of anyone going missing lately, not that that means anything. I'm with you, though. Let's hear it for another donor."

"Only if they don't want a quilt prize."

"I'm betting they don't get too many ten-thousand-dollar donations, and with three already this year, a fourth isn't too likely." Harriet unbuckled her seatbelt. "Enough stalling. Let's go get the metal detector and get out of here."

Lauren stopped a few steps from the door.

"Listen." She paused.

Harriet stopped and listened.

"I can't make out what they're saying, but someone sounds mad."

"You still want to go in?"

"We need the metal detector—it's the only way we can confirm or dispel the idea that there's a vent big enough to hold a five-year-old."

Lauren stepped aside.

"Lead the way."

Harriet opened the door to the reception area of the Center.

"I don't care how many people donated money, I don't care how many buildings were built, I don't care that it was Molly's last wish," Sandra Price shouted. "That woman has tormented my family for twenty years, and it seems like she's not going to stop just because she died.

"I don't know how else to tell you no. I don't want to come to your party, I don't want Amber's name on your building." She spoke slowly like she was talking to a child or someone who didn't have English as their first language. "I don't want anything else to do with you people. Is that clear enough for you?"

Sandra stood in the middle of the room, her fists balled at her sides, her face red. Patrice looked even paler than usual, and Carla's friend Sadie was backing her way toward the hall.

"Does this mean you aren't coming to the donor celebration?" Patrice stammered. She looked like she was about to cry.

Sandra threw her arms up in exasperation and caught sight of Harriet and Lauren. She spun to face them and made as though to speak. Then, she shook her head, let her arms fall to her sides, and, with one more glare at Patrice, stormed out the door, slamming it behind her.

Tears that had barely been held in check began to flow down Patrice's thin cheeks. Harriet looked at Lauren and, finding no help, picked up a box of tissues from the lamp table and crossed to hand them to the crying woman. Sadie hurried out from the hall and launched herself at Patrice, hugging her before stepping back.

"What are we going to do?" Patrice snuffled. "We were going to dedicate the new building in the name of Amber Price." She moaned. "Molly would have known what to do."

Harriet cleared her throat.

"Aren't you presenting your major donors with their quilts? Do you have anything for any of your other donors? Maybe you can make the ceremony be about the donors and the building they helped you build and just leave out the naming part."

"Not every building is named after somebody," Lauren added.

Patrice looked hopeful.

"Can we do that? Can we thank them without calling the building by its name?"

Sadie put her arm around Patrice's shoulders.

"Of course we can. We can worry about a name when the board gets to town. Let me make you a nice cup of tea, and then we can work on a new celebration plan." She looked over at Lauren and Harriet. "Would you like some tea?"

"No, thanks. We just came by to see if we can borrow the metal detector we saw here the other day," Harriet said.

"Sure," Sadie said and disappeared into the hallway.

"Well, that was weird," Lauren said when they were back in Harriet's car, the detector stowed in the back. Sadie had given them a quick tutorial on the unit before they left.

"Yeah, there's no winner in that little scenario. I mean, we only knew Molly for a couple of weeks, and she was driving *us* crazy with wanting us to solve her crime. You can just imagine what it's been like for Sandra Price, trying to get over the loss of a child with a survivor who won't let it go, hounding her for years."

Lauren gazed out her window.

"This just keeps getting better. And by the way, Molly never mentioned a new building to us."

"Molly never mentioned a lot of things. In fact, if it didn't have to do with Amber and her disappearance, she didn't tell us anything."

Harriet laughed.

"You're right. She could have had a whole secret life we didn't know about."

"Unfortunately, with her obsession, I don't think she had time for a secret life."

✂ --- ✂ --- ✂

Lauren wrestled the metal detector out of Harriet's car. They were parked near the restrooms in the lot at Fogg Park. It landed on the ground with a thunk.

"Do you want to carry it, or shall I?"

"I'll carry it, but I think we should swing by the homeless camp and see if we can get a better idea of where Molly was found the first time."

"Lead the way."

Harriet headed down the path behind the restroom building and into the woods. Joyce Elias met them a short distance into the trees, a reusable grocery tote in each hand.

"What brings you two into our fine forest today? And what is that contraption?" The faint English lilt to her voice seemed more pronounced than usual.

Harriet set the detector down.

"We're trying to help bring some closure to our friend DeAnn. Her sister Molly was obsessed with finding out what happened to her when she was five, and now, as you know, she's dead."

"We're well acquainted with that poor girl. Besides Max and me finding her body, she came out here many times since I've been here and probably before that, too."

"Lauren and I are on a bit of a wild goose chase. Just before she died, Molly told me she'd spoken to a psychic, and it had caused her to remember everything. Carla and I visited the psychic, but unfortunately, Molly didn't have her breakthrough until after she'd left.

"We asked the woman what she'd told Molly, but it was a bit vague. She said that Molly felt cold metal around her shoulders. She told us she couldn't tell what Molly was actually remembering and how much was fantasy based on *Alice in Wonderland*."

Lauren crossed her arms.

"Can we get to the point?" she finally said.

Harriet glared at her before continuing.

"Okay, okay. We got the idea maybe Molly was held somewhere that was connected by some kind of vent to the woods she was originally found in. We thought she might have crawled into the vent to hide and ended up coming out in the woods."

Joyce pointed at the metal detector.

"I suppose you were going to use that thing to find it?" she asked with a smirk.

Harriet put her hands in her jeans' back pockets.

"Well, we saw this at the Missing and Exploited Children Center and thought any vent pipe Molly crawled out of in the forest twenty years ago would be grown over with brush by now."

"Maybe yes, maybe no," Joyce said thoughtfully. "If it's been abandoned, yes, but if it's still being used to vent something, it might be obvious. Do you know where to start looking?"

Harriet smiled.

"Sort of."

"Tell you what. Let's go back to camp so I can put my groceries away, and while we're there, we can see if Max is around. If he is, we can ask him to show us where he found Molly. You can look around, and with any luck, you can find your vent without firing that thing up."

Lauren just looked at Harriet, who shrugged.

"Sounds good to us. If we don't find it that way, we can always use the metal detector." Harriet stopped. "Wait a minute. Max found Molly when she was killed. We're looking for the spot where she was found when she was five."

Joyce smiled at her.

"And that's why we need Max."

Lauren picked up the detector.

"You mean Max found her the first time, too?"

"Indeed, he did," Joyce said, and headed for her camp.

✂ --- ✂ --- ✂

Joyce roused Max from his afternoon nap, and they all waited while he went to the restroom then ate a granola bar from a plastic storage box that was chained to a tree in his sleeping area.

"Sure, I remember where I found that little girl," he told them. "I hope you're ready for a hike." He brushed past the women and headed deeper into the forest.

The trail led them diagonally across the park. Harriet was glad they weren't doing this in the winter as they jumped over a trickle of water that was probably knee-deep when the rains came. After the stream, they climbed steadily. She and Lauren passed the detector back and forth as their arms tired.

"Now that I see how much of a slope there is in this corner of the park, our vent scenario seems a little more plausible," she said to Lauren's back.

Lauren turned her head slightly but kept walking.

"Unfortunately, it also makes our detector less useful. If the vent is sticking out of the hillside, we may find the opening, but the depth of the dirt on the slope will prevent us from being able to tell which direction it goes in."

Harriet laughed.

"Makes me glad we lugged it all this way."

"Not much longer," Max called back to them.

Harriet blew out her breath and noticed he wasn't out of breath at all; she vowed to up her weekly running mileage.

"Okay," he said a few minutes later. They had reached the end of the trail and stood in a clearing facing a steep rocky bluff. To the left, the slope wasn't as steep or as rocky. It was, however, overgrown with blackberry bushes.

"She was in this clearing. I had just moved into the park—it wasn't as nice back then. None of the trails were developed like they are now. I figured I should know where the boundaries were and where people were able to enter the park. We didn't have lock-boxes back in those days, so security was always an issue, and anyway, I wanted to be sure I was in the most secure location before I set up a permanent camp."

Harriet and Lauren looked around.

"The alleged vent wouldn't have come out of rock, probably," Lauren said and turned to the left. Harriet had already begun poking into the blackberries with a stick she'd picked up along the trail.

Max waded into the blackberry thicket.

"If someone was digging a vent line, they wouldn't go very deep in this rocky soil. It'll probably be up near the top of the slope."

Harriet followed the path Max had tramped into the berry bushes and came up beside him, stomping berry canes down the way he was. Together, they worked their way slowly up to the top.

Max stopped as they neared the summit.

"You two can come up and help now," he called to Joyce and Lauren. "Pick up a stick if you can find one."

With four of them working, it only took another ten minutes before Joyce's stick clanged against metal.

"I think I've found something."

They stomped over to where she stood and watched as she probed with her stick then reached to pull stubborn vines from what she'd found. Harriet bent down to look into the small, smooth opening.

"If Molly was in that pipe, I can see why having her shoulders squeezed was what she remembered."

Lauren looked over Harriet's shoulder.

"We should ask DeAnn if Molly had dislocated shoulders when they found her."

Joyce bent over and looked.

"Children are quite small at that age, and they tend to be very flexible. I can imagine a small child fitting in there, especially if she were motivated by fear."

Harriet stepped back.

"Unfortunately, this could come from anywhere."

"Not really," Lauren said. "We know it didn't come from the park. And we know it didn't come in from that rocky bluff. At least, it's not likely."

"That still leaves a lot of possibilities," Harriet countered.

Lauren started back down the slope.

"We need to look at a map."

"We need to get back to the church and see if Aunt Beth and the others need help with the quilt." Harriet started for the trail.

Joyce sighed.

"You know, there is another possibility."

Harriet and Lauren stopped mid-step.

"Something besides Molly crawled out of this pipe?"

"Yes…well, no, not the crawling out part. What if someone thought they'd killed Molly and stuffed her in the end of this pipe? When she woke up, she crawled back out, and Max found her."

"Huh," Lauren said thoughtfully. "Did the psychic say she crawled a long distance?"

Harriet shook her head.

"I don't think so. I'd have to listen to the tape again to be sure, but I think she only said Molly felt pressure on her shoulders. Nothing about crawling."

Joyce turned back to the path.

"It's something to think about, anyway."

✂ --- ✂ --- ✂

Joyce led the way into the common area where the homeless camp residents took their meals together. She reached into a cooler that was tucked under one of the benches and pulled out four bottles of water.

"Will you let me know if you learn anything?" she asked.

Harriet took a long drink of water and recapped her bottle.

"Sure. If we learn anything. This seems like it's yet another dead end."

"I thought about what you said while we were walking back, and it does make more sense that someone could have stuffed Molly into that pipe. If the serial killer took Molly *and* Amber, he may have drugged them, and then, when he got them in his car, he may have thought Molly was already dead, so he 'buried' her in the pipe because it was relatively quick and easy compared to digging a hole. He then did whatever he wanted to do to Amber and later killed her and disposed of her somewhere else."

Joyce crossed her arms and rocked back on her heels.

"I'm trying to convince myself that Molly's killer doesn't care about a group of homeless people, but it is a worry."

"Can we do anything?" Harriet asked.

"No, it's not the first time a body has been found in these woods and likely won't be the last. It comes with the territory."

Lauren stepped closer to Joyce.

"I'm sure Pastor Mike could open the church gym the way he does when the weather is bad if you all wanted to sleep inside where it's safe. I could ask, if you want."

"Thank you, but I think we'll stay put. You know Lottie won't go inside for any reason, and if she won't go, Max won't go, and others will follow. We have our own precautions we take when things like this happen."

"Hopefully, things like this don't happen too often," Harriet said.

"More often than you think," Joyce said and looked from her to Lauren. "Not crazy murderers, but people who don't like homeless people in the park bother us sometimes, and people looking for their lost loved ones don't tend to respect our privacy."

"That's awful," Harriet said.

"Well, it's part of the lifestyle. If you can't handle it, you can always go to a shelter." Joyce said. She smiled again. "You should worry about yourselves more. We've been here a long time, and we'll be here longer still."

"I could bring you a battery-operated wireless security system for your space," Lauren offered.

"We have our own system. It's not fancy, but our tin cans and fishing line work fine. And we'll not let anyone sleep by themselves. Don't worry, we'll be quite safe."

"If you say so," Harriet said.

Joyce patted her on the back.

"I do say so. You worry about finishing your quilt and let the good detective catch the murderer."

"Now you sound like my aunt."

"I'll take that as a compliment," Joyce said with a chuckle.

"Thanks for helping us look," Lauren said and started toward the parking lot.

Chapter 26

$\mathcal{H}$arriet clicked the unlock button on her key fob. She glanced at the clock on the dash as she got in.

"Yikes, that took longer than I thought it would."

Lauren slid into the passenger seat.

"It always does. You aren't thinking of skipping our rice bowls, are you?"

"Not a chance."

✂ --- ✂ --- ✂

"You sure took your time," Aunt Beth scolded as they came down the stairs into the church basement. The quilters were gathered around one of the large cafeteria tables, putting the final stitches into the quilt binding.

"I hope you learned something while you were shirking your quilting duties," Mavis said.

Harriet sat down at the table.

"As a matter of fact, we learned two interesting things."

"Interesting, if irrelevant," Lauren interjected.

Harriet glared at her before continuing.

"First, we observed an interesting interaction between Sandra Price and the ladies at the Carey Bates Missing and Exploited Children Center. Apparently, they were going to name a building after Amber, and Sandra is not pleased."

"As I said, not really relevant," Lauren repeated.

"It does raise the question of, if Molly was running roughshod over Sandra Price, who else might she have been offending."

"The girl did seem obsessed," Mavis said. "And we only saw her obsession about Amber. Maybe she had other obsessions."

Harriet looked at her gratefully.

"My point exactly. The main thing we were doing is seeing if we could find the vent the psychic told us about."

"And," Aunt Beth asked, "did you?"

The two women explained their hike in the woods and the result.

"Sounds like Joyce brought up a good point," Connie said. "It makes sense that someone who knew about the vent could use it as a hiding place for a small girl."

"It's yet another scenario we can't prove or disprove," Lauren said.

Carla buried her thread under the binding and clipped her needle free, smoothing the fabric with her fingers.

"I've got to go take over with Wendy. Grandpa Rod has bowling."

Connie stood up.

"I promised Wendy mackie-cheese for her dinner." She put her needle back in a wooden needle tube and slipped it into her canvas quilt bag.

Aunt Beth sat back in her chair, which was pulled up to the end of the cafeteria table.

"I can't believe we finished with time to spare."

"You and me both," Mavis agreed. "I figured we'd be stitching the morning of the presentation."

Harriet's phone chimed the presence of a new text. She glanced at the message as she said, "I never doubted us for a minute."

Lauren read Harriet's phone screen over her shoulder.

"And here I thought you and I were going to watch movies tonight."

Harriet felt her face turned hot, and she clicked her screen off before Lauren could read the complete message.

"No, you didn't. You said you were working on a new computer program tonight."

Lauren laughed. "You're so easy I almost feel guilty yanking your chain."

"I take it that's your chef," Mavis commented.

"*We* didn't have plans, did we?" Harriet asked her.

"No, honey, we didn't, and if that young man wants to take you out, I think that would be real nice."

"He wants to watch movies at his house, which sounds pretty appealing right now."

Aunt Beth looked up from packing her quilt bag.

"Just don't stay out so late you're too tired for tomorrow's presentation."

"Hey, I'm not sixteen anymore."

Aunt Beth smiled.

"Well, then, you just act your age, and we'll all be fine. Now, Mavis, why don't you come have dinner with Jorge and me so you aren't sitting home alone? He's cooking Italian tonight."

180

Harriet shook her head as she got up and headed for the door. She found it amazing that her aunt organized the lives of everyone around her so effortlessly.

James set a bowl of homemade chicken noodle soup in front of Harriet. He'd laid his kitchen table for two with a red gingham tablecloth, white napkins and a basket of crusty rolls strategically placed in the center.

"How was your day?" he asked as he sat down with his own bowl of steaming soup.

Harriet sipped a spoonful of soup.

"This is really good. What am I saying? Everything you make is good. Better than good."

"It's a simple soup."

"You're much too humble." She reached across the table and took his free hand in hers. "You are an exceptional cook, and everything you make is beyond wonderful."

"Okay, fine, but let's talk about you. How was your day? Have the police caught Molly's killer yet? You know, I worry about you going around chasing baddies. I've kind of gotten used to having you around."

"Why, Chef James, I didn't know you cared." Harriet blushed as she smiled.

James gave her a knowing smile and picked up his spoon. She reminded herself she and he were snuggle-buddies and nothing more, but it didn't stop her heart from flip-flopping in her chest.

"I spent the afternoon on a wild goose chase," she said, trying to distract herself from James's impossibly long eyelashes.

"Where did you go?"

Harriet described her hike in the woods with Lauren and Joyce as they ate.

James put his spoon down.

"So, you know the vent couldn't have come from the bluff, or the park. Do you know who owns the rest of the property adjacent to the park and near the vent?"

"No. Joyce pointed out the park border, and frankly, I'd have never found it without her help. The land continues in the same woods and brush for ten or twenty yards, and then it went up a little and I couldn't see what was on the other side."

"If you can show me on a map what part of the park you were in, we can figure out what neighborhood backs up to it, and maybe we can figure out where the vent, if it really is a vent, originates."

"Where can we get a map of Fogg Park?"

James stood up and carried their soup bowls to the sink.

"If we're lucky, I have one. The local Chamber of Commerce printed a series of laminated maps a few years ago highlighting the various hiking trails in the area. If I remember right, there was one that covered Fogg Park and its surrounding environs. Let me finish clearing the table, and we can go up to my library and look."

"You have a library?"

He smiled and waggled his eyebrows at her.

"I am a man of many mysteries."

Harriet smiled.

"Follow me," he said a moment later, and led her out of the kitchen and up an oak stairway. His dachshund, Cyrano, assumed the invitation was for him and got up from his bed next to the floor vent in the kitchen.

"He loves the library," James explained as they climbed. "He has his own chair."

Harriet laughed when she saw the stair step unit that was pushed up against the chair to assist the little dachshund in climbing into the seat.

"I got tired of lifting him up and down every five minutes when we're up here. He's like a kid in a high chair. He drops his bone off the chair and then either jumps down and can't get back up, or he looks at it and whines until I get up and get it for him."

"You just need a cat. Fred and Scooter entertain each other."

James went to a bookshelf and picked up what at first glance appeared to be a large book but turned out to be a box. He opened it and sorted through a a sheaf of maps.

"Ah, here we go." He brought it to a library table that sat in the middle of the room and spread it out.

Harriet stood beside him and studied the map.

"Let's see," she put her finger on a spot within the area marked "Fogg Park." "This is the homeless camp." She traced the path she and the others had taken. She paused when the trail split three ways. "I know we went left, but I'm not sure which of the two lefts."

James looked where her finger touched the map. He put one arm around her and pulled her to him as he pointed with his other hand.

"If you ended up near the bluff, you must have taken the far left." He took her hand and traced the trail until it dead-ended near the border of the park.

Harriet breathed in and was overwhelmed by the scent of soap and a faint hint of lime. Had he put on aftershave? she wondered. She knew he didn't allow his workers to wear scent of any sort around the food.

He tapped the spot.

"Does this look like where you were?"

"Are you wearing aftershave?"

James turned to face her and pulled her closer. His voice was husky when he spoke.

"Would it bother you if I was?"

He nibbled at her neck, working his way toward her mouth.

"I think it's nice," she said just before his mouth captured hers in a gentle kiss.

"Shall we bring the map with us to the TV room?" he asked when they separated. "I think we'll be more comfortable there."

He grabbed the map without waiting for an answer and took Harriet's hand, leading her across the landing to what was originally the upstairs parlor. Two soft leather chairs with matching ottomans were separated by a large square side table. A goose-neck floor lamp stood behind the table, casting a soft yellow glow on a large bowl with two packages of microwave popcorn inside. A state-of-the-art flatscreen television hugged the wall opposite the chairs. James crossed to built-in cabinets next to the TV and opened a door, revealing a small microwave.

"Toss me the popcorn," he instructed and held out his hand.

She did as instructed.

"I think I'm embarrassed about my TV room now that I've seen yours. This is pretty nice."

Matching knitted afghans were draped over an arm of each chair, and once James had the first bag of popcorn cooking, he opened another door to reveal his library of movies.

"Hopefully, you'll find something you like in here. I try to buy one or two movies from each of the different award-nominee lists. Unfortunately, I almost never get to watch any of them. It's my fantasy to watch them all someday."

Harriet ran her finger over the line of DVD cases.

"Historical, drama, drama." She looked up at him. "Rom-com? I didn't see that coming."

He came over to see which one she was pointing at.

"I didn't know what it was. It had 'Die' in the title, so I thought it was a mystery."

Harriet closed her eyes and picked a movie from the middle of the group. She handed it to him without looking at it. He turned it over to read the back.

"A British woman's coming of age story...I like it."

She smiled.

"Me, too."

"Get comfortable while I finish the popcorn."

"That was really good," Harriet said as the credits rolled at the end of the movie.

"Double-header?"

Harriet glanced at her phone. The night was still young.

"I'm in."

"You pick the movie, I'll be right back."

She chose a zombie movie, and he came back with homemade ice cream sandwiches.

"Are you kidding me?" Harriet said as she peeled the wax paper from her treat.

"I was experimenting. I have to keep the menu fresh."

"This is delicious," she said when she finished her first bite.

He reached across the table between their chairs with his free hand and twined his fingers in hers.

"You know, I was thinking."

"That sounds dangerous."

He squeezed her hand.

"No, seriously. I was thinking about the map. You know that area along the border of Fogg Park you were looking at? I think it's near Lois's house. My mom's friend."

"I remember."

"I used to play with Lois's son while our moms did stuff. We went to some nearby woods to explore, and it went behind the houses in the neighborhood. I haven't been there in years, but I think it might be the same place. Anyway, I know you have to go to your big fundraiser tomorrow, but I've got a little time between the lunch and dinner crowds. I thought I'd drive over there and look around.

"There's been a lot of development in that part of Foggy Point since I was little, but I think the woods are still there, and I could stop by Lois's house and see if she'd let me go through her yard and walk along the creek. If there's anything there that could have a vent that comes out in the park, it should be pretty easy to spot."

"I couldn't ask you to do that," she protested.

"You didn't ask. I volunteered. Besides, I happen to know Lois is quite partial to my Death-by-Chocolate. I'll take her a piece, and she'll be putty in my hands."

"Is it safe?"

"Of course it's safe. It's practically Lois's back yard. And this way, you'll know whether there's anything to what the psychic said or not."

"I'm not sure it eliminates her information completely. She only said Molly felt like her shoulders were being squeezed in a narrow space. We concluded the vent hole we found was that space. We could be wrong."

"It seems like that would be a pretty big coincidence. I mean, the psychic said she was in a tight space, and you found a vent that could be that tight space right by where she was found. If you believe the psychic in the first place, it seems like that pipe was what she was talking about."

"The question at hand is whether Molly was stuffed in the end of a pipe or if the pipe is really a tunnel or vent or drain, and she crawled out from somewhere else. If you get farther away than those woods by Lois's house, the distance from Fogg Park becomes a problem."

Harriet looked down at their hands and then smiled up at him through her lashes.

"I *am* kind of curious."

"Consider it done. I'll bring the short one there." He lifted their hands and pointed to Cyrano, snoring on his chair, which sat against the side wall at right angles to the people chairs.. "We'll consider it his training walk."

James pointed the remote control at the DVD player and started the movie. When he saw the title, he pressed pause and tugged on Harriet's hand.

"If we're going to watch a scary movie, you're going to have to get a little closer."

His chair was big enough for two if she sat sideways and draped her legs across his lap. He wrapped his arms around her, and she leaned back against his chest.

"I think I like movie night at your house."

He smiled and pressed start.

Chapter 27

Connie, Lauren, and Beth joined Mavis and Harriet for breakfast the next morning. Mavis had made bread in her bread machine, setting it to bake during the night, and then making it into French toast before her guests arrived.

"I know French toast isn't on any of our diets, but I thought we should be fortified for the day's events."

Beth took a bite and savored it a moment before swallowing.

"You aren't going to hear any arguments from me."

Lauren smiled.

"What she said."

Harriet set her fork down on her plate.

"Do we need to wrap the quilts like a present?" she asked no one in particular.

Connie sighed and leaned back in her chair.

"I suppose we should. We can't just hand them to people, can we?"

Lauren sat up straight.

"We need to do it like they do on TV. You know—they wrap the bottom of the box and the top separately so when the person gets the package, they don't have to rip any paper, they just gracefully slide the lid off and reveal the contents."

"I think you watch too much TV," Aunt Beth told her.

Harriet poured maple syrup on her second piece of toast.

"I like the idea, though. And I have some plain lidded boxes in the right size. I use them to deliver finished quilts when they have dimensional work on the top or if they're particularly delicate."

"I've got a big roll of lavender wrapping paper left over from my son's wedding," Mavis said. "I'm sure there's enough to wrap all three."

Lauren leaned forward and made eye contact with Harriet.

"How was date night?"

Harriet rolled her eyes.

"I told you, it wasn't date night, it was movie night. We watched movies. I liked the zombie movie. It had a compelling plot."

"Like you'd know," Lauren smirked.

"James is a complete gentleman. We watched two movies, and I went home."

Harriet was thankful the only witness had been snoring in his dog chair the whole evening.

"Is your chef coming to the award ceremony?" Connie asked.

"I don't think so. He prepped the food for the event, but he has workers who do delivery and setup. He's working at the restaurant. You may have noticed he's always there whenever you go eat there."

"Like Jorge," Beth said, more to herself than anyone else.

When everyone was finished eating, Mavis served coffee and tea while Harriet and Lauren cleared the dishes. Then, she wiped her hands on a dish towel.

"Lauren, if you can go with Harriet to get the boxes from her place, I'll dig out the paper, and Beth and I can wrap them."

Connie sipped her coffee and set her mug on the table.

"I've got some inch-wide white grosgrain ribbon at home. I bought it for a Maypole project at school and got a better deal if I bought a dozen rolls."

"Sounds perfect," Beth said. She glanced at her watch. "Let's say we meet back here in an hour, and we can get these quilts wrapped up."

Harriet slipped her thumbs under the waistband of her black pants and wiggled them upward. Lauren rolled her eyes. The two women were standing in front of the Foggy Point Arts Center.

"Show-off."

"Hey, between my last project, the machine quilting on these first two quilts and then all the hand-quilting, I've lost a little weight. And that's in spite of James's best efforts."

"Speaking of the chef, how *did* movie night go?"

"It was nice. He's refreshingly uncomplicated. And he has a killer TV room." She described the room for her friend, including the custom dog chair.

"Why am I not surprised?"

"He spends a lot of time at the restaurant, where it's pretty hectic, so he decided to make his house a true sanctuary. Everything is set up for his interests and his comfort. I don't blame him."

"I didn't say there was anything wrong with it. It just sounds a little over the top."

"He also had a map of the hiking trails around Foggy Point, including in and out of the area where we were looking for the vent yesterday."

"Could you tell what was adjacent to the park border?"

"James used to play in that neighborhood when he was little, and his mom's friend still lives there. He said there used to be woods leading down to a creek."

Harriet slipped her phone from her pocket, pressed a button and looked at the time, then frowned.

"What's the matter?" Lauren asked. "You've checked the time four times since we got here, and I know you're not that anxious for this shindig to start."

"James was going to go into those woods behind his mom's friend Lois's house in the lull between the lunch and dinner crowds and see what's there."

"And?"

"I sort of thought he'd call and tell me what he'd found. It's a little past five-thirty, and he should have gotten back to the restaurant over an hour ago."

"And you thought he'd call you the minute he got back. It's just possible some disaster was happening in the kitchen, and when he's got it under control, he'll call you."

Harriet sighed.

"You're right. He never said he was going to call immediately. He's just busy."

Lauren pointed to their right.

"Here comes Jorge, delivering your aunt."

Jorge pulled up to the unloading area and helped Beth and her knee scooter out of his white truck.

"I will be so glad when I'm free of this contraption," she said.

"How much longer will that be?" Lauren asked.

"I see the doctor next Wednesday."

Mavis, Connie and Carla came up the sidewalk carrying the three lavender boxes.

"Shall we get this show on the road?" Mavis asked and led the way into the auditorium.

Harriet was checking her phone for the seventh time when the introductory remarks ended. She looked up to see who was taking the podium next and noticed Sandra Price sitting in the first row. Her hair was done in an old-fashioned beehive, and her back was ramrod straight. Tension radiated off the woman, even from three rows away. A muscular man in a gray suit sat beside her. She elbowed Lauren, sitting to her left.

"Look who's sitting in the front row," she whispered and glanced pointedly toward Sandra.

"I wonder what changed her mind." Lauren whispered back.

"I wonder who her date is."

Harriet studied the man in gray. His suit looked expensive—not a match for Sandra's Walmart look. She turned her attention back to the stage in time to see Stuart Jones adjusting the microphone.

"Like a rosebud plucked too soon…" he started, and Harriet had to look away as Lauren pointed her finger into her mouth and mimed gagging.

"Are we sure he's really a published poet?" she whispered.

"He said he was," Harriet whispered back."And I looked him up on Amazon. He does have a couple of books."

"Hush," Aunt Beth scolded from Lauren's other side.

Stewart droned on for another five minutes, and Harriet used the time to check her phone, which was now silenced. Still nothing.

Nancy returned to the podium and announced the naming of the Amber Price Annex, a new building that had just been erected adjacent to the strip mall where Carey Bates Center for Missing and Exploited Children was located. She called Sandra up to the stage.

Sandra climbed the four steps to the stage, and Stewart came from behind the curtain and escorted his foster mother to center stage, where Nancy Finely was joined by Patrice Orson.

"How much did she have to give to get a building?" Josh Phillips said in such a loud stage whisper that the entire audience fell silent. He looked around to be sure he had everyone's attention. "Come on, if I gave ten thousand dollars, and all I get is a homemade rag, how much did *she* give, huh?"

The quilters in the audience gasped, and the woman behind him leaned forward and whispered something Harriet couldn't hear. Judging by the woman's raw silk suit and conspicuous display of diamonds, she guessed she was one of the other quilt recipients. If this had been a movie, burly security guards would have come out of nowhere and taken him by the elbows and hustled him out of the auditorium before he could say anything else. But, this was Foggy Point. No guards dressed in black came out of the shadows.

The man in the gray suit hurried up to the stage and grabbed the microphone.

"We'll be taking a brief intermission. I hope you'll join us in the lobby for a glass of champagne." He then stepped off the stage in one leap and came up the aisle to confront Josh. She couldn't hear what the man said, but almost before she could see what he'd done, the anonymous man had twisted Josh's arm behind him and had Josh's fist held in the middle of his back. He pushed Josh forcefully up the aisle.

"You can leave quietly, or I can call the police, your choice." she heard the man say as they passed her aisle.

"Let me go, you gorilla! You have no right to hold an American citizen against my will. And what about free speech?" Josh was getting louder, and the man jerked his arm higher, causing him to cry out.

When they got past the auditorium seating area, the man turned Josh and directed him toward a side door that did not lead into the lobby. The door swung open from the other side, and the man in gray shoved Josh out. She wasn't sure, but she thought it was an exit directly out to the sidewalk. The door closed, and suit guy straightened his jacket and tie, relaxed the muscles in his face and disappeared into the lobby.

"Well, that was fun," Lauren said. "Want to go get some champagne?"

"No, I want this to be over. I'm getting kind of tired of these people and their drama."

Aunt Beth leaned forward.

"You and me both. I'd like to know who tampered with my car. When I know who did that and why, I can put all this…" She gestured toward her bandaged ankle. "…behind me and get on with life."

Connie stood up.

"I'm going out to the restroom. Does anyone want a snack while I'm out there?"

"Nothing for me. We haven't been here long enough to need anything," Lauren told her.

People dribbled back into the auditorium, and Nancy and Patrice returned to the podium. Sandra Price and her mysterious companion were not in the audience when Nancy welcomed everyone back. No mention was made of the now-absent Josh, or the naming of the new building.

Patrice was in the middle of a PowerPoint presentation telling all the scary statistics about human trafficking and about the success their program had achieved in bringing young people home when Harriet's phone vibrated. She glanced at the screen and was a little curious when it didn't say James's cell number but instead the land line at the restaurant.

"This is James," she whispered."I'm going out to call him back."

Aunt Beth's brows pulled together, and she pressed her lips tightly closed, but she didn't say anything. Harriet could tell her aunt disapproved, but she needed to talk to him.

She squeezed past Lauren and two other women and went as quietly up the aisle as she could manage, pressing redial on her phone as she went.

"Smuggler's Cove," a female voice said.

"Can I talk to James?"

"Is this Harriet? This is Yvonne. Do you know where James is?"

Harriet's heart felt like it had dropped to her feet. Yvonne was one of the restaurant's maître d's.

"I assumed he was at the restaurant. He went to check something out between crowds, but he was going to be back before the dinner rush."

"He left at two-thirty and told the students he'd be back in an hour. I got here at five, and he still wasn't back."

Harriet glanced at the time on her phone and put it back to her ear.

"So, you haven't heard from him in four hours?"

"We're really worried. So far, the students are managing to keep the food coming, but they're stressed to the breaking point. And this isn't like James."

"Let me see if I can find him."

"Hurry, please," Yvonne said and hung up.

Harriet tapped a quick text to Lauren.

James missing going to look.

Me 2 came back almost immediately, and a moment later, Lauren burst into the lobby.

"What do you mean missing?"

"That was the restaurant. He left to go check the woods next to Fogg Park at two-thirty, and he hasn't been back since."

"I'll drive," Lauren said. "My car's closer."

"I can't remember the name of the street. When we looked at the map it backed up to a green space that bordered the park."

"Didn't you say his mom's friend lived on the same street as Sandra Price?"

"Yes!" Harriet said and entered the Price address into the map program on her phone.

They drove through Foggy Point in grim silence until Lauren turned her car onto the street Sandra Price lived on and pulled to the curb several houses away.

"You don't happen to know Lois's last name do you?"

Harriet thought.

191

"I don't think anyone ever mentioned it."

Lauren pulled her tablet computer from her bag and opened the search function.

"What are you doing?" Harriet asked as Lauren rapidly tapped numbers onto the screen.

"I'm looking at the property maps on either side of the Prices. The city maps tell the ownership and tax history." She kept entering addresses. "And we have a winner. Two doors to the right."

Harriet got out and headed for Lois's door. It opened before she could knock.

"Are you James's friend Harriet?" A stocky gray-haired woman asked. She grabbed Harriet's hand and pulled her inside. "I'm so worried. James came here this afternoon and told me he was helping you follow up on something. He asked to go through our back gate to go into the woods behind our property. He said he'd stop back by on his way out. Only he never did."

Lauren followed Harriet into Lois's entryway.

"Maybe he was running late and left without stopping."

Lois pointed out the front window and down the street.

"My neighbor was hosting her bridge group, so James had to park down the street. Look, his car is still there. Besides, he left Cyrano here. He'd never leave without his dog."

Harriet and Lauren both looked, and sure enough, James's white catering van sat at the curb at the end of the street.

"What's in the woods?" Lauren asked.

"Behind our house, it's just trees and the creek. Years ago, Maudene Price lived on the part behind Sandra's house and the two houses beyond. I think the county took it over for back taxes when she died, and they deeded it over to the city to expand the creek restoration project. I think salmon come up the lower end of the creek. Nowhere near here, but the city is restoring the habitat anyway."

Harriet paced across the entry hall into the living room and back.

"Are there any structures back there?"

"The house pretty much fell apart before all the legal work was done. I think Sandra's husband tried to fight it in court. He wasn't successful, but he managed to drag it out quite a few years."

"Did they clear the site?"

"No, some kids set the remains on fire years ago. The foundation and stone fireplace are still there."

"Can we access that area from your yard?" Harriet asked.

"It's a little bushy in a couple of places, but you can get there. It'd be better if you were wearing jeans."

"Yeah, well. We don't have time for a wardrobe change." Harriet said.

Lois led them from the living room to the kitchen. Harriet's phone rang before they reached the back door. She glanced at the screen, prepared to send the caller to voicemail, but hesitated when she recognized Detective Morse's number.

"Hello?"

"Hey, I just wanted to let you know something happened at your cave. It was going to take so long to get surveillance equipment, I decided to buy a game-cam at the sporting goods store and strap it to a tree, pointed at the cave mouth."

"And?"

"You and Lauren stumbled across something major. My game cam wasn't sophisticated enough to be monitoring it real-time. It required me to take a thumb drive, download the data from the camera, and carry it back to a computer. I finally did that today, and it was a revelation.

"Someone stashed a group of people there for three days earlier this week. They brought them in on Monday morning and took them out Thursday morning. Unfortunately, the image of the vehicle they came in wasn't very clear—the techs are working on trying to clean it up, but for now we don't have anything. The people wielding the guns were wearing black clothes and black ski masks. I just wanted to reiterate that you and Lauren need to stay clear of that area."

"Wow."

"What?" Lauren asked.

"I'm putting you on speaker," Harriet told the detective. "Lauren's here, and we're with Lois…"

"Fletcher," Lois whispered.

"Lois Fletcher," Harriet said. "We've got a situation here ourselves."

"And that is?"

Harriet explained about the missing chef.

"Stay put, I'm coming over."

Chapter 28

Detective Morse took less than ten minutes to arrive. Harriet had spent the time pacing from the front room to the back door and back again, while Lauren texted Beth, Mavis and Connie.

Lois held the front door open as soon as Morse parked at the curb.

"I'm Lois. James is the son of my best friend. He came by today and asked if he could go through my yard to access the green space. He said he'd stop on his way back, and he never came, and his van is still parked down the street," she blurted without pausing for breath.

Morse looked at Harriet.

"And what, exactly, was he looking for?"

Harriet explained about the pipe, the vent theory, and their discovery that the green space bordered Fogg Park.

Morse looked thoughtful.

"That's all pretty preposterous. I mean, a vent coming from the green space to the park? I know there are stories of tunnels across the Mexican border or from taverns in a town to the shipping docks for shanghai purposes, but out in the middle of the woods? What would be the reason for that?"

No one said anything. Morse put her hands in her back pants pockets.

"Having said that, I wouldn't have guessed anyone was holding people in a cave in Foggy Point. There's nothing to connect that with Chef James, that I know of, but he does appear to be missing. I'm going to call for some backup to search the woods, and we'll start an official missing person report, even though it hasn't been twenty-four hours."

Harriet stepped over and stood toe-to-toe with her.

"I want to help."

"You know I can't let you do that. If James is out in the woods hurt, or if there's evidence that will help us find him, we need trained officers to handle it. The best thing you can do is go down to the station and tell the duty officer all you can about James's whereabouts before he disappeared. I need to call people and get things started. It's going to be dark soon."

Morse made a series of phone calls and barked orders to whoever was on the other end of them. Foggy Point PD cruisers pulled up in front of Lois's house, and a pair of evidence technicians walked down the street to James's van.

Harriet sat with Lauren and Lois in the living room.

"We can't just sit here."

Lois's eyes grew wide.

"The police told us to stay in here out of their way."

"Actually, she didn't," Lauren told her. "She wanted Harriet to go to the police station to tell them about James's disappearance. Only she didn't go, because she realized Morse was trying to get us out of here. She knew that because we've already told Morse everything we know about James's disappearance, which is pretty much nothing. We also have history with Jane. She tells us all the time to keep our noses out of police business."

Harriet sighed.

"I'd stick my nose in now if I thought it would help find James. Unfortunately, this time, Jane is right. They're professionals in searching, so we don't have much to contribute."

"I'm sure James isn't lying out there hurt," Lois said. "He knows every inch of those woods. Besides, they aren't that big—it's maybe eight acres. If he'd sprained his ankle, all he'd have to do is holler. We'd hear him from here if he was calling out."

"Or, to state the obvious," Lauren said, "he'd use his cell phone."

Harriet's shoulders slumped.

"I've been calling his cell phone since before we left the prize ceremony. It goes straight to voicemail."

"Would you gals like some tea or a soda?" Lois asked.

"I'd like some water," Lauren told her.

"I'll have tea," Harriet said.

Lauren turned in her seat so her body blocked Harriet from Lois in the kitchen and the police in the dining room.

"Okay, what are you thinking? I know you don't want tea at a time like this."

Harriet took a deep breath.

"This might be another wild-goose chase, but I can't help but think this has something to do with the vent or tunnel or whatever it is sticking out of the hill in Fogg Park. The fact that someone is using the cave to house people makes me believe even more that there could be an underground place of some sort."

"So, how does that help us with the James situation? Are we going to go to the vent and try to tap Morse code or something?"

"Be serious. I don't know Morse code, and I'm pretty sure you don't, either. But, am I remembering right—at dinner a couple of weeks ago you said you were working on software that went with a sewer-scoping camera?"

"I see where you're going. Yes, I still have one of the cameras to test the software with. It's currently in the sewer line in front of my apartment. My landlord has been letting me test my program. I can get it out but it will take fifteen minutes or so. You'll have to hose it off as I pull it out."

"Let's go get started."

"We don't know that the vent actually goes anywhere."

"There's only one way to find out."

Lois came back with their tea and water. Harriet took a sip then set the cup down on the coffee table.

"Thanks, we've got to go check something out."

✂ --- ✂ --- ✂

Lauren led the way back to the car.

"This all raises the question of what's going on. Who on earth would be trafficking people in Foggy Point?"

Harriet slid into the passenger seat.

"I've been thinking about that. Molly and Amber disappeared from this street, and now James has disappeared from the same street. Sandra Price's mother owned the property where he disappeared. Doesn't it seem like the Price name is coming up a lot in this whole situation?"

"It does seem weird, but Sandra Price? She always says how people keep harassing her because her daughter was killed and the body was never found. Are we joining the harassers? I mean, what about the whole serial-killer thing?"

"I don't know. Maybe all this has nothing to do with Amber and what happened to Molly before. Molly was trying to find out what happened back then, but maybe in the process she stumbled into something new and unrelated."

"And deadly?'

"Yes, and deadly."

Harriet tried to call James again. Again, nothing. She slammed her phone onto the seat beside her.

"James wouldn't be in this mess if he hadn't been trying to help me."

196

Lauren glanced over at her.

"Don't even go there. James is a big boy, and he's resourceful. You can't run a restaurant as well as he does and not know how to deal with difficult situations."

"This isn't a kale delivery that didn't come or table linens that are wrinkled. Someone has James, and that same someone probably killed Molly."

"Let's not borrow trouble. Let's just worry about getting the camera and sending it down the vent."

They drove the remainder of the trip in silence.

✂ --- ✂ --- ✂

Lauren slid the camera and its short cable connection into a pillowcase and handed Harriet a metal reel with the cable spooled around it.

"I'll have to burn this pillowcase when this adventure is over."

"Small price to pay if we find James. Let's go."

Lauren drove as fast as she dared, but it felt like an hour before she pulled her car to the curb next to the restrooms in Fogg Park. Harriet was out of the car before Lauren had killed the engine. She rushed down the path toward the homeless camp lugging the spool of camera cable. The sun had dipped below the horizon, and it was rapidly turning dark.

She nearly knocked Joyce down when she came around a bend in the path.

"What's the hurry?" Joyce asked. "And what it that?"

"We need to get back to the vent you showed us. My friend's life depends on it."

Thankfully she didn't ask any questions.

"Let me get a decent light." Joyce hurried back down the trail to her camp, returning a moment later with a large spotlight. "Follow me."

Lauren stumbled over a root and turned her ankle, but kept going as they followed Joyce through the woods for what seemed an eternity before they finally reached the clearing at the base of the bluff.

"Hopefully, we have enough cable to reach whatever is at the other end of this opening."

Lauren swung her messenger bag from her back and pulled out her laptop and the camera. Harriet brought the spool of cable over, and together they hooked the camera to one end of the cable and the laptop to the other. Joyce began clearing weeds and vines from the vent opening and the surrounding area.

"Can I help?" said a masculine voice from the trail.

Joyce put her hand to her heart.

"Oh, Max. You gave me a start."

"I was out looking for owls when I heard something crashing through the woods, so I took a deer trail over and came to investigate. And here you are, scaring the animals. Why are you in such a hurry?"

Joyce explained, and Max helped her finish clearing the opening.

Lauren brought the camera to the vent and set it down.

"Here goes nothing." She handed the cable to Harriet. "As soon as I get the image on my computer, start feeding the camera into the hole."

Lauren sat down and opened her computer, waking it from its sleeping state with four keystrokes.

"Okay, we're on board. Harriet, hold your hand at least a foot from the camera."

Harriet did as told; and when Lauren confirmed she could see the hand on the screen, she gave a thumbs-up, and Harriet fed the camera down the hole.

"Can you see anything?" she asked as she stood up.

Lauren began slowly uncoiling the spool of camera cable.

"If I could see anything interesting, we'd be standing on top of wherever this vent leads. So far, it looks amazingly similar to the sewer in front of my apartment."

Harriet came over and crouched behind her.

"What's that white thing that looks like a snake?"

"Based on my vast experience in the sewers, I'd say it's a root that worked its way through a seam in the vent lining."

Harriet ran her hands through her hair. Joyce came up behind her and put her hands on her shoulders, massaging as she did so.

"It's going to be okay. Take a deep breath. You have to believe this will work."

"If this leads to some sort of bomb shelter or something, won't it have filters in the vent?"

"Not necessarily," Lauren said without looking up from her screen. "First, if Molly crawled out this vent, it implies the filter, if there is one, is missing. Otherwise, she wouldn't have made it out. We're far enough in already to conclude it probably really is a vent.

"Second, depending on how the system works, it may rely on positive pressure. As long as the pressure in whatever this vent is attached to is greater than the outside pressure, the air inside will stay clean. I wouldn't count on that working in a nuclear holocaust, but if this leads to an underground still or a root cellar or something like that, they wouldn't need a sophisticated filtration system—or any filter at all, if we're lucky."

Harriet stood up and started pacing.

"Stop, already," Lauren said. "Or move farther back."

"How far has the camera gone?" Harriet said as she backed up.

Lauren glanced at the bottom corner of her screen.

"One hundred feet and counting."

Max came to stand by Harriet.

"The vent probably goes along the edge of the slope for twenty feet or so and then cuts out of the park and into the green space. It would be the easiest path to the area behind the houses down there."

Harriet strained to see.

"Can you see all that?"

Max chuckled.

"No, I've just studied every square foot of this park and its surrounding area over the years."

Lauren leaned closer to her screen.

"Something's changing here. The vent is getting bigger. The light isn't hitting both sides anymore."

"Whoa," Harriet exclaimed as the camera view spiraled, flashing a rapid series of images and then going dark. "What happened?"

"Hold on," Lauren said. She slowly reversed the direction of the spool, backing the camera out by a foot. The LED camera illuminated the area it was looking at. It appeared to be a flat, rough surface. "I think we're looking at the floor of wherever our vent terminates." She backed the camera slowly, waiting each time for it to auto-focus.

Harriet leaned closer and reached over Lauren's shoulder to point.

"That looks like the toe of a shoe."

Joyce and Max joined them, and they all studied the screen.

Harriet startled when the foot moved.

"Can you move the camera up and down a little to make sure whoever belongs to that foot is seeing us?"

Lauren did as requested, moving the camera first a little then, eventually, three feet up and down, repeating several times. On the fourth try, the image went crazy, flashing light and dark. A blurry image pulsed on the screen as the auto-focus tried to sharpen it. The cable went taut, and Harriet reached over and fed more cable into the hole.

"I think someone just grabbed the camera."

James's face came into focus as she spoke. He had figured out it was a camera and was holding it at arms-length. They could see his mouth moving but couldn't tell what he was saying.

"Anyone read lips?" Lauren asked.

Harriet pulled her phone from her pocket and speed-dialed him. The call went to voicemail without any reaction from him.

He looked up at the ceiling and then down. They watched as he crouched and, with his free hand, attempted to write in the dirt on the floor, but the floor was too rough. They also noticed as he moved the camera around that he wasn't alone.

"Write a note on your phone and hold it up to the camera," Harriet told the image on the screen.

James turned around, the camera pointing at three young women cowering on a filthy mattress. Their lips moved. He must have asked them something. The middle one shook her head and looked at the woman beside her, her lips moving as she did so. The second woman shook her head also. James shone the camera back on himself, a look of frustration on his face.

"You cell phone," Harriet repeated.

He pressed his lips together.

"Whoever put him there probably took his phone." Lauren said.

"No, they didn't, I can see the shape in his front pocket. They probably knew he wouldn't get a signal underground, so they didn't worry about it."

James looked off-screen in the direction of the women, and then reached into his pocket. One of the women must have prompted him about his phone.

The group collectively held their breath as James typed on the little screen.

"Good grief, is he writing a novel?" Lauren said in frustration.

Finally, he held his phone in one hand and the camera in the other, spreading them several feet apart. Lauren adjusted the focus with her computer. Harriet leaned even closer to the screen. He had typed a message using the notepad function on his phone.

"'Exploring foundation behind and between Lois's and Price house,'" she read. "'Hit from behind. Woke in dark, chained to bed. Not alone.'"

Harriet's own phone was still in her hand. She dialed Morse.

"We found James," she said when Morse answered.

"Where is he?"

"I don't know—not exactly. He says he was exploring the burned-out foundation behind Lois's house, and someone hit him on the head. He woke up in a dark place that's connected to the vent in the park."

"Slow down," Morse said. "You're not making sense. We searched the foundation. There's nothing there."

Harriet recounted how they'd discovered James. Lauren pointed at the screen.

"Look, James is showing us around the space."

He pointed the camera across the room to a ladder that disappeared upward into the dark. He wasn't able to get close enough to it, and the camera's light range was sufficiently small, that they couldn't see where it went other than up.

He tapped a note on his phone and held it to the screen.

Only entrance ladder up into ceiling. Round pipe?

Harriet relayed the message to Morse.

"I'm headed back to the foundation, and I called in the K-Nine unit."

Chapter 29

Harriet watched James on Lauren's laptop.

"I wish we could talk to him."

His lips would move, then one or more of the women would move her lips. It was clear they were talking to each other, but no communication was taking place. He looked like he was trying to explain the camera and that help was coming. Their eyes got wide, and they squeezed together and away from him whenever he gestured. Clearly, they were terrified.

"Has anyone called his family?"

Harriet gasped.

"I didn't even think about his family. And I don't have his mother's number."

Lauren opened a new search window on top of the camera view.

"Got it," she said and turned the screen more squarely to Harriet.

Harriet dialed his parents' house. No one answered. She left a brief message requesting a call back.

"Don't you think you should have given them a little more than 'call me please'?" Lauren asked.

"I don't think this is the sort of thing that should be left in a message."

"Whatever."

Lauren turned away from the screen.

"Are we going to sit here and watch and wait to see if Morse finds him?"

"I'd like to go look for him, but the police and the dogs are already searching the foundation area."

Max held his right elbow in his left hand, resting his chin on his right fist. His brow furrowed as he thought.

"What is it, Max?" Joyce asked him.

"I was thinking." He paused and then started again. "I've not mea-sured it with a device, but I don't think the amount of cable you let into that little tunnel is enough to reach that foundation."

Harriet and Lauren spun around at the same time to look at him.

"What?" Harriet said.

Lauren turned back to her computer and started furiously typing.

"I'm still working on this part of the software, but I think I have enough…"

The view of James in the underground room disappeared and was re-placed by a white screen with blue grid lines on it and a curvy red line su-perimposed on the grid. The grid was marked in feet.

"Eventually, this will show the actually terrain," she said. "He's right. This is the route the camera took."

Max leaned over and pointed.

"See where it turns left and then right? That's where it had to go be-tween two boulders that are just beyond the park."

"Max," Harriet asked, "do you think you could follow this line and lead us to where the camera is?"

"Sure."

Joyce held out her big spotlight.

"You'll be needing this," she said and handed it to Harriet. She turned to Lauren. "I'll stand watch over your computer if you want to go with them."

Lauren stood up.

"Guard it with your life."

"Nothing less," Joyce said and smiled.

✂ --- ✂ --- ✂

Max led the way out of the park, stopping occasionally and studying the ground around them. The moon had come out, and while not full, it was sufficient to make the spotlight unnecessary once they got out of the trees.

"We're about halfway—" Max stopped abruptly, holding his hand out to block Harriet and Lauren. "Down!" he ordered, and they all crouched below the weeds and berry vines. "Someone's coming," he whispered.

Lauren leaned around him.

"I don't see anyone."

"Hush," he scolded and pointed to his ear.

When the trio was perfectly still, Harriet could hear what Max had heard. He was right—something or someone was coming toward them from the green space direction. She held her breath as the rustling got louder. She sneaked a look and saw a smallish figure in dark clothing approaching. The figure stopped and squatted.

"That should be right where the camera is," Max whispered.

The figure picked up a bundle of something and moved it to the side, then repeated the motion. Lauren stretched up to look.

"He's clearing a hatch cover," she whispered. "He's about to go down."

Harriet stood, turned the spotlight on the figure, and hurried through the brush. Max and Lauren followed.

"What are we doing here?" Lauren gasped as they went.

"Stopping whoever that is from getting to James. Stop!" she shouted.

The figure held an arm up to block the light but kept reaching down to the ground with its other hand.

"Stewart?" Harriet asked in a loud voice."What are you doing?"

"Get that light out of my eyes," he shouted back.

Harriet lowered the light slightly, and Stewart took the opportunity to pull an ugly-looking black gun from the small of his back.

"Turn the light off and walk this way slowly, and no one will get hurt."

Lauren pressed a couple of keys on her cell phone and hit enter. The phone chirped when she hit send.

"Toss your phones on the ground," he directed. Harriet and Lauren complied. "And the light."

Stewart motioned the two women to the small clearing he was standing in. Harriet noticed Max had disappeared. He must have faded into the background before she lowered the light.

"Why are you holding James prisoner?" Harriet pressed. "He's a chef. What did he ever do to you?"

"He got in the way, that's what he did." He pushed the two women together. "This is all your fault, you know. You couldn't leave things alone, could you? I'm supposed to be reading poetry tonight at a new club, and instead, I'm out here with you two."

"Nothing's happened yet. You could let us go, and we wouldn't tell anyone," Harriet said.

"And if you hadn't mentioned the chef, I might have considered it. If you know about the chef, you know about the women, and we can't have that."

Lauren glared at him.

"Who is 'we'?"

Stewart spread his hands, palms up, gun dangling from the right one. He started laughing and then said in a singsong voice.

"I am me and you are she, and she is he, and we are all together…see how you run in front of my gun, you better run…"

Harriet looked at Lauren, not sure if he expected them to try to run away so he could shoot them, or if he was having some sort of breakdown.

Stewart raised the gun and took aim.

They heard a soft *whoosh*, and Stewart dropped the gun and started screaming. He crumpled to the ground, his left hand clutching his right forearm, dark liquid dripping from between his fingers.

Harriet grabbed the spotlight from where she dropped it and shone it on him. A nasty-looking knife was embedded in his right arm. Judging by the flow of blood oozing from around his hand in spite of the pressure he was applying, if he let go of his arm to pick up the gun, he could bleed to death.

"Don't just stand there, call me an ambulance. And give me a belt or some-thing."

Lauren stepped back to the spot where they had first stopped and felt around on the ground for her phone. When she found it, she dialed 911.

"We need an ambulance, and police and probably a firetruck, too. We're in the green space behind Fogg Meadows and the park."

Max was standing a few feet away. He waited until the faint sound of sirens was audible and then backed slowly away and faded into the woods.

Harriet crouched down next to Stewart.

"What's a nice poet like you doing with a bunch of captive women and a chained-up chef?"

"I don't have to tell you anything."

"You're right, but I'm probably your last chance to tell your story to someone who cares even remotely about your side of things."

Stewart started crying.

"All I ever wanted to be was a poet. I wrote my first poem when I was seven years old. You know what my parents did?"

He looked at Harriet. She shook her head.

"My mother laughed. She laughed, and my dad beat me. When I went to school the next day, my teacher reported my parents to Children's Ser-vices, and I got put in foster care. Sandra had lost Amber a couple of years before and had applied to be a foster parent. She didn't laugh at my poems."

Harriet looked over her shoulder at the approaching flashing lights and then turned back to Stewart.

"They're going to be here in a minute or less, and being Sandra Price's foster child doesn't explain why you're holding four people hostage in a hole in the ground."

"I'm trying to tell you…"

Harriet glanced at Lauren, who was yanking on a handle she'd pried up from the trapdoor.

"I'm not holding anyone hostage—Sandra is. Or the people she works for. She's just a step in the process."

Lauren stopped pulling on the door.

"Whoa!" she said in a stage whisper. "Talk about a big reveal."

Stewart was crying in earnest.

"Sandra was involved in this business before I even went to live with her. All I did was feed and water them sometimes."

Lauren came and stood over him.

"I'm no lawyer, but maybe you can turn state's evidence or something."

Stewart tipped his head to his shoulder and attempted to wipe his tears.

"Do you really think they'll let me do that?"

Lauren shrugged.

"Like I said, I'm not a lawyer, but if I were you, I'd hire the best one you can afford and don't say another word until you do."

"Lauren!" Harriet shouted. "Why are you helping him?"

"I believe him. He's not a criminal mastermind. He's a poet."

"He tried to shoot us."

Stewart looked up embarrassed.

"It wasn't loaded."

"We didn't know that," Harriet yelled at him.

A fireman and two paramedics stormed up with multiple boxes of equipment. Two more people arrived carrying an aluminum tubing basket that replaced the usual gurney when a victim was injured away from a passable roadway.

Detective Morse then joined the group, accompanied by two uniformed officers carrying crowbars.

Harriet bent down and pulled on the door, but it didn't budge.

"Stand back," Morse told her.

The two officers wedged their tools on either side of the hatch cover and pried it open. They set their tools down and drew their guns before climbing down into the hole.

"James!" Harriet yelled.

"Down here," a disembodied voice said from underground.

Less than a minute later, James climbed up the ladder and out into the field. He rushed to Harriet and wrapped his arms around her.

"Hey, I'm fine," he said softly as she held him and cried.

"I was so worried," she said into his shoulder.

"I was worried, too," Lauren said in a dry tone.

Three of the paramedics carried Stewart away on the portable gurney, and the fourth one stepped over to James and handed him a bottle of water.

"Are you hurt anywhere?" he asked.

"Someone whacked me in the head with something."

The EMT looked at the back of his head.

"You've got a nasty lump back there. I'm afraid concussion protocol says we've got to take you to the hospital and check you out."

"I need to check the restaurant. I'll sign a release or something."

James continued to plead, but the man had already spoken to the guys in the ambulance, and the fireman was returning already with another carry basket. They loaded James onto the portable stretcher and hauled him away.

"I'll come find you at the hospital," Harriet called after them.

"That'll be after you and this one…" Morse pointed at Lauren. "…do some explaining down at the station."

The uniformed officers led three bedraggled women from the underground bunker. More uniformed officers arrived, followed by two four-wheeled all-terrain vehicles.

Morse walked Lauren and Harriet to her unmarked car and when everyone was in, headed for the station. The third time Harriet complained about not being able to go to James, Morse turned on the lights and sirens.

Chapter 30

Lauren burst through the door of Harriet's studio, dropped her messenger bag then bent to pull a bottle of champagne from its interior. She joined the group standing around the brand-new long-arm quilting machine that had just been delivered and set up.

"Am I late?" She held up the bottle. "I wasn't sure if this was like a ship christening or not, so I brought a bottle to break on its…whatever the long-arm equivalent of a ship's bow is."

Harriet looked at her.

"You're not breaking that on any part of this machine. I haven't decided if I'm keeping it or not."

Aunt Beth's face turned red.

"What? Of course you'll keep it. You're being childish. This is a much better machine than the one that was damaged. The fact that your parents had a hand in it being here doesn't change that fact."

"They wouldn't even have known I needed a machine if you hadn't told them," Harriet countered.

"That's where you're wrong. *They* called *me*. You may not talk to them very often—and that *is* as much them as it is you—but they do care about you, and they keep track of you much more than you believe. They called me when they found out something had happened here, and asked what they could do. Their first instinct was to write you a check, but I told them they needed to put a little more effort into it. To their credit, buying you a top-of-the-line quilting machine was their idea."

"You'd be foolish to return such a nice machine just because you have unresolved issues with your parents," Connie told her.

The Loose Threads were standing around the machine, all eyes on Harriet.

"Okay, fine. It can stay."

The group collectively let out its breath.

The outside studio door opened again, this time letting James in. He carried a foil-wrapped pan.

"Anyone hungry?"

Harriet went over to him.

"I thought you were supposed to be resting this week."

"I've passed all my concussion milestones so far so they let me resume a little of my normal activity. They said no restaurant yet—I'm still banned from doing anything that requires too much thinking or too much energy. Lucky for you, I can make brownies in my sleep."

"Let's put on the tea kettle and coffeepot," Mavis said and led the way to the kitchen.

✂ --- ✂ --- ✂

Jenny wiped her mouth and set her napkin beside her tea mug on Harriet's dining room table.

"Those brownies were incredible."

Mavis sipped her tea.

"I'm glad James is still around to bake them."

"James is glad, too," he said. "I wasn't sure I would be for a while there."

A tap sounded on the studio door, and shortly thereafter, Detective Morse entered the dining room. Harriet stood up and went into the kitchen to get another plate and mug.

"I'm glad you could make it." she said.

Mavis stood up and picked up the coffee carafe with a questioning expression. Morse nodded, and Mavis filled her mug.

"I'm sure you all would like some answers. I can't tell you everything, and in fact, since the FBI took over, I'm not sure I even know everything that's happened."

Harriet sat back down.

"I'm still in shock about Sandra Price."

Morse set her cup down after taking a long drink of coffee.

"Everyone's in shock about that. The FBI and pretty much all the local jurisdictions up and down the I-Five corridor have known for a long time that the freeway was a major human trafficking route. It goes from Mexico to Canada, with major ports all along the way. They also know that it takes a lot of support to move that many people. There are lots of regional and national task forces working on breaking it.

"The existence of the trafficking is no surprise. It's the idea that a middle-class mother living in a nice, small-town neighborhood is a major link in the chain that's got everyone rethinking what they're doing."

Mavis leaned forward in her chair.

"How long do they think this has been going on?"

"No one knows for sure," Morse answered her. "From records they found in an office in the underground bunker, it's been decades."

Harriet thought for a moment.

"So, is Amber's disappearance related to this?"

"That seems likely, now. The investigation into her disappearance has been reopened. The working theory is that Amber and Molly stumbled on to the bunker. Maybe they followed Sandra, or maybe they just were playing and found it. If the hatch was open, they probably climbed down the ladder and surprised either Sandra or one of her employees.

"As you've probably guessed, Molly got free and climbed out through the vent. Amber wasn't so lucky and was either killed or sent off to who knows where to become part of the trade. I'm sure they kept an eye on Molly, and when it turned out she didn't remember what had happened to her, they forgot about her...or tried to."

Robin tapped her pen on the table. She wasn't taking notes this time, but the pen had found its way to her hand anyway.

"It must have really bothered them when Molly grew up and came back to town trying to figure out what had happened."

"Before her attorney arrived, Sandra was in a holding cell, and she had a little fit. She was ranting and raving and apparently unaware that everything said in those cells is recorded. She was mad at herself for going so easy on 'those idiotic quilters and their amateur detecting.' She outlined in great detail what she *should* have done to Beth's car—which, by the way, she thought was Harriet's. And she cursed her inept minions over the fact that they didn't trash your place worse or even burn it to the ground."

"That snake," Aunt Beth hissed.

"Will she ever get out of jail?" Harriet asked.

"No. It's clear from her meticulous record-keeping she was a major player. The poet might be able to strike a deal—he grew up the foster child of traffickers, and as near as they can tell so far, he made some effort to distance himself from them." Morse looked down, studying a coffee spill on the tablecloth.

"It's hard to tell how they'll treat him. After he reached adulthood, he could have left, but if he has a good lawyer, they could bring in psychologists to argue how much damage was done to him, and they'll undoubtedly argue Stockholm syndrome."

"Do they know who killed Molly?" Harriet asked.

"I don't think that's sorted out yet. It probably wasn't Sandra herself. They've arrested at least half a dozen of her associates, and it could have been any of them. One will eventually take a deal and turn on the rest. The first one to talk gets the best deal, and they all know that."

Beth stood up and stretched her healing arm.

"I'm just glad it's all over. Things could have been worse."

James had been quietly listening to Morse's information.

"I'm glad it's over, too. I'll be happier when they let me back in the restaurant, but in the meantime, I have a surprise that I think will put a smile on all your faces. Harriet, will you help me?"

"I've got to see this," Lauren said. "It will take a lot to top those brownies."

James led Harriet out of the dining room, through the kitchen and studio and out the door.

"Are we running away?" she asked him.

"No, but it's a good idea." He pulled her into his arms and kissed her soundly. "I really do have a surprise." He led her to his van. "Open the door and pull out that cooler."

She did as told and set the cooler on the ground.

"Okay, don't say anything in case anyone can hear us, but look inside."

Harriet again did as instructed. She found a large white laundry bag, opened the drawstring and looked inside.

"Oh, my gosh. Where did you get this?"

"One of my mom's friends was volunteering at Goodwill, and it came in from a donation box. She checked to be sure it was a documented donation, then talked to the manager. Under the circumstances, they were able to work out a deal."

"We have to show the others."

Harriet took the bundle from the cooler and carried it back inside. People had gotten up from the table and were clearing dishes and making more coffee.

"Come on back in here, everyone, you have to see this." She waited until they were all seated around the table again. "Lauren, can you help me here?"

She loosened the strings on the bag and put a handful of fabric in her friend's hand then, taking a handful herself, pulled the bag away with her free hand. The hand-quilted disappearing nine-patch quilt unfolded as they stepped apart and held it up for all to see.

"Where did that come from?" Aunt Beth asked.

James repeated his story.

"Apparently, Josh was so mad after he was marched out of the presentation ceremony that, when his quilt was delivered, he took it to the nearest Goodwill donation box. Fortunately, one of my mom's friends was volunteering when it came through and was able to negotiate for it. She thought you all might want to re-gift it or use it as a raffle quilt or something, so here it is."

Connie stood up.

"I for one am glad that jerk doesn't have our nice quilt."

"Well," Mavis said, "we'll have to decide what a proper disposition is for it. For now, I think getting it back is a fitting end to this unfortunate adventure."

END

Acknowledgments

My books are not written in a vacuum but rather push their way into daily life, causing me to miss dinner, keep the lights on too late and to ask random questions, often of a grisly nature, at coffee break. Thanks to my friends and family for putting up with that. I also appreciate the flexibility of my knitting groups who always understand when I have to miss class for book related activities.

My sister-in-law, the real Beth, deserves sainthood for all the driving, cooking and the unfailing support of my writing activities. Her friends Sally and Kay also help when I'm in Texas and to them also, thank you.

Jack and Linne Lindquist of Craftsman's Touch Books have opened a whole new world of opportunity for me by providing a venue for me to promote and sell my books and for being so kind and supportive. Thanks Jack and Linne.

Barb Stillman at the *Country Register* is a wonderful supporter—thank you Barb, I love the drawings and the winners.

A huge thank you to Deon Stonehouse, owner of Sunriver Books and Music in Sunriver, Oregon and also to Diana Portwood, manager of Bob's Beach Books in Lincoln City, Oregon. Both stores host wonderful author events and have been gracious enough to include me.

A huge shout out to my cover artist April Martinez—the covers just keep getting better.

Last and most important, thanks to Liz for making it all happen.

About The Author

After working nearly 30 years in the high tech industry, where her writing consisted of performance reviews, process specs and a scintillating proprietary tome on electronics assembly, **ARLENE SACHITANO** wrote her first mystery novel, *Chip and Die*.

Inspired by the success of the popular Block of the Month quilting pattern program *Seams Like Murder* for Storyquilts.com, Inc., she wrote *Quilt As Desired*, the first Harriet Truman/Loose Threads mystery, which was published in the fall of 2007. *Disappearing Nine Patch* is the ninth episode in the highly-successful series.

Arlene is aided in her writing endeavors by her canine companion Navarre. When not writing, she is on the board of directors of the Harriet Vane Chapter of Sisters In Crime as well as Latimer Quilt and Textile Center in Tillamook. She teaches knitting at Latimer and, of course, is a quilter.

She's been married to Jack for more than thirty years, splitting their time between Tillamook and Multnomah Village in Portland. They have three lovely children and three brilliant grandchildren. She also has two wonderful friends named Susan.

About The Artist

APRIL MARTINEZ was born in the Philippines and raised in San Diego, California, daughter to a US Navy chef and a US postal worker, sibling to one younger sister. For years, she went from job to job, dissatisfied that she couldn't make use of her creative tendencies, until she started working as an imaging specialist for a big book and magazine publishing house in Irvine and began learning the trade of graphic design.

From that point on, she worked as a graphic designer and webmaster at subsequent day jobs while doing freelance art and illustration at night. April lives with her cat in Orange County, California, as a full-time freelance artist/illustrator and graphic designer.

CPSIA information can be obtained
at www.ICGtesting.com
Printed in the USA
LVOW10s1526141216

517259LV00003B/540/P